Closing In

SUE FORTIN

D0332560

A division of HarperCollins*Publishers*
www.harpercollins.co.uk

HarperImpulse an imprint of
HarperCollins*Publishers* Ltd
77–85 Fulham Palace Road
Hammersmith, London W6 8JB

www.harpercollins.co.uk

A Paperback Original 2014

First published in Great Britain in ebook format by HarperImpulse 2014

Cover images © Shutterstock.com

Sue Fortin asserts the moral right
to be identified as the author of this work

A catalogue record for this book is
available from the British Library

ISBN: 9780008104412

This novel is entirely a work of fiction.
The names, characters and incidents portrayed in it are
the work of the author's imagination. Any resemblance to
actual persons, living or dead, events or localities is
entirely coincidental.

Automatically produced by Atomik ePublisher from Easypress

To The Romaniacs for eternal encouragement,
sublime support, words of wisdom and
lashings of laughter.

Prologue

The bag had been hidden at the back of the loft for several weeks now. Packed and ready to go. Helen checked the contents. The all-important papers were there. Deed poll, change of name. New bank account. New bank card. New passport. She ran her finger over the gold-embossed coat of arms of the little red book before flicking through the green pages, pausing at the photograph. The face that had stared back at her all these years was the same; shoulder-length blonde hair, hazel eyes and fair complexion but the name betrayed the picture. Helen Matthews was no more.

'Hello, Ellen Newman.' It was a whisper. Helen barely dared to say her new name out loud. The past twelve months had taught her caution at all times. She had been waiting for this opportunity for what seemed like forever; like a sleeper cell, her escape plan could finally be activated. Her hand shook at the thought of what lay ahead. A mixture of anticipation and fear. She took a moment to calm her breathing and bring the rush of adrenalin under control. She needed to keep a clear head and not panic. She had rehearsed this over and over again in her mind for several months. The anxiety passed, allowing the control to take its place. She closed the passport and stuffed it back into the holdall. 'Come on, Ellen, let's get you out of here.'

'What do you mean, you don't know where she is, Kate?' He squeezed his mobile phone tightly, feeling the frustration rise but fought to keep it in check. 'You're her best friend. Surely she told you where she was going?'

'Look, Toby, I honestly don't know where she is.'

Toby didn't miss the guarded note in Kate's voice. She wasn't going to tell him anything. He took a deep breath and forced a conciliatory tone. 'I don't even know why she took off. I got back from a weekend away clay-pigeon shooting and found a note. I'm worried about her. That's all. Please, Kate?' Jesus, was he going to have to beg?

'Okay,' Kate relented. 'If I hear from her, I'll tell her to ring you or something.'

'Thanks. I really appreciate it. I feel lost without her.' Finishing the call he dropped his phone on to the sofa and picked up the note Helen had left.

Toby, by the time you read this, I will be gone. I am leaving you for good and not coming back. Things between us have become too bad. Please don't try to find me. It's over between us. Helen

P.S. Please remember to feed Scruffs. I've stocked the cupboard up with cat food so you don't need to buy any more for at least a week.

He looked at Scruffs stretched out on the sofa next to him. Toby reached over and ran his fingers up and down the cat's neck. He could feel all the tiny bones of its skeleton beneath the fur and skin. Scrawny little thing. Helen adored that cat and, yet, she had left it. This was all so out of character for her. Running out on him, on the cat, on their life together. It was the last thing he thought she would do. How had he not seen this coming and where in God's name could she have gone? He was sure Kate knew. In fact, he'd stake his Square Mile bankers' salary on it. Scooping the cat up, Toby continued to stroke the tortoiseshell fur as he walked over to the full-length window. He stood looking out over the Islington skyline.

His finger and thumb massaged the back of the cat's neck, before sliding all the way around, meeting under its chin.

'You're out there somewhere, Helen.' He dropped Scruffs to the floor, ignoring the squeak of protest at the rather unceremonious dismissal. Toby pressed his forehead against the glass, the palms of his hands following suit. 'I'm not letting you go without a fight, that's for sure, sweetheart.'

Chapter One

Six months later

Ellen checked the address on the piece of paper in her hand. The Lodge, Sea Lane, Felpham, West Sussex. She looked up at the flint-built house, with its imposing black front door, flanked each side by two sets of Georgian-style paned windows. Her gaze followed the building up to the roof, where a pair of dormer windows looked out like eyes peering across the rooftops. Ellen wondered if you could see the beach from up there. It would be nice if that was going to be her room. Her eyes travelled back down the building, locating the circular brass bell embedded in the flintwork. She pushed it in for a couple of seconds, hearing the buzz coming from inside before releasing it. She took a polite step back from the door. Ellen felt uncomfortable and self-conscious as she waited. A little bubble of nerves bounced around her stomach as she heard the lock being turned from the other side, shortly followed by the door being opened.

'Can I help you?' A woman stood before Ellen. She was probably in her early forties, hair tied back neatly and she was wearing a business-like skirt and jacket.

'Hello, I'm Ellen Newman.' Ellen hoped she sounded casual, as if she'd being saying her name all her life, rather than just the past six months. Choosing a name so close to her original one, Helen, had made the transition easier. There hadn't been many times when she had missed someone addressing her as Ellen. She forced herself to exhale slowly. The woman said nothing but cast her eyes over her. Ellen pushed on. 'I've come from Cherubs Nanny Agency. Mr Donovan should be expecting me.' She tried a smile.

'Oh, yes. That's right. Come in.' The woman opened the door wider and stepped back to reveal a spacious, almost square hall, black and white tiles covering the floor and a dark oak staircase sweeping up and round. 'I'm Mr Donovan's PA. Carla Grosvenor. But we just call him Donovan. No need for the Mr.' Ellen nodded as the PA continued. 'Do you have a letter of introduction from the agency? I have your file with your photo ID; I need to confirm you are who you say you are.'

Ellen took the letter from the agency out of her bag and handed it over. She was relieved to see her hand was steady, even though her heart was racing. Carla read the letter.

'That all seems in order,' she said. 'If you follow me, I'll show you to your room. I'll leave you to sort your things out and then a bit later I can give you a tour of the house.'

Ellen nodded. She was about to ask after the child she was going to be nanny to, when a movement caught her attention. Ellen looked around the PA down the hallway. A little dark head bobbed behind a doorway out of sight and then, after a second or two, slowly looked around the corner. Two big brown eyes met with Ellen's before once again disappearing from view.

'Oh, that must be Izzy,' said Carla. 'She's very shy. Izzy! Izzy! Come and meet your new nanny … err,' she looked at the letter in her hand. 'Ellen.'

'Don't worry about it now. I can meet her in a little while,' said Ellen. She didn't quite like the sharp tone of voice Carla was adopting.

'Izzy! I said, come here. Now,' continued Carla without acknowledging Ellen at all.

'Please, it's really not a problem,' said Ellen. 'Don't force her. There's plenty of time.'

Carla let out an impatient sigh. 'No, I've asked her to do something. She shouldn't ignore me.'

At that moment, another woman appeared from around the doorway. She was in her late sixties, Ellen estimated.

'Come on Izzy.' The woman gently pulled the child out into the hallway and led her to where Ellen and Carla were standing. 'Hello, I'm Mrs Holloway. Housekeeper.'

She extended a hand to Ellen. 'Pleased to meet you,' said Ellen, shaking the pudgy digits of the housekeeper.

'This, here, is Izzy.'

Automatically, Ellen crouched down so she was level with the little girl and hopefully would seem less intimidating. 'Hello, Izzy,' she said. 'My name's Ellen. I'm going to be your nanny.' She waited for a response but wasn't particularly surprised when none was given. 'I've just got here, so I'm going to go up to my room and unpack my things and then later perhaps we can do something together. Yes?' Still no response.

'Don't be rude, Izzy,' said Carla. 'Say hello.'

'Really, it's okay,' insisted Ellen.

After sending Izzy on her way back to the kitchen with Mrs Holloway, Carla proceeded to show Ellen up to her room.

'You're up on the top floor. Your bedroom is next door to the playroom. Izzy sleeps on the middle floor. She doesn't usually wake up so it doesn't matter that you are sleeping on a different floor.'

Ellen's room did indeed have a sea view, albeit a glimpse through the trees and rooftop of the house on the opposite side of the private road. All the houses on the Sea Lane estate were individual affairs; some more subtly designed than others, but all very expensive-looking. Her room itself had a double bed, covered in a pretty flowery, very French-looking eiderdown, next to a dressing table and a wardrobe on the opposite wall. A further door led to a small, but modern, shower room.

Ellen began unpacking her case. It didn't take long. After all, her life had only begun six months ago. If it had been Helen Matthews standing here, then there might be a whole lot more stuff to unpack. A little flutter of unease flew through her but she fought it down. She'd been safe for the past six months. The longer the time passed, the more distance she put between Helen Matthews and Ellen Newman, the safer she was. If anything was going to happen, surely it would have done so by now. She unzipped her handbag and took out the little brown bottle of tablets; they rattled against each other and the plastic bottle as she shook out one small white pill. She popped it into her mouth and swallowed, the film coating making the journey to her stomach easier. Ellen replaced the bottle in her bag, taking deep breaths, allowing the moment of fear to pass over her. She noted with satisfaction that these anxiety attacks were becoming less frequent and passing quicker. She was still safe.

Chapter Two

An hour later, Ellen was following Carla around the house for her guided tour. The middle floor comprised bedrooms for Izzy, Donovan and for Carla.

'I don't stay very often,' explained Carla. 'I prefer to go home these days. Things to do.'

The house was immaculately kept, noted Ellen, as they trawled through the rooms. A formal dining room led off one side of the entrance hall and a large sitting room on the other. Halfway down the hall on the right was Carla's office, which had an interlocking door into the sitting room on one side and on the other, another door, which led into Donovan's office.

'Donovan has consulting rooms he uses. They are over at Chichester. If he's not there, then he's down at the police station. I'm based either here or at the consulting rooms, depending on whether he has a clinic that day or not.' Carla paused. 'Did they tell you what he does?'

'He's a psychologist, I think they said.'

'That's right. A criminal psychologist for Sussex Police. Hence the reason for spending a lot of time there.'

'Is that where he is now?' asked Ellen.

'Yes, they called him in earlier. I don't know what time he will be back; these things can drag on for hours. You will probably have to wait until tomorrow to meet him.' Carla strode down the black and white-tiled hallway to the back of the house where Ellen had first seen Izzy that morning. Ellen followed her down the corridor and into the kitchen.

Izzy was bent over a mixing bowl at the kitchen table, attempting to knead a piece of dough about the size of a tennis ball.

Mrs Holloway was standing on the other side of the table doing the same with her much larger piece of dough. She looked up as Ellen and Carla entered the room.

'Hello,' she said, smiling at them. Then she spoke to the child. 'Izzy, you've got visitors.' She nodded towards the doorway.

Izzy gave a quick glance in Ellen's direction but then immediately turned her attention back to the piece of dough. Ellen sat down beside her at the table. 'Hello, Izzy,' she spoke gently and with warmth. 'What have you got there? Dough? What are you making with that?'

Izzy shrugged and let the dough drop into the bowl. She began picking at her fingers. Ellen carried on, understanding that it was going to take a while before she earned the child's trust

Ellen picked up the dough ball. 'Eww, it's all sticky. Look, if we sprinkle some more flour into the bowl and roll the dough around, it will stop it being so gooey. Here, you do it.'

Izzy hesitated for a moment before putting her hand into the bag of flour and taking a handful, sprinkling it into the bowl. Ellen dropped the dough ball into it. A puff of flour ballooned into the air, showering them both in white dust. Ellen made an exaggerated yelp of surprise, followed by some spluttering noises.

It had the desired effect. Izzy giggled. 'Oh my word,' said Ellen. 'What a mess I've made.' She wiped her hand across her face, purposefully leaving a trail of flour over her nose and her cheek. This was rewarded by more giggling from Izzy.

'You've got it on your face,' said Izzy.

'Have I? Where?' Ellen wiped her face, knowing full well she was making it worse.

'There!' Izzy laughed out loud, pointing at Ellen's chin.

'Here?' More flour on her face.

'No! There!'

The two of them were now laughing together, as was Mrs Holloway. Only Carla remained immune to the fun. 'Don't make too much mess,' said Carla. 'It will be your bedtime soon.'

Immediately, Izzy's face fell and she lapsed back into a subdued silence. Ellen bit down the urge to say something to Carla. Now wasn't the time, not in front of Izzy and certainly not in the first few hours of her new job.

'Doesn't she stay up to see her father?' said Ellen instead.

'Izzy needs routine,' explained Carla. 'Donovan likes it that way. And truth be told, the child does too. In fact, while I think about it, there's a folder up in the nursery I should have told you about. It's got Izzy's routine set out. When she has her meals, how she spends her time. If you can acquaint yourself with that, then it will make the transition easier and create minimum disruption for Izzy.'

Poor Izzy, it made her sound like some sort of Stepford child. Every minute of her day planned out. Where was the fun in that?

'I'll have a look. It may be that I make a few changes once I get used to everything,' said Ellen, trying to keep her voice casual.

'Not too much. We like things to run smoothly around here.' There was a distinctly challenging tone to Carla's voice.

Once again, Ellen resisted the urge to argue but nevertheless, she resolved to make changes as she saw fit. Carla could take a running jump with her timetable. Ellen contemplated her new employer. Was he a stickler for routine as well? Maybe that was why the previous nanny had left; too much control? She shuddered to herself as this idea nudged painful, not too distant memories, to the fore. Control like that was never a good thing. She couldn't help but wonder if that's why there was no Mrs Donovan. The agency had said that the mother had left three years ago but had offered no explanation as to why. What would make a mother leave her young child? It must have been bad. Was it as bad for Mrs

Donovan as it had been for herself? A slither of mistrust towards her new employer coiled itself in her stomach.

The French Marseillaise sounded out on Donovan's phone; the tune he had specifically assigned to Amanda, his soon to be ex-wife. As he drove into Felpham village, he flirted with the idea of ignoring it. However, previous experience told him this would be futile. She would simply keep ringing. With much reluctance, Donovan hit the accept button for the hands-free kit.

'Amanda.'

'Donovan.' Their usual minimalistic greeting. 'I'm in the UK this week. In fact, I'm going to be in the UK a lot more. Sebastian and I are relocating to London.'

Donovan's eyes snapped to the handset as if it would confirm what he had just heard. 'London? Permanently?' He tried to keep the surprise out of his voice. It never did to let Amanda think she had the upper hand on anything.

'That's right. Now, I expect to be able to see Isobel far more often. In fact, it's something my solicitor will be writing to your solicitor about. I envisage joint custody, Isobel to spend equal time with both of us and in the long term, I'm looking to her living with me.'

Donovan brought the car to halt worthy of emergency-stop status. 'What?' He managed to grind out. Joint custody. Izzy living with Amanda. No way.

'It's really quite simple, Donovan,' replied Amanda, her tone clipped and matter of fact. 'I'm Isobel's mother. I'm going to be back in the UK and I want her living with me. It's how it should be. An eight-year-old girl living with her father may be nice now, but as she grows up she will need her mother for all sorts of reasons. You're an intelligent man, Donovan, use your brains.'

'Wait a minute. When did you decide all this? What's wrong with France and lover boy's chateau all of a sudden? You can't just announce you're coming back and Izzy is going to live with you. As

11

I have sole custody I don't think it's a case of simply handing her over. She's with me for a very good reason.' Donovan manoeuvred his car over to the side of the road.

'All that's in the past now,' snapped Amanda. 'I'm not going to get into an argument with you, Donovan. I'll be in touch about seeing Isobel soon.'

The line went dead.

Donovan cursed out loud. Amanda back on the scene. Great. Exactly what he could do without. He pinched the bridge of his nose, closing his eyes for a moment. Then taking his usual pragmatic approach, Donovan decided there was little he could do about it tonight. He needed to get home. It had been a long day and he was shattered. However, Amanda's words refused to fade from their continuous loop replaying in his mind.

Chapter Three

Toby squeezed the remote key to his Audi TT, the clonk of the central locking reassuring him it was secure. As he approached Kate's front door, he caught sight of his reflection in the glass panel. He looked dishevelled, his hair was ruffled and his tie dragged to one side, where he had snatched at his top button to undo it. He hated looking a mess. The front door swung open before he reached it.

'Toby. What are you doing here?' Kate's voice was wary. She stepped into the doorway and pulled the door tightly to her body. Entry most definitely denied.

'Hello, Kate. How are you?' His voice sounded lifeless.

She gave him a quizzical look. 'I'm fine, thanks.'

He nodded and cast a downward look, shuffling from one foot to another. 'Good. That's good.'

'Are you all right?' she asked.

Toby shrugged. 'Yeah. Well, no. Not really.' He looked up, raking his hand through his hair. 'It's Helen's birthday next week and I … er … I wanted …' He threw a glance down the road. 'Oh, look, I shouldn't have come. Sorry to bother you.' He turned and began a slow retreat down the path, shoulders slumped.

'Toby! Wait.' He paused to give himself time to keep his composure. Facial muscles under control he returned to the front door.

13

Kate had the door wide open now and was standing on the step. 'What's up?'

'Helen.' Even to his own ears, he sounded monotone. 'I thought I'd got over her leaving but I can't stop thinking about her. I'm worried about her, Kate. Really worried. I thought she would be in touch by now. I know the police told me she was okay and that she didn't want to be contacted but …' He sniffed and wiped at his eyes. 'I miss her. I need to speak to her. I want her back, Kate. So badly.'

'After what happened? She didn't run away without a reason.' He winced at the incredulous tone in her voice and took a moment before answering.

'It wasn't like she said. You know that.'

'Do I?'

'Yes, you do.' He looked her straight in the eye and held her gaze. She broke away first. He pushed on, sensing she was faltering. He pulled out an envelope from his jacket pocket. 'Can you give this to her, please?'

Kate kept her arms folded and eyed the envelope. 'I can't.'

'Please … It's a birthday card and, here, a small present too.' He took the slim brown box from his other pocket. A solid-gold bangle with Italian Murano glass beads. Blue ones. Her favourite colour. He pushed the case into Kate's hand.

'I can't give these to her because I don't know where she is. I don't see her and that's the truth,' insisted Kate.

He believed her. It was what he suspected. He also suspected that she did keep in touch, even if they didn't actually see each other. If he could just get into Kate's house and have a poke around, he'd be sure to find something. Drastic times called for drastic measures.

Making it seem as though he was indecisive and didn't know whether to stay or go, Toby schooled his face into the bleakest expression he could muster, looking at Kate, then down the path and then back to her again. He went to speak, stopped and then ran his hand down his face in what he hoped looked something like desperation. Sensing Kate's resolve weakening, with a flourish he flung his arm up against the wall of the house and buried his head in the crook of his elbow. This was followed by a loud and drawn-out exhalation of air, which morphed into a groan.

'Why don't you come in for a moment,' said Kate. He felt her tug at his sleeve and allowed himself to be taken indoors. Her voice was softer. The ice maiden was thawing. 'You can't stand out there in that state. Mrs Howard, next door, is already twitching at her curtain to see what's going on.'

'Sorry, Kate. Really, I don't want to be any trouble.' He followed her into the lounge.

'Sit there, I'll make you a coffee but then you'll have to go.'

He nodded and sat down on the sofa. The TV was on and although Toby had no interest in the soap, he feigned interest. Out of his peripheral vision he noted Kate hastily scoop up an envelope from the coffee table. He pretended not to notice. He gave it a couple of seconds before turning to look over his shoulder. His timing was perfect. Kate was just placing the envelope between two hardbacks on the bookshelf. A look of guilt swept over her face and she hurriedly pushed the novels back into place.

'Sugar?' she asked as she went into the kitchen.

The bookcase was by the side of the doorway to the kitchen. Toby got up and leaned against the door frame, making small talk with Kate while she made the coffee. It wasn't going to be easy getting hold of that envelope but, with a bit of luck, he should manage it. He took out his phone, and whilst pretending to check for messages, he switched the camera on and muted the sound, all the time continuing to bemoan the loss of Helen. He placed his phone on the bookshelf and while Kate was pouring the boiling water into the cups, he reached out and gave the envelope a quick tug so it was sticking out further from the books.

Kate passed his cup to him. Right, this was it. Time to sacrifice a good suit but it would be worth it. Toby fumbled with the cup and dropped it onto the tiled kitchen floor. Obligingly the cup broke and coffee spewed everywhere, splashing his trousers in the process.

Kate gave a small yelp and hopped back out of the way.

'Oh shit! I'm so sorry,' said Toby, surveying the broken china and the rapidly spreading brown liquid. Kate grabbed some kitchen roll and began tearing off sheets and laying them on the floor, first as a dam and then to soak up the mess. 'Here, let me.' Toby offered. Fortunately, Kate refused.

'No, it's okay. I'll do it. Don't worry, it's only a cup.'

While she was distracted, Toby moved back into the living room as if trying to stay out of Kate's way. Standing at the bookcase, he pulled the card out from between the books, laying it flat on the shelf. Checking Kate was still preoccupied, he picked up his phone and took a couple of shots of the address on the envelope. He didn't have time to study what it said, but if his hunch was right, this was something to do with Helen. 'I'm so clumsy,' he said as Kate retrieved a dustpan and brush from under the sink. 'I'm like it all the time now. A bundle of nerves. This business with Helen, it's really getting to me.' He turned away from her, so she couldn't see his face. Glancing at the envelope, he slid it back between the books and then dropped his phone into his pocket. He wanted to get home. All thoughts of coffee were relegated. 'I'd better go. I'm sorry about the mess.' He fashioned a regretful smile, which was met by a nod.

Once sitting in the safety of his car, Toby looked at the photos on his phone. Shit. The first one was a bit blurred and the second one had completely missed the address. He flicked to the final one. It was slightly out of focus, but he could make out the writing. A frown folded across his face.

Ellen Newman
The Lodge,
Sea Lane,

Felpham,
West Sussex.

It wasn't the name he was expecting. He'd got it wrong. What a waste of time and a good pair of trousers. He thumped the steering wheel in frustration.

Chapter Four

Donovan parked his black Range Rover outside his house. He looked up at the top-floor windows. All was dark. Izzy would, of course, be fast asleep by now. He let out a long sigh and promised himself that he would make time to take her out at the weekend. Entering the house, he was greeted by Carla.

'Good evening, Donovan.' She smiled, taking his coat from him and handing him the day's post. 'Have you had a good day?'

'It was okay, thank you.' He turned to Carla. 'How is Izzy?'

'She's fine. The new nanny arrived today.' Carla followed him into the study. 'Ellen Newman.'

'Great, she turned up then. That's good. And what do you think of her?'

'Too early to say yet.'

Donovan didn't miss the coolness in Carla's voice. He wondered if they were going to regret taking on a new nanny without actually interviewing her and purely going on the recommendation of the agency. He sat at his desk, dropping the unopened envelopes onto the lacquered walnut. 'You don't sound very convinced.'

'As I say, it's early days. Now, I'll get you a coffee and see what Mrs Holloway has left for supper. Would you like to eat in here?'

Carla was fussing too much. He didn't want to offend her, he'd be lost without her most of the time. She was a fantastic PA and a loyal friend but, sometimes, he felt as though he was married to her.

'I'll sort supper and coffee out for myself. Thank you, Carla. I don't think I will be doing much work this evening, I'm too tired. You go home now.'

'As you wish, Donovan,' replied Carla. 'Just one thing, the new nanny. When would you like to meet her?'

'Where is she now?'

'She took Izzy to bed and said she was going to her room afterwards.'

'Okay, don't disturb her now. I'll see her in the morning at some point.' Donovan smiled up at his PA. 'You look tired, Carla. Let me call a cab for you.'

'Thank you but I can do it.' Carla went to leave, but paused in the doorway. 'You should get some rest too, you look very tired yourself. I'll see myself out. Goodnight.'

'Goodnight,' he said as he flicked through the pile of letters. He went to open one, then changed his mind and tossed it back onto the pile. He was too tired for all this tonight. It was past ten o'clock. Far too late to be reading referral letters and police reports. He lent back in his chair and closed his eyes for a moment, letting the thoughts of the day drift to the back of his mind. He needed to stop thinking about Amanda. He breathed deep and slow, concentrating on relaxing his mind, body and soul. Relax. That was better.

Donovan wasn't quite sure how long he had sat in his chair for and suspected he had probably drifted off into a near-sleep. He checked his watch. It was almost eleven and his stomach was complaining at the lack of food.

'Right, something to eat,' he said out loud, as he loosened his tie and undid his top button.

Stopping in the hallway, Donovan thought of Izzy asleep in her room. Slipping off his shoes at the foot of the stairs, he began the ascent of the oak staircase.

Reaching the landing, he padded lightly down the hall to the first door. It was slightly ajar.

Izzy was fast asleep, as he'd expected. Her toy teddy, Mr Snuggles, was on the floor. Donovan picked up the well-loved bear and slipped it under the cover. Izzy stirred, her eyes fluttering open.

'Daddy?'

'Yes, it's Daddy,' whispered Donovan. He leant over and dropped a kiss on her dark hair. 'Go back to sleep, angel. Daddy loves you.'

Donovan stayed for a minute, just watching her, drawing on the feeling of contentment to soothe away the sourness of the day.

Less frayed, he made his way back downstairs to the kitchen; his appetite piqued now he felt more relaxed.

He hadn't expected anyone to be in there and was startled to see the back of a woman at the sink. It didn't appear that she had noticed him, his stocking feet making no announcement of his arrival. He took the moment to cast his eye over the slim figure, encased in jeans and a long-sleeved t-shirt, with fair hair resting on narrow shoulders. The new nanny, he presumed. Donovan gave a subtle cough.

Startled, she spun round.

Donovan smiled, held out his hand and stepped forward. 'Good evening. I'm Donovan. You must be …'

'Ellen Newman.' She quickly wiped her hands on a tea towel.

With her sleeves pushed up to the elbow, Donovan couldn't help but notice several reddish circular marks on her right forearm. Eczema perhaps?

Ellen withdrew her hand and pulled her sleeves down. 'I was just making myself a coffee. Would you like one?' Her voice was calm but her eyes were anxious.

'If you're making one, that would be great. Thank you. Black, no sugar,' Donovan replied, moving over to the oven and lifting the lid on a saucepan. 'Ah, butternut squash soup. Mrs Holloway's speciality. Would you like some?' She seemed to hesitate. Donovan sensed she probably wanted to say yes, but was too polite. He took two bowls out of the cupboard. 'It really is delicious. You'll love it, I promise. And I'd be glad of the company. It will give us a chance to get to know each other, seeing as you're working for me now. ' Without giving her a chance to say no, he set two places at the table and ladled the creamy orange liquid into the bowls.

Getting out some bread and buttering several slices, he sat down at the table and was satisfied to see Ellen sit down opposite him.

'Thank you,' she said. 'It does smell lovely.'

'I'm sorry we haven't had the chance to meet before,' said Donovan. 'I usually like to interview staff myself but it was an emergency and I know Cherubs Nanny Agency is very thorough with its checks. You came with very good references.'

Ellen nodded. 'Yes, I must admit it is a little unusual not to meet the parents first, but as you say, it was exceptional circumstances. The agency said your previous nanny left because of a family bereavement back in Scotland, is that right?'

Donovan nodded. 'Yes. She didn't want to come back, said it was too far away from her family. I suppose the bereavement made her take stock of things. You haven't come quite so far, have you?'

'No, only from London. I've been here, well, West Sussex and the south coast, before. When I was a child, but not for a long time. You know, family holidays.'

'And your family now, where are they?'

He watched as she hesitated and toyed the spoon in circular motions through the soup. 'My mum died when I was young. I'm an only child. My dad is remarried with his own young family. I don't see him much.'

He sensed she wasn't comfortable talking about it and, not wanting to make her feel uneasy, he let the subject drop. 'How long have you worked for Cherubs?'

'Seven years, now. They have always placed me with very good families so I had no reason to doubt them this time, despite not having met you beforehand.'

'And is your room okay?'

'Yes, it's really nice. Thank you.'

'I know you're a bit out of the way on the top floor, but it's nice for Izzy to have the run of it. Downstairs isn't quite so child-friendly. I don't want her to have to creep around all day simply because I'm working.' He watched her face take on a slightly surprised look.

'Oh, right,' she said. 'It's nice she has a big playroom on the top floor.'

'Exactly. And you've met Carla, my long-suffering PA of over ten years?' A nod and what Donovan suspected was a forced smile. Ellen had obviously already felt the brusqueness of her colleague. 'Carla can sometimes come across as a little starchy. Please don't take offence. It's just her way.'

'Okay. I'll bear that in mind.' Ellen pushed her empty bowl away from her. 'You were right, the soup was lovely.'

She looked as if she was preparing to leave, but Donovan wanted to question her a bit more, call it a post-employment interview. Okay, it was probably a bit late now, but he would feel better if he knew a bit more about her.

'Ellen, tell me, how was it you were able to start here at such short notice?'

'I've been working abroad for the last six months. I've had a spell in France at a campsite, running their children's club. Now the high season has finished, I'm back here in the UK. The timing couldn't have been better.'

It was a simple and very plausible explanation. 'Where were you working before in the UK? Were you live-in? Sorry for all the questions.' He smiled at her.

She smiled back, although he still sensed a slight unease. 'It's okay. I was working for a family in London and, no, it wasn't a live-in position.' He didn't say anything but looked encouragingly at her, allowing the silence to give a sense of expectation. A technique he often used with his clients to get them to speak. Invariably it worked. Ellen was not immune to this tactic. 'I had a flat in North London with my boyfriend but we split up. That's how I ended up working abroad.'

She stood up and took her bowl and cup over to the dishwasher, clearly not wanting to pursue the conversation.

'Any chance you'll get back together?'

'No.'

The reply was out almost before he had time to finish his sentence. She sure was definite about that.

'Amicable break-up, was it?' Donovan knew he was verging on the point of being nosy but he felt his questions justified. He was, after all, entrusting his most precious thing, his daughter, in her safe keeping. She was facing him now and looked as if she was contemplating telling him to mind his own business. He felt compelled to explain his questioning. 'Look, Ellen, I don't mean to pry but it's just I like to know who is looking after my daughter. I don't want you running off back to your boyfriend if you suddenly decided the grass wasn't greener after all.' For a moment he thought she was going to take offence, the indignation clear on her face. He watched as she visibly reined in her emotions, letting out a breath before speaking.

'Of course, you're absolutely right to ask. I understand.' Her voice was calm. 'I can assure you, there is absolutely no chance whatsoever that I will be going back to my boyfriend. That was all over six months ago and I haven't been tempted once since then to reconsider my decision. This job is a new start for me and I am fully committed to looking after your daughter. I have her best interest at heart. I really do.'

'Thank you,' said Donovan. 'That's what I wanted to hear.'

'Good. If you'll excuse me, I'm going to bed. Goodnight, Donovan.'

Ellen firmly closed the door to her room and sank down onto her bed, her legs suddenly feeling weak and her shoulders heavy. She ran her fingers over the circular marks on her right arm. They were rough under her fingertips but no longer hurt. The physical pain had gone. The pain she felt inside, in her mind, was not so eager to leave.

Chapter Five

Still feeling bad tempered from his wasted efforts Toby crashed around the kitchen of his apartment whilst making a decent cup of coffee. One which he had no intention of throwing on the floor this time. He had been sure from the guilty look on Kate's face that the envelope held the key to Helen's whereabouts. He leaned back against the counter and sipped his coffee, his eyes idly wandering over the notice board on the wall opposite. It was a pink quilted heart that Helen had made and proudly hung in place herself, since he had refused to. It wasn't his style but he relented and left it there since it was round the corner and not in full view. It still had her stuff on it. A photo of them on holiday in St Lucia last year. Another photo of Scruffs in his usual position; sprawled out across the sofa. His eyes moved over the board. A couple of receipts. A shopping list. A retro black and white postcard of the Hollywood actor Paul Newman, an icon Helen adored, shared the same pin as a dental appointment card alongside a takeaway menu for the local Chinese.

He stopped in mid-thought. His eyes flicked back to the dental card. When was the appointment? Maybe he could wait outside the dentist, just in case she attended. Putting his cup down, his attention firmly fixed on the card, he walked over and unpinned it, ignoring the picture of Paul Newman, which fell to the floor.

He turned the appointment card over and was disappointed to see that the routine check-up had been and gone. He wondered if they would give him any information as to a new address for her. It was too late to ring them now; he'd contact them in the morning. He placed the card in his wallet. As he went to finish making his coffee, his foot kicked the postcard, which had landed face down on the floor. Toby bent to retrieve the card. Absently he glanced at the message on the back, written to Helen from Kate.

I know you said you fancied a new man but this is the best I could come up with.
Lol.
Kate xxx

Toby reread the message. Turned the card over and then back again. New man. Paul Newman. Newman.

He pulled his iPhone from his pocket and hastily located the picture he had taken of the envelope at Kate's flat. Ellen Newman.

A warm feeling of victory ebbed over him.

'Clever, sweetheart,' he muttered, 'but not that clever.'

Ellen woke early the next morning after a night of restless sleep. She showered and dressed before making her way downstairs to Izzy's room. Poking her head around the corner of the door, she expected to see the little girl fast asleep, it was so quiet in there. Instead, Izzy was sitting up in her bed looking at a book.

'Good morning, Izzy,' said Ellen. 'You're up early. You should have come and woken me.'

'But I'm not allowed. Carla says I must stay in bed until someone comes to get me for breakfast. Is it breakfast time?'

'Not yet but we can get you dressed and go downstairs, if you want.'

'We're not allowed to until breakfast time,' said Izzy, looking up at Ellen. 'It's the rules.'

'The rules? Whose rules are those?' Ellen felt her hackles go up. Carla and her rules. Whose house was this? Then, noticing the anxious look on Izzy's face, she felt bad about asking the child. 'Hey, don't worry. We can have some of our own rules. In fact, my first new rule is ... we can get up early and go exploring. How does that sound? You can show me the garden. I haven't been out there yet.'

Izzy looked delighted at the suggestion. 'The garden? Really?' Discarding her book with abandonment, she threw back her duvet and jumped onto the floor. 'I can show you my trampoline.'

'Excellent! Let's get you washed and dressed then.'

The grass was still a little damp from the morning dew. Trees shielded the garden from the sight of neighbouring properties, their long shadows cast across the lawn.

The trampoline was at the far end of the garden, next to a wooden climbing frame and swing.

'Race you to the trampoline,' said Ellen. 'Ready, steady ... hey! You're supposed to wait for me to say go!' She laughed as Izzy sped off down the neatly kept lawn. Ellen ran after her but made sure she didn't catch up.

'I win! I win!' sang out Izzy as she scampered up the steps of the trampoline and through the opening of the safety net. 'Look at me. I can bounce really high, just like Tigger. Bounce! Bounce! Bounce!'

Ellen wriggled in through the opening, zipping up the net behind her. Wobbling against the spring of the mat, she laughed as she staggered towards Izzy. Holding hands, they bounced up and down, laughing and shrieking as they jumped higher, before Ellen lost her footing and landed in a heap, bringing Izzy down on top of her. Ellen wasn't quite sure if she was laughing at herself or whether Izzy's infectious giggling was making her just as bad. Getting to her feet again, she hauled Izzy up.

'Come on, Tigger,' she said. 'Let's try again. See if we can bounce higher this time.

Ellen didn't hear Carla at first, but noticing the sudden look of concern on Izzy's face, she stopped jumping and turned to look back at the house. Carla was marching down the garden towards them.

'Oh dear,' said Ellen, looking back at Izzy and pulling an *eek* sort of face. 'Carla doesn't look too happy.'

'What are you doing out here this time of the morning, making all this noise?' demanded Carla, as she reached the trampoline. 'You will have the whole street awake at this rate. Come inside at once.'

'We were only having a bit of fun, seeing as we were up early,' replied Ellen, attempting a graceful exit from the trampoline. She lifted Izzy down onto the grass and sensing the child's unease, picked her up again and began carrying her back towards the house.

'That's not how we do things here.' Carla turned to Izzy. 'You should have told Miss Newman that you're not allowed out here until after breakfast.'

'Ellen. Izzy doesn't have to call me Miss Newman.' Ellen couldn't hide the annoyance in her voice. All these rules for an eight-year-old. What sort of place was this, for goodness sake? She felt Izzy bury her head into her shoulder. Probably frightened of what could potentially turn into an argument. Ellen purposefully put a spring in her stride and started singing a nursery rhyme. She felt Izzy relax against her and was pleased when she joined in with the song.

As they reached the patio, something made Ellen glance up to the first-floor window. Donovan was standing there looking down at them. 'Oh, Izzy, there's Daddy. Wave. Hello, Daddy!' They both waved up at Donovan, who smiled broadly at his daughter and waved furiously back. Then, for a second, his gaze switched to Ellen and he smiled directly at her. Why it made her tummy give a little flutter, Ellen wasn't sure. She distracted herself by putting Izzy down and, taking her hand, led her indoors.

Sitting at the breakfast table with Izzy, Ellen was disappointed when Carla sat down opposite them.

'I'd appreciate it if you stick to how things are done here, please,' said Carla, fixing her gaze on Ellen. 'It's important Izzy keeps to a routine; that way when you leave there is minimum disruption for her. Your replacement can fit in easily.'

'My replacement? When I leave?' Ellen met Carla's gaze with equal intensity. She wouldn't let herself be bullied. Those days were long gone. She'd let that happen with Toby and had sworn never again. 'I'm not planning on going anywhere soon.'

'I'm sure Carla was thinking longterm.' Donovan entered the kitchen. 'Morning, ladies, and good morning, my beautiful princess.' Izzy slipped down from her seat and ran to her father, who scooped her up into a big hug, kissing her on the nose.

'Good morning, Donovan.' Carla smiled warmly. Ellen couldn't help but notice the change in demeanour of the PA. 'I was merely pointing out to Miss Newman that nannies come and go, but it must always be Izzy's best interest kept at heart, hence the routine we like to stick to.'

'We were just having a bit of fun. It's such a nice morning for this time of year, we thought we'd take advantage of it.' Ellen defended herself.

'Quite right too, nothing like a bit of spontaneity,' Donovan replied cheerfully. Ellen revelled in his obvious approval of her actions but this feeling of triumph was soon diminished by his next sentence. 'However, Carla does have a point. It's best for Izzy if we stick to something of a routine.'

'Of course,' she said after a moment, and then immediately wanted to kick herself when she saw the disappointed look sweep over Izzy's face.

Breakfast passed without further confrontation and soon it was time to take Izzy to school.

'Let's do your coat up, Izzy,' said Ellen, crouching down and fastening the zip. 'It's a bit windy out there today.'

'Are you taking me to school?'

29

'Yes, that's right but Daddy's coming as well. He needs to show me the way.'

As Ellen stood up, Donovan came out from his study. 'Are we all ready, then?

'Yippee!' cried Izzy. 'Can we go in your car, Daddy?'

'I don't see any reason why not,' replied Donovan, running his hand across his daughter's head.

The clipping of heels on the tiled floor signalled the arrival of Carla. 'Did I hear you say you were going out, Donovan?' she said, joining the group in the hallway.

'That's right. I thought I'd take the opportunity of driving Izzy to school.'

'In that case,' she turned to Ellen, 'you won't be needed. Why don't you go and see if Mrs Holloway wants a hand in the kitchen?'

'I don't mean to be rude, Carla, but I'm employed as a nanny, not a domestic help. It does state that clearly in the contract from the agency,' said Ellen. She didn't mind helping out now and again, but she didn't want it to be a foregone conclusion. 'Anything I do is supposed to be related to Izzy.'

Ellen watched Carla's eyebrows rise so high, she thought for a moment they would disappear into her hairline. Fortunately, Donovan spoke first.

'Ellen does have a point,' he said. 'Besides, I want her to come with me so she can learn the route before having to do the school run alone.'

'As you wish, Donovan,' replied Carla, her smile so obviously forced. The telephone ringing in the study was a timely interruption. 'I'll get that. Have a good day at school, Izzy.' Carla clipped her way back down the hall to attend to the telephone.

'Carla doesn't like you,' said Izzy.

'Izzy!' reprimanded Donovan. 'That's not true. Of course Carla likes Ellen.'

'It is true,' said Izzy, matter-of-factly, in the way only a child could. 'You can tell by the way she screws her eyes up at Ellen and her mouth all scrunches up like she's eaten Brussels sprouts. Like this.'

Ellen couldn't help laughing. That had to be the perfect impression of Carla. Glancing across at Donovan, she was met by serious-looking eyes. Oh dear, he clearly didn't share her appreciation of the joke. Ellen fought to control herself but then Donovan's face erupted into a huge grin. He shook his head and looked down at his daughter.

'Izzy, sometimes it's best to say things in your head rather than out loud. You could upset people. Remember, we've had this discussion before?' Izzy pouted slightly at the admonishment but then graciously nodded before homing in for a cuddle.

Walking out to the car, Donovan leant in toward Ellen. 'Sorry about that.'

Ellen smiled at him. 'That's okay, really don't worry.' She opened the rear door of the Range Rover and lifted Izzy up into the seat. 'Can you do your seat belt? My, you are a big girl.' She closed the door and, turning round, was surprised to find Donovan standing right behind her. She could smell the freshness of his aftershave and the fabric softener on his clothes.

'But I do worry. Please ignore Carla. As I said before …'

'I know, she's just a bit frosty. Hopefully, it won't be too long before the thaw sets in,' finished off Ellen, good-humouredly. She wanted to add that Izzy was probably right about Carla not liking her, but she kept the thought to herself. Ellen went to move around the back of the vehicle to sit alongside Izzy but Donovan blocked her way.

'Sit in the front,' he said. 'You'll get a better idea of where you're going then.' Reaching past her with his left hand, he opened the passenger door and, taking hold of her elbow, turned her in the direction of the front seat.

The Range Rover was huge compared to Toby's sporty TT. She hadn't driven regularly for three years now; living in London she had forgone a car. Toby had his car, which she had only been allowed to drive when he was too drunk. Her role as designated driver was automatically assumed without question. Well, she had questioned it once. Toby made sure she never questioned it again.

'Will I be using this car to drive Izzy to school?' she asked.

'If I said yes, would it worry you?' he asked.

Ellen looked across and could see him reining in a grin. 'It wouldn't worry me, but it might worry you.'

Donovan let out a small laugh, which danced around the confined space of the vehicle. It was a warming feeling, one which she realised she hadn't experienced for a long time.

'In that case then,' said Donovan, 'you can use the Fiesta that's parked in the garage.'

'That's a relief.' Ellen was aware that she was grinning, probably wider than necessary, but her facial muscles seemed intent on exercising themselves to their full potential.

'For both of us,' he replied with a wink.

Chapter Six

They drove in silence out of the private beach estate, towards the nearby town of Chichester. The traffic was heavy and it took some time before they reached the north of city, where they then headed to Oakdale School, an independent school nestled in the rolling countryside of the Sussex Downs.

The drop-off routine was efficient and impeccably carried out. Pull up in the car park, walk over to the classroom, a kiss and a hug for both Ellen and Donovan, before Izzy was rounded up by her class teacher and whisked off into Blueberry Class.

'Well, that seems pretty straightforward,' said Ellen, fastening her seat belt as Donovan pulled out of the car park. The narrow village lane was busy with school-run traffic.

'Yes, Izzy's very good. Very adaptable,' he replied.

'Has she had to adapt to a lot then?' pried Ellen. She knew she shouldn't really, but hadn't he been doing the same the previous evening? Not only that, she somehow felt comfortable in his company. She didn't think he would take offence. She stole a glance at him. His lips pursed as if thinking about his response.

'If I'm honest, we've had several nannies recently. I know it's not ideal for Izzy. Just as she gets used to one, they leave, then a replacement comes and she has to try and build up a rapport all over again.' They were out on the dual carriageway now, heading back towards Felpham. 'And before you ask, because I'm certain you're going to … the nannies haven't lasted for a variety of reasons.'

'What about Izzy's mother?' The question was out before Ellen had time to check herself. Now she really was pushing the boundaries. 'Sorry, you don't have to answer, it's none of my business.' Damage limitation.

'Remember when I said to Izzy that sometimes it's best to say things in your head and not out loud?' He gave Ellen a sideways glance, his eyebrow raised. 'Well, that.'

There was no dancing feeling of words this time. The silence that filled the rest of the car journey was more like a funeral march. Donovan clearly had no intention of talking about Izzy's mother and Ellen cursed herself for mentioning it.

Ellen's thoughts turned to Kate and how she was going to get to a computer.

'Do you know if there are any internet cafés in Felpham?' she asked breaking the silence.

'We're not exactly a bustling metropolis. We can do the cafés but it's more likely they will have blackboard and chalk than Wi-Fi.'

'I suppose I could use the library. I take it there is a library here?'

'In the main town but you don't have to do that. You can use my laptop. I'll sort it out for you when we get in.'

Ellen thanked Donovan. She was pretty sure the IP address couldn't be traced unless she actually sent an email. She had set up a new email account and shared the details with Kate. They had agreed to communicate by email but, rather than sending the electronic messages and thereby leaving a cyber-trail, they were saving the emails to draft without actually sending them. Once Ellen had saved an email, Kate could log onto the account from her own computer and read the draft email. She would then delete it and compose a reply, which would be left in the draft box for Ellen to pick up. This way there was no footprint or record of their communications. Not that Toby was some computer geek who could trace these things, but she wasn't taking any chances.

Once they had got back to *The Lodge*, it didn't take Donovan long to produce the laptop for Ellen. 'It needs charging, I'm afraid,' he said.

'Oh, thank you,' said Ellen. 'I really appreciate this. I'll give it back to you as soon as I'm done.'

'No rush. I don't use it that often. I prefer the main computer in my office.' Donovan passed the laptop to her, wrapping up the lead and placing it on top. 'My documents are all password protected so you're safe using it. You won't stumble across any confidential information or client details.'

Carla came out of the office. 'Oh, Donovan. I've just had DCI Froames on the line. He wants to know if you can go down and interview a suspect. Apparently, he mentioned it to you yesterday?'

Donovan frowned for a moment while he recalled the conversation. 'That's right. To do with an attack on a young woman in her home. Okay, tell Ken I'm on my way.'

'That doesn't sound very nice,' commented Ellen.

'No, it's not, but if it means it leads to someone's arrest and conviction, then I regard it as a positive thing.'

'I suppose that's the best way to look at it.'

'Definitely. Something good out of something bad. Justice for the victim and punishment for the criminal.' He smiled at her. A smile that Ellen found hard to match to the job he was about to undertake.

Chapter Seven

As much as Donovan loved his job, he hated it too. He loved the analysis, the breakdown of potential suspects, the building up of criminal psychological profiles but hated the scenarios; the often skin-crawling and despicable crimes this role brought him into contact with.

He fixed his gaze on Oscar Lampard across the interview desk. Donovan looked for any signs, any body language that would give a clue as to whether Lampard was telling the truth or even uncomfortable with his responses. Lampard held Donovan's gaze equally, a look of defiance lingering behind his eyes, his arms folded as he sat back in the chair, his ankle casually hooked over his opposite knee. He toyed with a brown asthma inhaler, turning it up one way and then the other. So far Donovan hadn't managed to get Lampard to so much as break into a sweat. He doubted very much the inhaler was going to be needed.

'So, how am I doing, Doc?' said Lampard. 'Have I passed?'

'Passed?' Donovan raised his eyebrows in question.

'Yeah, passed your tests, like. Have I answered all your questions properly or have I let slip something that can tell you all about me?' said Lampard beginning to look as though he was enjoying himself. 'Have you been able to work out if I'm some psycho nutter who had a poor relationship with his mother? Did my mother dress me up as a girl and, as a result, I hate women, which means I attacked my neighbour. That's how it goes, doesn't it?'

Gut instinct played a big part in Donovan's work. Today his gut was shouting loud and clear. Oscar Lampard had something to hide but was he hiding the attempted murder of his neighbour Stella Harris? Time to play hardball.

'You've got the general idea,' said Donovan. 'However, I'd probably go down the route of what was your first sexual encounter like? Was it with a girl or a boy?' Donovan paused looking for a reaction. Yep, there it was. Subtle but it was there. Lampard's face remained impassive but the inhaler was now clenched in a firm grip, no longer being casually worked up and down on his knee. Donovan continued. 'A member of your family even. Or one of your mum's special friends, you know, an uncle who's not really an uncle.'

Lampard was clearly fighting to prevent his smile turning to a sneer. 'Maggie Harting. Behind the youth club. I was fourteen she was fifteen. Big tits. In fact, big everything. She wasn't shy about putting it out.'

'Too big for you?' said Donovan. He continued without giving Lampard a chance to voice his obvious displeasure at the innuendo. 'Did she have a laugh at your expense afterwards? Tell everyone what a little boy you really were?'

The sneer broke free and Lampard leaned forward in his chair. 'Piss. Off.'

Donovan didn't flinch. 'All the other kids laughed at you after that, I expect. You were the spotty, lanky kid who none of the girls fancied and you only got a chance with Maggie because, as you said yourself, she wasn't shy putting it out. Kind of backfired didn't it? Instead of the girls thinking you're some sort of hotshot, turns out Oscar Lampard is, in fact, a let-down.'

Lampard sat back in his chair, apparently in control again. He waved a dismissive hand in Donovan's direction. 'Whatever you say, Doc.'

Donovan flicked open the file in front of him. He didn't really need to look at it but he wanted to give Lampard a few moments to let what had been said settle in his mind.

'So, Oscar, it's all right if I call you that, isn't it?' Oscar shrugged. Donovan continued. 'Stella Harris, the girl who was attacked. You told my colleagues that you were on first-name terms with her and chatted when your paths crossed, but that was about it.'

'Yeah and what of it?'

'Fancy her, did you? She's quite a looker, well she was, before her face became a punch bag. Lovely blonde hair, pretty delicate features, great figure. Come on, you must have fancied her.'

'She's pretty. So what? Doesn't mean I attacked her,' said Lampard. He put his leg down and shuffled in his seat. 'She's stuck-up anyway. Not my type.'

'Snotty bitch, eh, Oscar? Is that what you thought? Prissy cow. Marching in and out of the flat like Lady Muck, parading around in her short skirts and high heels. Flashing her thighs. I bet she was asking for it really.'

Lampard thumped his hand down on the table, the plastic inhaler clashing with the Formica. He jumped to his feet. Donovan matched his action and the two men leaned across the desk, their faces inches apart.

The police officer, who had been patiently standing by the door observing, took a step towards them, ordering Lampard to sit back down. He cast Donovan a disapproving look. Donovan cursed under his breath. He was just about to move in for the killer blow in his verbal assault. Lampard was on the brink of cracking, then the sodding PC had taken it upon himself to act as a referee. Brilliant.

Oscar Lampard was sitting back down. Composed. Calm. In control. He slid the inhaler into his pocket and in an angelic-like way, brought his hands together on his lap. Donovan took his seat, throwing the PC a scowl as he did so. He'd have a word with DCI Ken Froames later to make sure this plod wasn't in on future interviews. A rookie who didn't know Donovan's style. He turned his attention back to Lampard, who appeared relaxed, a smile settling on his face. Lampard leaned in and gestured with his hand for Donovan to move forward. Donovan obliged.

'You're going to be sorry you messed with me,' he muttered quietly so only Donovan could hear.

Donovan remained unruffled. It wasn't the first time he had been threatened in this line of work. It held no fear for him. It was all talk. However, sensing he had lost this particular battle, but certainly not the war, Donovan stood up. A coffee was definitely needed. He was sure Lampard was guilty. He matched the profile but without any hard evidence from the police, it wasn't enough to charge him.

'Oi, Doc,' said Lampard as Donovan reached the interview room door. 'Watch your back now. It's dangerous out there.'

Chapter Eight

With the laptop charged, Ellen sat propped up against the head-rest of her bed. She logged onto the email account she and Kate had set up. One message in the draft box. Ellen clicked it open.

Hi lovely

Just wishing you good luck in your new job. So glad you're back in the UK now. When things have settled down for you, we will have to meet up. Sussex is only a train ride away. I've got some post to send off today so you should get it tomorrow or the day after. I think it's only bank stuff.

There is one thing. Toby. Don't be alarmed, everything is okay. He called by the other day and left a card and present for you. I told him I didn't know where you were and he seemed to accept it. What do you want me to do with the gift?

Right, I must go and get ready. It's Patrick's 13th birthday today and we are all going out for a family tea. Thanks for his card and the money, he was delighted with it. I can't believe my little brother is a teenager now! Hormones, testosterone – ew!

Love, hugs and kisses.

xx

Ellen smiled at the thought of Kate's little brother becoming a hormonal teenager. Patrick, a rather late addition to the Gibson family, was doted upon and thoroughly spoilt by everyone. A small chord of homesickness plucked at her. She wished she could be there.

Deleting the email from the draft box, Ellen began a new one.

Hello yourself!

I can't believe it either, little baby Patrick is 13 already – wow! Wish him happy birthday from me. Glad the card got there safely. By the time you read this, you will have already been out for his birthday. Hope you all had a lovely time and I'm really sorry I couldn't be there.

As for Toby and his card/present – do with it what you like. I don't want it at all. I hope he was okay when he called round and didn't give you any trouble. It goes without saying, don't trust him, you know what he's like.

Everything is good here. My boss, Donovan, seems really nice, his daughter Izzy is lovely, so sweet. The PA on the other hand – can't say I'm won over yet, but it's early days. It's great being by the sea. I am glad to be back in the UK. We will definitely catch up soon. Give me a few weeks and we will sort something out.

Love, hugs and kisses coming back your way.

Xx

Ignoring the frostiness from Carla, Ellen soon began to feel comfortable and at ease in the Donovan household. Despite her reluctance at the word *routine*, she had to acknowledge, she had settled into a regular pattern of getting Izzy ready for school and driving her in before taking a stroll along the seafront or around the village and then returning to the house. There wasn't a great deal to do while Izzy was at school and once the playroom was clean and tidy, she had time on her hands. In recent days, Ellen had found herself in the kitchen with Mrs Holloway, helping to prepare the tea. Again, this was despite her statement that she wasn't there to do domestic duties. Ellen liked Mrs Holloway and from chatting to the older woman she had learnt more about the Donovan family.

'Mrs Donovan, oh she was a right one,' said Mrs Holloway, as Ellen helped her peel the potatoes. 'Liked a tipple or two, I can tell you.'

'Don't we all?' said Ellen with a smile.

Mrs Holloway put down the potato peeler. She eyed Ellen. 'That's as may be, but not quite to the extent that Mrs D drank. It caused no end of problems between her and the boss. He hated her drinking. She used to get legless. Many a time, he'd have to put her to bed and cancel guests at the last minute or worse still, sit through the whole meal while herself was upstairs in a drunken slumber.'

'How awful,' said Ellen. 'Couldn't she get any help for her drinking?'

'Didn't want none.' It was said with disdain. Mrs Holloway picked up the peeler and began stripping another potato. 'It all came to a head one day when Mrs D insisted on driving up to the school to collect Izzy. Been on the G&T all afternoon. Luckily, the class teacher had the sense to call Donovan. Apparently, he got up there with Carla just as Mrs D was bundling Izzy into the car. Had every intention of driving off in that state. The teacher had tried to stall for time but Mrs D had got fed up. Dread to think what would have happened if Donovan hadn't got there when he did.'

'Oh, my God, that's terrible,' said Ellen, genuinely shocked at the thought.

'The next day, Donovan had Mrs D checked into a private clinic, changed the locks and applied for sole custody of Izzy.'

'I suppose Mrs Donovan couldn't object, not after what had happened.'

'Oh good God, no. Best thing for the poor child too. Not wishing to speak out of turn, but that Mrs D isn't fit to be a mother.'

'Is she still like it?'

42

Mrs Holloway shrugged as she dropped a halved potato into the pot of water. 'Says she's not. She got herself sorted and then ran off to Paris with some French bloke. More fool him.'

'I've yet to have the pleasure of meeting her,' said Ellen.

'Don't rush yourself on that score.' Mrs Holloway lifted the saucepan of potatoes over to the hob. 'Now, a little birdy tells me it's your birthday tomorrow.'

'I didn't realise anyone knew,' said Ellen in surprise.

'That will be Carla for you. She's extremely organised. Nothing gets past her.'

'I'm not sure she would worry about my birthday.'

'She wouldn't want to let Donovan down. He's been very good to her,' said Mrs Holloway, turning to look at Ellen. 'Besides, she's not that bad really. Her bark is worse than her bite. Right, clear those peelings away for me and I'll show you how to make puff pastry.'

The next morning, Ellen was practically dragged downstairs by Izzy and was greeted in the kitchen by the rest of the household singing *Happy Birthday*. Even Carla appeared to join in.

'Thank you,' said Ellen, a smile stretching across her face. 'What a lovely way to start the day.'

'We've bought you presents,' said Izzy excitedly. She grabbed a beautifully wrapped pink box from the table. 'It's chocolates.'

'Izzy!' chorused Donovan, Carla and Mrs Holloway.

'What?' said Izzy looking round.

'You're supposed to wait for Ellen to open the present herself otherwise there's no surprise.' Donovan gave a laugh and turned to Ellen, mouthing *sorry* across the top of Izzy.

'It's fine,' said Ellen. She bent down to Izzy, who was looking embarrassed. 'Hey, want to help me unwrap these lovely chocolates then?' Awkward moment over.

'Happy birthday,' said Mrs Holloway, taking a chocolate from the box Ellen offered round. 'Don't mind if I do.'

'Not for me, thank you,' said Carla. 'Too early in the day. Oh, and happy birthday.'

'Donovan?' Ellen held the box towards her boss.

'Well, seeing as it's your birthday.' He took a chocolate and then slipped it to Izzy with a wink and a stage whisper. 'Don't let Ellen see I've given you another chocolate.'

'Are you going to give Ellen the other present?' said Izzy as she stuffed the second chocolate into her mouth. 'You know the …'

'No! Don't say anything. Remember, it's a surprise.' Donovan pressed his finger to his daughter's mouth. 'You concentrate on eating.' He picked up another beautifully wrapped box and held it out to Ellen. 'This is from all of us. Happy birthday.' He stepped forward and leant in, kissing her on the cheek.

Ellen hoped she hadn't blushed as much as she felt she probably had; her face definitely warm. 'Thank you.' She took the box and unwrapped it. 'Oh, I can't believe it. Really, you shouldn't have. I can't accept this. It's too much.'

Donovan held up his hand. 'Shhh…'

'No, really Donovan, it's very generous but I couldn't possibly …'

'You're as bad as Izzy.' Donovan picked up a chocolate and popped it in Ellen's mouth. 'Be quiet, eat your chocolate and enjoy your present. You haven't got a laptop and this is only a small notebook. It's not expensive, but it will do the job for what you need. Now I don't want to hear another word about it.'

Ellen guessed that objecting any further would be futile and might possibly offend. She concentrated on swallowing the chocolate before speaking. 'Thank you. I'm delighted and extremely grateful. It's very kind of you.'

'Right, well I must get off. I've got a very important meeting with the local constabulary this morning.'

'One that might involve eggs and bacon?' said Ellen.

'You've got the idea. A breakfast meeting with the DCI.' He scooped Izzy up and kissed her. 'That's Uncle Ken to you. Now be a good girl, have a lovely day at school and when I get home tonight, we will all have birthday cake!'

It was a touching scene, if you liked that sort of thing. If you didn't know any better you'd think they were one big happy family. He shifted from his spot in the bushes, his legs beginning to get pins and needles where he had stood still for so long observing the early morning birthday celebrations. Time to take his leave. He'd seen enough. His suspicions were confirmed. He now had plans to make. He was going to enjoy himself.

Chapter Nine

'Morning, Ken,' said Donovan, shaking his friend's hand. 'Are we going for a full house today?' Donovan sat down at the table of the café with the DCI. 'The sea looks calm this morning.' He looked out of the window. It was a bright day for October and the sun was warming through the glass nicely where they sat. Donovan could see a lone figure standing on the edge of the seafront promenade. The fact that the man had his hood up and a scarf covering his mouth and nose belied the warmth that Donovan felt. 'Nippy out there though, nevertheless.'

'Yep, summer has definitely gone,' replied Ken following Donovan's gaze. 'Even so, that's a bit over the top.'

'What's that?'

'Hood and scarf.'

'Takes all sorts, I suppose,' said Donovan. 'Ah, here comes the waitress.' After placing their orders, Donovan look out of the window again. A sixth-sense feeling was drawing his eyes away from his companion. Donovan frowned.

'You all right?' asked Ken.

'Mmm, I think so. Probably nothing.' Donovan was talking to himself more than to Ken. The man wrapped in the scarf was still standing there – looking right at the café. At himself and Ken. Donovan turned to Ken. 'Friend of yours, is he?'

'What?'

'That bloke, out there.' Donovan looked again, his eyes locking with the voyeur.

'Nothing to do with me,' said Ken. 'At least I don't think so. Hard to tell.'

The man then raised his arm and made a pistol with his hand, two fingers pointing straight at Donovan and Ken. With his other hand he pretended to cock the gun and fire it, flicking his hand slightly to signify the bang.

'What the ...?' Donovan stood up, his chair scraping noisily on the floor.

The man turned and sprinted off out of sight.

'Sit down, mate,' said Ken. 'No point running after him. Just some bloody idiot. Take no notice.'

'What was that all about?' A rhetorical question.

'Look, here comes our breakfast,' said Ken, flapping his napkin open and laying it across his lap. 'Come on, tuck in.'

Donovan sat back down. The breakfast was a far more tempting option.

'So, any progress on the Stella Harris case? Have you been able to find any evidence against Lampard?' Donovan spoke in a quiet voice. The café wasn't busy but you could never tell who was eavesdropping, albeit unintentionally.

Ken swallowed and putting his cutlery down, dabbed at his mouth with his napkin. 'In a word, no.' He let out a sigh. 'All circumstantial evidence at the moment. We're hoping that Stella Harris regains consciousness and can remember something. It's not looking good, though. Lampard's prints are at the scene; on the door, on the furniture, etc. and her blood is on his clothing, but his explanation for that is that he found her. At the moment we have nothing to suggest otherwise.' Ken shifted in his seat and Donovan sensed his friend wasn't telling him everything.

'What else?' he prompted.

'Lampard's being a bit elusive.'

'Elusive? As in you can't get hold of him?'

'Yes, exactly that. We needed to check something with him yesterday but he wasn't at his home address and he hadn't turned up for work either.'

'So now you have a probable murderer on the loose.'

'The girl's not dead yet,' said Ken. 'We haven't been able to charge him with anything so couldn't arrest him. Asked him to make sure he didn't go anywhere. We're on the lookout for him, naturally.'

'You need to find him fast. He's dangerous.'

'Innocent until proven guilty,' said Ken.

'Bollocks,' said Donovan, picking up his mug of tea. 'You know as well as I do, that bastard attacked Stella Harris. Have you got any leads as to where he might be?'

'We're looking into a few. Just thought I'd give you the heads up.'

Donovan frowned as he recalled his meeting with Lampard. The frown deepened slightly. 'Ah, yes. The "watch your back" threat.' Donovan shrugged. 'I've had them before. It's just bullshit. Comes from low self-esteem. Designed to intimidate others and make the perpetrator feel empowered.' He smiled at his friend, who rolled his eyes. 'Do you want me to continue with a more in-depth analysis?'

'Spare me the psychobabble,' said Ken. 'We've got more serious things to deal with, like a fresh brew.'

'My thoughts exactly.'

After a rather longer breakfast than planned, Ellen was anxious to get Izzy to school. The traffic around Chichester was always heavy and particularly so at school drop-off time.

'Come on, Izzy, time to go,' said Ellen. She adjusted the emerald-green ribbon on Izzy's school hat. 'There, you look beautiful. Bye, Carla! Bye, Mrs Holloway!'

Ellen gave a small shiver as they crunched across the gravel drive to the carport where the little blue Fiesta was parked. Despite the sun being out, there was definitely a chilly autumnal feel in the air today. Izzy skipped on ahead, reaching the car first.

'Ellen!'

'What's up?'

'Come here, look what's on your car.'

Under the windscreen wiper was a single red rose. Ellen lifted the wiper and retrieved the bloom. She looked for a note but there appeared to be none.

'Can I smell it?' said Izzy reaching up to take it.

Ellen handed it to her. 'I don't think it smells of much. I wonder who left it there.' Was it Donovan? It wouldn't be anyone else – she didn't know anyone else. She took the rose back from Izzy and unlocked the vehicle. 'In you get, Izzy. That's it. Sit back and fasten your seat belt. Good girl.' Getting in the car, Ellen placed the rose on the passenger seat. It must be from Donovan. She wasn't quite sure how she felt about that. A rose was something associated with love. Why would Donovan do that?

Ellen switched on the engine and drove out onto the road, her thoughts still very much on the rose. She didn't know Donovan in any great depth, but, somehow, leaving a rose on her car didn't seem his style.

Ellen drove on, turning out of the beach estate and onto the road leading to Chichester. The only logical explanation was that he was testing the water. A good response from her would give him the encouragement to pursue things.

The lights at the end of the village were on red and Ellen drew to a stop, first in the queue. She glanced down at the rose. If she gave a negative response to the gesture, then Donovan could simply deny any knowledge of it and claim he hadn't put it there. It was a clever plan, she decided. He couldn't lose.

The blaring of a car horn made Ellen jump. The lights had turned to green and she was just sitting there. She shoved the car into first gear and jerked forward, kangaroo-hopped and stalled the hatchback in the middle of the set of traffic lights.

'Shit,' muttered Ellen as she started the engine again, trying to ignore more hooting from the car behind. She glanced in the rear-view mirror. Some impatient boy racer sporting a beanie hat and sunglasses.

'You said a naughty word,' Izzy piped up. 'Daddy says it's rude to say shit.'

Oh no, just what Ellen needed; a reprimand from Izzy about swearing, especially when she was struggling to start the blasted car whilst holding up the traffic and incurring the wrath of Boy Racer. 'I'm sorry. I shouldn't have said it. Daddy is right. Come on car! Please … Yes!' Another sudden jerk forwards and they were moving again. Ellen took a deep breath and settled herself. She looked once again in her rear-view mirror.

Great. Boy Racer was now tailgating her. What was his problem? Ellen checked her speed. A steady thirty. Right on the button of the speed limit. Boy Racer could get himself all worked up if he wanted, she on the other hand wouldn't. In fact, she would pull over at the next convenient place and let him pass.

The petrol station a few minutes down the road provided her with this opportunity. Ellen turned onto the forecourt and pulled round past the pumps. She looked over to the road waiting to see Boy Racer go by. He didn't. So where was he? Surely he hadn't needed petrol too? She turned in her seat and looked through the back window. Her heart gave a nervous jump. Boy Racer had pulled his Astra on to the forecourt too and was sitting on the other side of the pumps. She strained to get a better look at him but couldn't make anything out from this far away. Ellen toyed with going over to confront him but dismissed the idea almost immediately.

'What are you looking at?' asked Izzy, trying to twist around on her booster seat to look out of the window.

'Nothing, don't worry. Thought I saw someone I knew.' It was a rubbish excuse but apparently plausible for an eight-year-old. Izzy didn't ask any more questions. Ellen turned back and put the car into first gear. 'Right, we're late as it is, let's get off to school. Your teacher will be wondering where you are.'

The traffic was building up and as Ellen pulled into the stream of cars, she was relieved to note that Boy Racer was still sitting on the forecourt. The rest of the journey to school proved uneventful and Ellen was glad nothing more had come of the incident.

Chapter Ten

'Ellen got a rose on her car,' said Izzy across the kitchen table that evening when they were sitting eating tea.

Ellen wasn't sure whether to be grateful for Izzy's announcement or not. She looked up from her pasta at Donovan. He raised his eyebrows in question. 'A rose? From an admirer?'

Ellen shrugged. 'It didn't have a name on it.' She couldn't read his expression. Perhaps a look of mild surprise. Definitely no form of recognition.

'A secret admirer, then,' he said.

'It was on her car,' said Izzy. 'And, Ellen said a rude word.'

Ellen cringed inwardly and felt her face heat up, she looked apologetically over at Donovan.

'If Ellen said a rude word, then I'm sure it was an accident and she won't say it again,' said Donovan. He met Ellen's eyes. 'Will you Ellen?'

She shook her head in reply wondering exactly how much further she could cringe. At this current moment, it seemed to be a great deal further.

'Another car went beep! Beeeeepppp! BEEEEEPPPP!!!' Izzy's impression of the car horn was effective in changing the course of the conversation, for which Ellen was grateful.

'Okay, okay, I get the idea,' said Donovan good humouredly.

'Why was the car beeping?'

Ellen felt that now was a good time to intervene. 'I stalled the Fiesta at the traffic lights and the other driver got really impatient. Some young boy racer, you know the sort.'

'You can rule him out as your admirer, then,' replied Donovan and gave a chuckle. 'Right, where's this birthday cake? I've been looking forward to a slice all day.'

'Birthday cake! Birthday cake!' chanted Izzy.

Whilst Ellen was relieved that Donovan didn't seem overly concerned about her slip of the tongue, equally, he appeared just as uninterested in the rose. Surely if he had left it there, then he would have said something or at least dropped a hint. However, it was something she would have to consider later as everyone was now demanding her attention to blow out the candles on the cake Mrs Holloway had produced at that moment.

The next few days passed uneventfully and Ellen took the opportunity to do some exploring of the local area, Coronation Park at the top of Sea Lane became her favourite spot. A winding pathway trailed a circuit around the edge of the park, taking in a children's play area, a basketball court and two football pitches. These different areas were separated by shrubs, bushes and trees; Ellen particularly liked the majestic oak tree that stood at a turn in the path.

Sundays were deemed to be Ellen's day off as Donovan liked to have at least one day a week to devote to his daughter. Although Ellen had tended to spend a lot of her free time either pottering around the house or reading in her bedroom, more often than not, she would end up joining in with whatever Donovan and Izzy were doing. Ellen enjoyed being part of the household and they appeared to have accepted her, albeit to varying degrees. Carla was still spiky but Ellen was getting used to that and it was bothering her less and less.

So far the weather had been pleasant but as October rolled on, it was definitely beginning to turn more wintery. Monday morning had greeted them with a blustery wind and a light drizzle. Ellen and Izzy had spent most of the previous day indoors doing jigsaw puzzles and colouring. Donovan had asked Ellen if she could look after Izzy the previous day, despite it being a Sunday, as he needed to complete some urgent reports

'It's not very nice out there today,' said Ellen as she gathered Izzy's book bag and lunch box up. 'You ready? Go and say goodbye to Daddy.'

Right on cue, Donovan came out of his office as he always did to see his daughter before she went to school. Ellen was surprised to see him dressed casually in a pair of jeans and a jumper.

Donovan smiled at her. 'Thought I'd join you two ladies this morning, if that's okay?'

'Yippee!' squealed Izzy. She gave her father a big hug. She had missed Donovan over the last few days, thought Ellen, and judging by the expression on Donovan's face, it was a mutual feeling. It was a warming thought.

'We'll take my car,' said Donovan. 'Come on, let's go.' He scooped Izzy up. 'Bye Carla! Bye Mrs Holloway!'

The journey to school was chatty and laughter-filled. Izzy clearly delighted to have Donovan with them, which was having a contagious effect on Ellen. She dismissed the fact that she might be buoyed by his company herself. No, it was definitely Izzy's enthusiasm.

Surprisingly, Izzy went into school quite happily. Ellen had almost expected her to be reluctant to leave her father but that wasn't the case.

'She enjoyed you taking her today,' said Ellen as they drove out of the school grounds.

'I've been really busy over the last few days and I know I've neglected her a bit,' said Donovan. 'Thanks for stepping in despite the fact that Sundays are supposed to be your own. I really appreciate it.'

'It was no problem. I didn't have anything planned and I enjoy Izzy's company.'

'I won't make a habit of it. If you need any extra time off to see your friends or family, just shout and we can sort something out. Don't want people to think I'm making you work all day, every day.'

Ellen didn't reply. She couldn't exactly say that she wasn't in contact with anyone, except for Kate, and that was only by secret email. Instead, she simply smiled at Donovan, mumbled thanks and turned her attention to the passing scenery.

As they reached Felpham, Ellen realised that instead of turning onto the Sea Lane estate, where Donovan's house was, he had driven into the village itself. He brought the car to a stop near the seafront and cut the engine.

'Come on,' he said hopping out of the vehicle. 'We're going for a walk.'

Ellen looked through the windscreen at the grey clouds stalking the sun across the sky. The drizzle had stopped but it still didn't look very nice out there. From where she was sitting, high up in the four by four, she could see the beach. The sea itself didn't look a dissimilar colour to the sky, only broken now and again by the waves crashing over and turning the caps of the water white.

'You really want to go for a walk on a day like this?' she said, as Donovan paused midway through closing his door.

He grinned. 'Come on, don't be a wimp. It's great walking along the beach on squally days and, besides, it will be practically deserted. Just how I like it.' He pushed his door closed and, looking back through the window, gestured with his head for Ellen to follow.

'I'd sooner be walking along here in my shorts and t-shirt with an ice cream in my hand and the sun blazing down,' Ellen said, as they strode along the seafront against the wind.

'Stop moaning,' said Donovan good-humouredly.

'It's freezing too.'

'What do you expect? You've only got a little fleece on. You really are a townie, aren't you? Nothing like a bit of sea air to clear the lungs, or would you sooner be breathing in exhaust fumes and jostling for pavement space with commuters?'

Ellen could hear the amusement in his voice. He had a point. They walked along the path, Ellen spending most of her time admiring the beautiful gardens of the houses that backed onto the beach. They were all very large and grand, much like Donovan's. As they walked further along, they passed some pretty blue and yellow beach huts. Another five minutes round a small spit in the shoreline and some rather less-attractive beach huts greeted them.

'They don't look very nice,' said Ellen, taking in the dreary grey colour of the wooden huts with peeling paint and broken windows. Pieces of roofing-felt flapped in the wind, hanging down like depressed bunting, where stormy winds had ripped them from their fixings.

Donovan explained that the beach huts were disused and in the pipeline to be demolished. 'More picture-postcard blue and yellow ones will follow in their place,' he said.

'So where exactly are we now?' asked Ellen.

'This is called Old Point,' said Donovan. 'No one comes down here much as it's a bit isolated. You can only access the shoreline from one road that, back in the 1930's, used to service a small holiday camp. You know, *Hi-De-Hi* sort of thing. It finally closed down about twenty years ago.'

'Why hasn't anyone developed it in all that time?' said Ellen, looking beyond the battered wooden huts to where boarded-up rows of chalets stood, alongside larger buildings, which she assumed were once the dining hall, ballroom and entertainment lounge. 'It's a shame to let something that was once so full of life fall into such a neglected and dead state.'

'There's been so many different plans put forward for developing the whole site. It's been the topic of heated public debates. Finally, though, last year plans and funding were agreed and they intend to start work on it next spring. These old beach huts don't really fit in, as you can imagine.'

'You can say that again.'

'Let's go down onto the beach,' said Donovan, steering her in the direction of the pebbles.

The tide was on its way out. Crunching over the stones and shingle, holding on to Donovan's arm for support, Ellen allowed herself to be guided onto the gritty dark-brown sand. Donovan picked up a pebble and skimmed it across the water, the stone bouncing twice before disappearing below the surface. 'Only twice?' remarked Ellen, giving her best unimpressed look.

'I would like to see you do better,' said Donovan, tossing another stone in the palm of his hand. He threw it to her.

Ellen caught it and mirrored his actions, making out she was weighing the stone up, before rubbing it against her sleeve and pretending to spit on it. 'More than two bounces? Easy peasy, lemon squeezy.'

Donovan laughed out loud. 'You sound like Izzy. Again.'

'You won't be laughing in a minute,' said Ellen. She pulled her arm back and, crouching slightly, she flicked the stone out across the water. 'One, two, three! Oh, yes!' Ellen jumped up and clapped her hands together. 'Beat that.' She bent down picked up another pebble and chucked it in Donovan's direction.

Donovan caught the pebble and turned it over in his hand a couple of times, before throwing it underarm into the sea. Ellen could tell by the look on his face the game was over. What had she done wrong? Was he really that bad a loser? Without turning his gaze from the English Channel, he spoke.

'You made me think about Izzy's mother and how different you are. Amanda, my estranged wife, has never been particularly light-hearted or maternal.' He dug his hands into the pockets of his jacket. 'Swap the "n" of maternal for an "I" and that's more like her.'

Ellen did the alphabetical gymnastics. 'Material.'

'Exactly. Much more material. Especially if it comes in the form of alcohol, handbags, shoes or clothes, in that order.'

'Oh, I see,' said Ellen, fully aware of the angst in his voice. 'How long has Amanda been in France?'

'Three years but she's moving back to the UK.'

'Is that not a good thing, though? Won't Izzy be able to see her mother more?'

She watched Donovan's face as he continued to stare at a fixed spot on the horizon. 'No, it's not a good thing. She wants custody of Izzy.' Now he turned to face Ellen. 'And that is going to happen over my dead body.'

Ellen had no doubt that he meant exactly what he said. That it was no idle threat or cliché. She watched as he stomped his way back up the shingle incline, every footstep planting into the stones with purpose.

Sighing to herself that the good mood of the day was broken, Ellen followed him back up to the promenade. She took the hand he extended to hoick her up from the stones and, offering a murmur of gratitude in return, was gifted a small smile. The grouchiness was apparently over. She liked this about him. It didn't seem he sulked for long. Unlike Toby. This turn of thought made her shudder involuntarily. She blinked her eyes slowly and swallowed, to regain her equilibrium. She mustn't think about him. She needed to stay calm and exorcise him and his actions from her mind. She had managed this quite well when she had been abroad, so she could continue it now.

'You all right?' Donovan's concerned voice pierced her thoughts. 'You look very pale. It must be the cold getting to you. You really should invest in a warmer coat.'

Ellen managed a nod. 'Yes, I must.' She was quite happy for him to believe it was the cold sending a shiver down her spine and taking the colour from her face. She realised she was rubbing her right forearm agitatedly, and quickly stuffed her hands in her pockets. Looking out the corner of her eye, she was met by Donovan's gaze. He looked down at her arm and then back at her again without saying a word. His eyes looked right into her own, as if they could read the memories unwillingly forming in her mind. When he stopped walking and turned to face her, Ellen knew what was coming next.

'There's something I need to ask you. I wouldn't normally pry but I have Izzy and her wellbeing to think of. My daughter is my number-one priority. Do you understand?' He paused and Ellen obliged with a small nod. He continued. 'The marks on your arms … what are they from?'

Ellen could feel her breath quicken and a small rush of adrenalin zip to her fingertips. She pulled the zip on her fleece up to the top. 'Psoriasis,' she said.

'You see, the thing is, Ellen, as a psychologist, I'm an expert in body language. That also includes the eyes. Now if a person looks up and to the left, neurophysiology tells us they are accessing visually constructed images. Things that have happened, that they can recall. This tells us they are telling the truth. However, if they look up and to the right before they answer a question, they are activating the creative censors in the brain. They are constructing an image to fit the question. In other words, they are lying.'

'I believe this is a theory rather than a fact. If it was that easy, there would be no need for lawyers. Or criminal psychologists,' said Ellen.

'True, there's a whole lot more to it than just that,' said Donovan. 'Four things happened before you answered me. One. Your eyes shot upwards and to the right. Two. Your breathing quickened. Three. Your face went ever so slightly pink. Four. You fiddled with the zip on your jacket.'

'Thanks for the psychology lesson.'

'That was a very brief introduction. Do you want me to continue? Or would you like to say something?'

'I really don't want to talk about it.' And she really didn't. The story of her scars was not something she had shared with anyone. Ellen felt uncomfortable with his persistence.

'What are they from, Ellen?' He placed his hands on her

shoulders so she couldn't turn away. She had to answer him.

Chapter Eleven

Ellen could feel the shame and anger bubbling up inside her. She fought to control her reaction. One of her pills wouldn't go amiss right now, but she absolutely couldn't take any in front of Donovan. She focused her mind on delivering a calm response.

'I said, I don't want to talk about it. If you're worried about Izzy's safety around me then you have two choices. Either believe me when I say that your daughter is at no risk whatsoever, or if you don't believe me, then sack me.' She felt sick at the thought of being sacked. Where would she go, for God's sake? Who would employ her once they knew she had been fired because her boss thought she was a danger to his child?

Donovan dropped his hands from her shoulders. 'Okay,' he said with a shrug.

Ellen's eyes raced around his face, trying to read the implication of that simple, non-committal response. What the hell did that mean? 'Okay? Okay what? You believe me or I'm sacked?'

Donovan was already walking on towards the car. 'Okay, you're not sacked,' he called back over his shoulder.

Ellen jogged to catch up with him, falling into step at his side. 'So you believe me?'

They reached the Range Rover. Donovan pressed the remote lock and with a blip and a clonk the vehicle unlocked. He opened

Ellen's door for her.

'I didn't say that.' He flicked the door shut behind her and she sat in the passenger seat watching him walk around the front of the car to the driver's side. He got in and fastened his seat belt. 'And before you say anything, if I were you, I'd remember that old saying of quitting while you're ahead.'

With that he started the engine. Conversation ended, it would appear. Although, Ellen suspected that it was more like conversation suspended until further notice. She didn't believe for one moment that Donovan was satisfied with her answer.

Carla was at the door before Donovan had even time to switch off the engine. Ellen could feel the PA's eyes, like laser beams, searing into her.

'There's Carla,' she said, needlessly glancing at Donovan. His eyes turned to the front door.

'So it is.' Then he looked back at Ellen. The smile he flashed at Ellen was followed by a small pat on her knee, which although was the lightest and fleeting of touches, felt as if it had seared through her jeans, heating her skin underneath.

As Ellen got out of the car and followed Donovan up to the door, she found herself wondering what it would be like to feel his hands on her bare skin for real. This thought was quickly dispelled. Donovan was her boss, who was probably merely being friendly. The touch wouldn't have meant anything to him.

The sound of Carla cooing at Donovan broke her reverie.

'Is everything all right, Donovan? I was concerned when you didn't come straight back.'

'We stopped off at the beach for a bit of fresh air. Sorry, Carla, I should have let you know.'

Ellen watched as Donovan smiled engagingly at Carla and apologised winningly. Sweet as it was, Ellen couldn't help wondering why Donovan felt the need to grovel to Carla like that. He was, after all, the boss.

Ellen smiled at Carla as she closed the door behind the trio. A smile that she so didn't mean and she suspected Carla knew it.

'I suppose I'd better get back to the coalface,' said Donovan. 'Thank you for your company this morning. I'll catch you later.'

'Bye,' said Ellen, aware of the feeling of disappointment creeping through her that he would be shut away in his office now for the rest of the day.

Sighing to herself, Ellen went up to her room and plugged the laptop in. It was completely dead, so while she waited for some life to be fed back into it, she decided she needed to do something constructive to keep herself busy.

Izzy's playroom was a good place to start. It could do with brightening up and making into more of a child's room rather than a sterile medical waiting room. White, plain walls, white shutters and matching white furniture made it feel very clinical. What the room needed, no, correction, what Izzy needed, was brighter colours, pictures, posters, pretty curtains, a rug to cheer the room up and make it a place that a young girl would want to spend time in. It all looked very chic as it was now, but it really wasn't any fun. Ellen began to make a note of things she wanted to change. Needing a tape measure, she went downstairs to see if Mrs Holloway had one.

At the foot of the stairs, Ellen noticed a white folded piece of paper on the doormat. She was sure it hadn't been there when they had come in as someone would have noticed it. She picked it up and, seeing no name on it, opened it out.

It took a moment for the black, handwritten words to make any sense but when they did, an uneasy feeling of fear launched itself from somewhere in the pit of her stomach.

SAW YOU AT THE BEACH

Ellen stared at the words. Obviously it was referring to her and Donovan that morning, but who had seen them? Questions raced each other to the front of her mind. Why had this been sent? What

63

was the purpose of this note? Was it a warning of some kind? And exactly who was it meant for – her or Donovan?

The door to the office opened and Donovan appeared in the hallway, his mobile to his ear.

'No, it definitely wasn't me or my secretary. I'm just going to check with the nanny, although she's been with me all morning, so I can't see how it could have been.' He moved the phone away from his mouth. 'Ellen, you didn't ring Izzy's school this morning to make sure she was all right, did you?'

'No,' replied Ellen. She frowned and shrugged. Donovan gave a small nod of acknowledgement and turned his attention back to the caller. Ellen slowly folded the paper back in half and discreetly slid her hand and the note behind her back. She didn't know why, but for some reason she didn't want Donovan to see it, not yet anyway. Not until she had time to think about it. She didn't want him to be any more twitchy about her presence in the house. She needed this job.

'No. It wasn't anyone here, Mrs Hudson. Have you checked with Izzy's mother? Maybe she … Oh, you already have. And it wasn't her either … well, I can't really explain it then … Okay. Thank you. Goodbye.' Donovan ended the call.

'Something wrong?' asked Ellen.

Donovan pursed his lips and then shook his head. 'No. I think the school must have got muddled up with another parent or something. For some reason they thought I had rung to make sure Izzy was okay.'

'But we only left her an hour or so ago.'

'Exactly. And she's fine so I don't really know what all the fuss is.' He turned to go back to his office, then paused, apparently changing his mind, and walked over to Ellen. 'What's that you're hiding?' His voice sounded light-hearted but Ellen got the distinct feeling he wasn't actually joking. Obediently, she held the piece of paper out to him.

'I came down just now and found it on the doormat,' she said.

Donovan opened the paper and read it. His eyes flicked from the paper to Ellen and back again. 'Are you sure there's nothing I should know about you?' His voice matched the deadpan look on his face.

'It might not be for me,' she replied nodding towards the note.

A raise of his dark eyebrows. 'So you think it's for me?'

Ellen shrugged. 'That could be one theory. Maybe one of your clients?'

'True. And what do you think the purpose of it is?'

'I suppose it depends who it's for.'

Donovan appeared to consider this for a moment before folding the paper up again. 'All very odd.' This time he eyes rested on her as if he was studying her; trying to make up his mind about something. After a long moment, he spoke. 'I tell you what, have a little think about things today and come and see me after Izzy's gone to bed. We'll have a chat. There might be something you've forgotten to mention.'

Ellen nodded. She didn't like the cold look in his eyes that perfectly matched the temperature of his voice. She also didn't like the fact that she may have to tell him more than she wanted.

Chapter Twelve

Donovan sat at his desk and looked again at the note he had taken from Ellen. If you could call it a note. He wasn't sure five words constituted a note. What the hell was it all about? Someone was playing games. What with the hoax telephone call to the school and now this, he didn't believe in coincidences. Things happened for a reason.

The sound of his mobile going off and the distinctive tune of the French Marseillaise ringing out told him it was Amanda. Slipping the note into his desk drawer, he answered the call.

'Donovan. I've just had a phone call from Isobel's school. Is everything okay? What's happening? Is there something wrong?' Donovan sat patiently waiting for Amanda to pause for breath. 'The school said Isobel has a new nanny. Is that right? Why haven't you told me about this?'

The pause came.

'One question at a time,' said Donovan. 'Now listen. Izzy is fine. There is nothing to worry about. The school simply got a message muddled up. Yes, Izzy has a new nanny and I was going to tell you about her the next time we spoke.'

'Really?'

He could detect her sarcasm in just that one word, but Donovan took a deep breath and made a conscious effort to retain his civility.

'Yes, really. Her name is Ellen and she's from the agency. Izzy likes her and she seems very nice. She's great with Izzy. It's nice to see the pair of them playing together.'

'It sounds like Isobel is not the only one to like her.'

Donovan chose to ignore this typically barbed Amanda remark. 'Is there anything else? Only I've got a meeting shortly.'

'Text me this girl's number so I have it in case of emergencies. I'll be over next weekend to meet her.'

Amanda finished the call in the same abrupt manner in which she started, leaving Donovan to ponder next weekend's meeting. He'd better give Ellen the heads up as to what to expect from Amanda. Carla was one thing, but Izzy's mother was in a different league. That was assuming he hadn't sacked Ellen by then. It all depended on what she said tonight. She'd only been here a few weeks and she had raised far more questions and concerns than Donovan was comfortable with.

He buzzed through to Carla in the adjoining office.

'Carla, have you got Ellen's CV, please?'

A few minutes later, Carla appeared in his office with a manila file in her hand. She passed it across the desk to him.

'Is anything wrong?' she asked.

'No, no. Nothing at all.' Donovan smiled to reassure his PA. 'Amanda is coming over at the weekend and wants to meet Ellen. I just wanted to get up to date with Ellen's employment history and so on.'

The file told him nothing other than the official line. Ellen was twenty-eight, had worked as a nanny for over nine years, the past seven of those with Cherubs Nanny Agency. She was a qualified nursery nurse. She had been working abroad recently. Came with excellent references. She seemed perfect. That was if you believed in perfect. Donovan didn't.

Ellen had been hoping that Donovan wasn't totally serious about wanting to talk to her that night. However, after sitting through a rather subdued evening meal at the table with him and Izzy, Donovan reminded her of their meeting, as he took Izzy upstairs to read her a story.

'I'll put Izzy to bed tonight and I will see you at about eight thirty in the living room.'

It was less of a request, than an order. Ellen nodded her head and mumbled an *okay*. She gave Izzy a smile and blew her a kiss goodnight.

'I want Ellen to read me a story,' said Izzy.

Ellen glanced at Donovan; his face was expressionless. 'Daddy's going to sort you out tonight. He's going to bath you, read you a story and put you to bed. Now, isn't that nice?'

Izzy shrugged. Ellen suppressed a groan. She didn't want Donovan to feel pushed out by his own daughter. She tried again, remembering Donovan had told her about a late business meeting he had scheduled the following day. 'I'll do it tomorrow night. Promise.'

'Possibly,' said Donovan under his breath. Ellen pretended not to notice. He continued. 'Half eight then, Ellen.' He picked his daughter up and blew a raspberry on the side of her neck. 'Come on, gorgeous, let's get you sorted.' Izzy giggled in delight. Her apparent desire to have Ellen put her to bed was forgotten.

The allotted time came round far too quickly for Ellen's liking. She had decided she would tell Donovan some of the things, but not everything. She would play it by ear and see how much she could get away with not saying. The fact that he was a criminal psychologist could put a bit of a dampener on her plan. She rather suspected he would know far more than she realised.

Going downstairs, she tapped gently on the living-room door, which was slightly ajar.

'Come in.' Donovan was sitting on one of the large pale-blue sofas situated either side of the fireplace. The far wall housed built-in white shelving stocked with books. An array of scatter cushions filled the seating in the bay window and French doors opened onto the side garden. The room was decorated in neutral, pastel tones, creating a calming and airy feeling which, together with the high ceilings, made it seem twice as big as it was. Ellen had only been in here once before, choosing to spend her evenings in her room or the kitchen. She noted with approval the original coving and the ornate ceiling rose. Very tasteful. Although, it was no different to what she would have expected. The rest of the house was exactly the same. Understated, but expensive.

Donovan stood up. 'You didn't have to knock. Please, sit down.' He indicated one of the sofas before making his way over to the cabinet on the right of the oak fireplace. 'Would you like a drink? Gin? Vodka? Wine?'

'A glass of white wine would be nice, thank you,' said Ellen, perching on the edge of the seat. She'd only have one glass, it would take the edge off her nerves but wouldn't loosen her tongue.

Donovan passed Ellen her drink and then sat down opposite her with what looked like a whiskey. He took a mouthful then spoke. 'I've been looking at your CV, Ellen. It's very impressive. Both agencies speak very highly of you.'

'Thank you.' Ellen said, guardedly.

'But, if I'm honest, it doesn't really tell me a lot about you. About Ellen Newman.' He sat forward, resting his arms on his knees, swirling the amber liquid around in the crystal tumbler. He looked at her expectantly.

Ellen shrugged. 'What do you want to know? I grew up in London. Went through college. Got a job…' She stopped as Donovan held up his hand.

'I can see that from your CV.' Again, his steely grey eyes fixed on her. 'Maybe it will be easier if I just ask the questions.'

'Okay.' Why she said okay, when it really wasn't, Ellen didn't know, but it seemed she had no choice.

'What's with the scars on your arms? That's not psoriasis.'

Straight for the jugular. No messing around. Ellen felt her throat dry up and was aware that her breathing was getting heavier.

'Splash marks. Boiling water from a kettle.'

'Wrong. Eyes went to the right, Ellen,' said Donovan. 'I'm very patient and my rules are that I don't have to accept your first answer. Or your second one for that matter. Try again.'

'It's not really any of your business,' said Ellen, not daring to make eye contact in any form. She stared into her wine glass. For a psychologist, he wasn't very subtle. It was a wonder he had any clients.

'That's wrong again. Three strikes and you're out. Did I forget that rule?' He took another sip of his whiskey and then let out a sigh. 'Look Ellen, I don't mean to sound rude and uncaring. In fact, I'm anything but uncaring. I care a great deal. As I've said all along, Izzy is my number-one priority and I can't have her surrounded by people I don't feel one hundred per cent positive about. I really like you and so does Izzy. I want you to stay. Normally, I'm not very tolerant of things like this, but if you let me know a bit more of your background, I will feel happier and can make a better judgement.'

It was Ellen's turn to let out a long sigh. She was in a no-win situation. If she didn't tell him, he'd sack her, and if she did tell him, well, he'd still sack her – probably. Should she gamble? She came to a decision.

'I'm sorry, Donovan, but maybe I should leave. I'm not sure we can work together.' She put her glass on the table. 'I would like to say goodbye to Izzy in the morning, if that's okay with you? I don't want to just abandon her.'

'Before you make any rash decisions, let me reassure you that anything you say to me will go no further than the two of us. I promise.'

Donovan came and sat beside her. He was close. Closer than he needed to be. It felt unnerving, or was it exciting? Ellen couldn't make up her mind. She could feel his eyes trained upon her. She wanted to move away. But she couldn't. She continued her examination of the contents of her wine glass. His hand slid over hers.

Long slender fingers that were as soft as his voice when he spoke.

'Please, think carefully before running away. Eventually, whatever it is you're running from will catch you up. If it hasn't already.'

'I'm not running away from anything,' she managed to croak out, while the word *liar* screamed inside her head.

He inched closer. Their bodies were against each other and Donovan slipped his arm around her shoulders, pulling her into him. Her head resting under the crook of his chin as he ran a strand of her hair through his fingers. The kiss he dropped on top of her head sent a zing right through her body. She could hear his heart beating a steady rhythm, whilst acutely aware hers was all over the place like a scat-fest. Ellen allowed herself the luxury of being held; a haven of safety.

'We all run from something at some point in our lives,' said Donovan, tipping her face up to look at him.

'Even you?' Ellen found it hard to imagine that Donovan would do anything other than meet life head on. She couldn't imagine him running.

'Even me.' There was a momentary flash of vulnerability in his eyes. 'Amanda and her drinking. I ignored it for far too long.'

Ellen understood but any notion of pursuing this thought was wiped away as he kissed her on the mouth with such tenderness, Ellen wasn't sure she had experienced anything like it before. Her body was way ahead of the game as she kissed him back. Her mind, however, had other ideas.

Disentangling herself, Ellen pulled away. 'This isn't right.'

'Who said?'

She shrugged. Despondent. 'Maybe, just not right at this moment.'

He nodded. 'Okay.'

She hated his okay. She couldn't decipher it. Neither could she decipher her own feelings. She needed space. Everything was closing in around her.

'I must go,' said Ellen standing up.

'Don't run, Ellen,' said Donovan.

She took a step back as he rose from the sofa. She had to be strong and not give in. She couldn't let herself become attached to Donovan. She'd done that before with Toby, and look how that had turned out. The thought frightened her.

'I'm sorry. I can't stay. Goodnight, Donovan.' Somehow her legs obeyed her brain and carried her steadily out of the living room and up the two flights of stairs to her bedroom. Locking the door, she rushed to the en-suite and grabbed her wash bag. With no regard for the contents, she tipped everything out into the sink and snatched at the bottle of pills. She could feel the clamminess of her body as a cold bead of perspiration streaked down her spine. Her eyes felt heavy and her head light. Anxiety fought to take hold of her and the walls seemed to be closing in around her. With a herculean effort, she focused on the bottle, tipped several pills out into the palm of her hand. She grappled to get two between her fingers, finally managing to keep hold, as the rest dropped into the sink. She popped them in her mouth and washed them down with a tumbler of water. Just the knowledge that she had taken two of them was enough to begin the calming process.

She caught sight of her reflection in the cabinet mirror. Helen Matthews looked back at her. Tears she had been unaware of were chasing down her face. Ellen couldn't bear to look. She didn't want that person to come back again. Helen was weak. Ellen was strong.

Bowing her head, Ellen rested her hands on the sink and concentrated on making her breathing deep and controlled. Gradually, the haze in her mind cleared and her thoughts became more cohesive.

He was wrong. She could run. She'd done it before and she'd do it again. She had no choice.

Chapter Thirteen

'Damn it!' Donovan slumped back into the sofa. That didn't go well. He hadn't planned to kiss her, it had just kind of happened. And he didn't do just *kind of* anything. Not until now, anyway.

On top of his impulsive action, he had underestimated her fear. Not purely of her past, but fear of her future too. He'd been way off the mark and now she was leaving. He closed his eyes. What the hell was wrong with him? He didn't want Ellen to go. Why, because of Izzy, or for his own reasons? Both, truth be told. Ellen had *trouble* written all over her, yet he felt as though he hadn't had nearly enough of her.

This was no good, thought Donovan, as he slugged back another whiskey. He wasn't known for being passive and just letting things happen. He was a doer. Time to be proactive.

Within a minute, he was outside Ellen's door, waiting for her to answer his knock. He could hear movement from inside the room. He tapped again, this time a bit harder. 'Ellen? It's me, Donovan.' As though he needed to introduce himself. Who else would it be? He felt slightly stupid. 'Ellen. I'm sorry for upsetting you. Could you open the door, please?' He waited patiently and was rewarded by the sound of her footsteps crossing the room and the bolt sliding on the other side of the door. She opened it wide enough for him not to feel like a deranged axe man, but not so wide that she made him feel like Prince Charming and was inviting him in. Her eyes looked red. She'd been crying. He felt guilty, despite suspecting the tears were for the fear she felt, whatever the fear was.

'I'm sorry I upset you,' he repeated. 'I was being very clumsy. I'd like to blame it on a difficult day, if that's all right with you?' He smiled, hoping it would look unassuming and warm.

'Okay, we'll stick with a difficult day excuse.' She returned his smile.

'I've got a busy couple of days coming up. Tomorrow I'm in London, giving evidence in a court case. There's a possibility it may run on and I'll have to be away overnight.'

'So, you'd like me to stay until you get back?'

'Pretty much, yes.' He pursed his lips, taking time to choose the next words carefully. He didn't want to put pressure on her. She needed to feel she was in control and making her own decisions. 'Maybe you could reconsider leaving? Not now, but while I'm away. We could chat when I get back. Both Izzy and I would really miss you if you left. But, if you're intent on leaving, I'll do everything I can so you are safe.'

Despite the dim lighting of the table lamp in her room, he could see tears threatening to tip the rims of her eyes. She swallowed hard and blinked them back before speaking.

'Okay, I'll think about it.'

He wasn't entirely convinced but he'd have to accept it for now. He kissed his first two fingers and then pressed them briefly to her mouth.

She caught his hand and held it to her face. Closing her eyes, a stray tear cascaded down her cheek and mingled with their entwined fingers. Stepping forwards, he instinctively wrapped her in his arms, holding her close and breathing in the coconut scent of her hair. He could feel her body sink into his and for a moment he felt as if he had soaked up all her fears and anxieties. She needed to trust him. Not just him, but herself as well. There was definitely

74

a feeling between them but she was scared. He knew he needed to exercise patience. Some things were easier said than done, though.

'Hey, it's okay,' Donovan whispered into her hair. He kissed the top of her head and pulled away slightly so he could see her face. He moved the strand of her hair that had fallen across her eye. The watery eyes that met his own made his stomach flip. He felt he could read them like a book as they skipped between fear, shyness and desire. He smiled what he hoped was reassurance. 'Listen to me, Ellen,' he began, 'Don't panic. No knee-jerk reactions. No running. Promise?'

She appeared to consider for a few seconds. A small smile accompanied the nod of her head. 'Okay, I promise.'

'Good. I'll be back in a day or two and we can talk then,' he said. 'You've nothing to be frightened of. You're safe here.'

Christ, he hoped he was right.

Ellen sat down in the kitchen with a cup of tea. Mrs Holloway was having a day off and Izzy was at school. Other than Carla, who had tucked herself away in her office all day, Ellen was alone with the house. Ellen looked at the photograph on the kitchen windowsill of Donovan and Izzy, both standing proudly beside a snowman they had built. It was probably only last year, mused Ellen, Izzy didn't look much younger than she did now. Her eyes rested on Donovan. He was due back that evening. She was looking forward to seeing him; somehow, the house wasn't the same without him. The last few days had given her time to calm down and to think rationally. He had been right; her reaction the other night had been knee jerk. The need to flee had been quelled by his reassuring words, which had twirled around in Ellen's head time and time again. Nearly as often as the memory of his body close to hers, his arms, his hands and the sweet sensation of his kisses, albeit the latter only briefly. The desire to trust him, to believe him was so strong, but it was rather ironic that it was this very strength that was frightening her. She didn't really know Donovan that well. She had only worked for him for a short time. She thought she had known Toby, but how wrong she had been there and she had paid a high price.

A movement beyond the window somewhere in the garden caught Ellen's attention. She looked down the green lawn, strewn with autumn leaves, which were being gently bowled around by the wind. She was sure she had seen something dart beyond the hydrangea bush. A person? As far as she was aware Donovan didn't have a gardener and, besides, he would have made himself known and there would be signs of someone actually gardening. She stood up and walked over to the bank of full-length glass that separated the outside space from inside. Her eyes scanned the length and breadth of the garden. Nothing. No one.

Ellen was about to go and sit back down when she noticed something on the grass. Something that didn't belong there. Putting her cup on the table, she went out to investigate.

Lying in the middle of the lawn, the blue object stood out against the dead, brown leaves. As Ellen approached it, a sense of foreboding unfurled itself from within her and, despite the thickness of her jumper, she shivered. A rustle from the bushes startled her. Her eyes flicked towards the sound. The hydrangea flower heads were dead now and the leaves were dropping from the plant. Whoever had originally planted the shrubs must have known their stuff for there were also evergreen bushes and plants in the flowerbed ready to fill the space; their green and heavy foliage making it impossible to see through.

She looked the length of the garden. Empty of anybody, not least a gardener. She was letting her imagination get the better of her.

A scrambling sound broke through the rustle of leaves and whistle of the wind. Ellen jumped and let out a yelp. She spun round, trying to locate the sound.

A cat ran along the top of the fence, before leaping into next door's garden.

'Oh, for goodness sake,' sighed Ellen, holding her hand to her fast-beating heart. 'Get a grip of yourself, girl.'

The wind gave an extra whip and the leaves tumbled across the grass. Ellen turned her attention back to the foreign object and walked over to it.

A thin, blue leather collar. She stooped and picked it up. A cat collar. Like the one Scruffs, her cat, had. Scruffs, who she had left with Toby. A small pang of guilt spiked at her. She looked towards the fence where the cat had disappeared. Had it been wearing a collar? It had probably come off, especially if it hadn't been fastened properly. There was a little ID barrel, which Ellen unscrewed. Maybe she could return it to the owner.

After a bit of fiddling, Ellen managed to pluck the tightly rolled piece of paper from the barrel and open it out.

She read the typed words and frowned, putting her finger to her lip in thought. She noticed a sickly sweet smell. She inspected her fingers but they were clean. She brought the note up and sniffed. It stung her nose and she stepped back, a light-headed feeling rushing through her. She took a moment to recover before turning her attention back to the words on the note.

Ding dong bell, Pussy's in the well.

This was weird. This was wrong. Ellen wondered about the strange sickly aroma. Holding her hair back from her face as the wind uncaringly tossed it around, she raised the note and breathed in.

'Urgh.' It was no better second time around. She closed her eyes to try and overcome the head rush and opening them, refocused on her surroundings. It was then she heard a slosh of something slipping into water, swiftly followed by a frantic scratching and splashing noise coming from somewhere to her right. She swung around. The lid of the water butt was resting against the side of the greenhouse. *Ding dong bell, Pussy's in the well.* The words of the note repeated in her mind and slowly her eyes scaled the plastic tub.

She felt slightly giddy, not only from the smell on the tag but from fear. Ellen broke out into a staggering, swaying run, somehow managing to stay on her feet. *Ding dong bell, Pussy's in the well.*

She smashed into the water butt, dropping the collar and note as she put her hands out to break her stumble. The splashing was subsiding. A dark shape flailed in the water. Ellen dove her hand into the water. It touched something furry. Something bony. Not knowing what part of the creature she was grabbing, she tried to catch hold. It turned in the water and she felt sharp claws scratch at her arm through her jumper. The pain made her snatch her hand away.

Her head felt woozy, almost drunken. She refocused her eyes and forced herself to concentrate.

This time she propelled both hands into the water and scooped up the animal. Lifting it out in one swift movement, a wet, bedraggled and distressed cat appeared. It turned and hissed, clearly frightened. Ellen dropped it to the ground before falling to her hands and knees, as the light-headed feeling engulfed her. When she looked up, the cat had gone. She gripped onto the side of the water butt and hauled herself to her feet.

A deluge of fear swamped her. She could feel her heart racing, her breathing becoming shorter. Her pulse was throbbing in her neck and her throat constricted. She recognised the signs. She was having a panic attack. A bad one. She needed to get out of the garden. Away.

Stumbling blindly, she made for the house, staggering through the rose arch that led onto the patio, her jumper catching on the thorns as she struggled to negotiate the iron framework. Everything was swaying in front of her eyes. She felt dizzy. Her limbs felt heavy, as though her feet were encased in concrete blocks.

Her peripheral vision caught sight of someone standing near the fence. She turned her head in what seemed like slow motion. She could hear the blood pumping through her, a *womp, womp, womp* throb, blocking out all other noise. The effort of merely turning her head sapped her strength; it was as if an invisible force was pushing against her every movement. She couldn't focus properly. The figure moved out of her vision. She had no energy to turn to follow it. Ellen wanted to call out but her mouth had ceased taking orders from her brain. Her feet were having a similar problem. She was aware of her foot catching on something and that she was falling. The Italian travertine patio slowly rising to meet her. Or was she on her way down to it? She couldn't decipher the sensation.

Somewhere in the distance, a muffled voice shouted her name. Hands grabbed her and then everything went black.

Chapter Fourteen

Donovan watched Ellen sip the hot, sweet tea Carla had just made. Sitting on the sofa with a blanket around her, Ellen looked pale and drawn. Her jumper, with soaking-wet sleeves, had been discarded as soon as he had carried her in from the garden in a semi-conscious and clearly distressed state.

He glanced at Carla, who was perched next to Ellen, supervising the tea-drinking process. Donovan had arrived home early and wandering through the seemingly empty house from the kitchen had come across Carla in the garden, kneeling beside Ellen.

'So,' he began softly, 'do you know what happened?'

She lowered the cup, resting it on her knees, her hands shaking slightly. Carla took the cup and placed it on the coffee table, where Donovan was now sitting directly opposite Ellen.

'I … er … there was something on the lawn. A cat's collar. I went out to get it.' She pulled the blanket tighter around her, keeping her arms covered. 'I looked at the name tag and it said *Ding dong bell, Pussy's in the well.*'

Donovan exchanged a look with Carla and was then instantly annoyed with himself, as he realised Ellen had caught the exchange. She sat up straighter, a look of indignation on her face. He cut in before she could say anything. 'Go on. What happened next?'

Her demeanour remained defiant, daring him to disbelieve her.

'I heard a splash. I knew it was the water butt. There was a cat in it. I grabbed it. It scratched me. I dropped it and it ran away.'

'And then you fainted,' said Carla.

'It wasn't quite like that. Maybe it was. I don't really know. I felt frightened. Something wasn't right. It was like everything was swaying and I couldn't get my balance. A bit like being on a boat in a rough sea.'

'Like I said, you fainted.'

'I don't know,' repeated Ellen.

'The cat's collar,' said Donovan. 'What happened to that?'

Ellen looked blankly, then at Carla. 'I can't remember. I had it in my hand.' She frowned as if she was thinking hard. 'Yes, I definitely had it. I remember, because it smelt funny. My fingers smelt strange.'

'Strange, in what way?' Donovan wondered if she was getting a bit confused.

'Like a sweet sort of alcohol smell.' She put her fingers to her nose. 'It's gone now. Was the cat okay?'

Donovan looked to Carla for the answer. She shrugged. 'I didn't see any cat. And I didn't notice any collar either. Sorry.'

'I didn't imagine it,' shot back Ellen.

'I'll go and look in the garden,' said Donovan getting up. 'See if I can find the collar.'

'It's all right. I'll go,' said Carla. 'You stay with Ellen.' She raised her eyebrows slightly at him. She clearly felt Ellen was imagining the whole thing. Maybe she was, but somehow it didn't seem Ellen's style and, even if she was, to what end? He nodded to Carla and she left the room, he manoeuvred himself to Ellen's side, putting a comforting arm around her shoulders.

'I didn't imagine it,' said Ellen. Donovan felt her relax slightly as she allowed him to pull her closer. Donovan sat stroking her hair, saying nothing, until Carla came back in.

'I can't see anything out there at all,' she said standing in the doorway.

Ellen sat bolt upright. 'It must be there.'

Carla shook her head. 'Nothing,' she said. She looked directly at Donovan. Another raise of the eyebrows.

'I'm telling the truth.' Ellen's voice was insistent. 'Donovan, look at me. Ask me about the cat. Look at my eyes. Left or right? You'll know if I'm telling the truth.' She was shaking his arm.

'Stop, Ellen. Calm down.' He held her shoulders firmly.

'Do it. Ask me!'

She looked so agitated and desperate. 'Please, Ellen, listen to me,' he said. 'Whatever happened out there has been a nasty shock. I have absolutely no intention of doing the whole eyes to the right, eyes to the left thing. Anyway, like you said, it's only a theory. It doesn't prove anything.'

'I can prove it,' she said, an anxious look sweeping over her face.

'Ellen, please …'

'No. I can.' Her voice was firm. The anxiety replaced by a look of determination. She threw off the blanket and thrust out her right arm. 'Look.'

Donovan's eyes dropped to her arm. Four fresh, angry scratches, about two inches long, graced Ellen skin. These, coupled with the circular scars already on her arm made him inwardly wince.

Carla came over and looked at Ellen's arms. 'Thorns,' she said.

'What?' Donovan wasn't following.

'The roses. Ellen, you fell into the archway just before you fainted. They must be scratches from the thorns.'

Carla didn't mention the scarring, for which Donovan was grateful. Ellen covered her arms back up with the blanket. 'It was the cat,' she mumbled, the conviction from her voice gone.

Carla gave him an apologetic look. 'I'll be in the office if you need me.' She put a hand on Ellen's shoulder. 'And you as well.'

'Thank you, Carla,' he said, aware that the gratitude was more for her gesture towards Ellen. He waited for his PA to leave the room before lifting Ellen's arm out from the blanket. He ran his index finger lightly over the marks.

'What happened, Ellen?' It was almost a whisper.

She looked at him for what felt like an eternity.

'I'm sorry, Donovan. I can't tell you.'

Before he could respond she was standing up, grabbing her wet jumper and heading towards the door.

'Ellen! Wait!' Donovan sprang to his feet, catching the top of her arm in his hand. He went to turn her around but stilled as he saw her flinch, shying away from him. An automatic reaction? One she must have performed many a time and now was her natural response if she was grabbed. He let go of her instantly. She took a good two steps away from him.

'Don't touch me!' It was a shout he hadn't been expecting.

'I wouldn't hurt you. I was merely …,' his words faded away as she ran from the room and up the stairs.

By the time she had reached her room, Ellen knew it was an over-reaction. She had no reason to be frightened of Donovan; he had never given her cause to doubt him once. Things were different. He was different.

What a mess this was turning out to be. She didn't understand what was going on or why. Who would have done that to her earlier? She mulled this over. The logical explanation seemed to be Carla. No one else was in the house this afternoon. Carla had 'found' her. Carla had been out looking for the cat collar and apparently not been able to locate it. This was added to the fact that Carla didn't actually like her. Perhaps this was her way of getting rid of her. But then Carla had been almost kind to her at the end.

Then there was Toby to take into consideration. And, of course, any one of Donovan's mad clients or suspects he'd interviewed.

She buried her face in her hands and rubbed her eyes. Definitely a mess. She felt her emotions swinging one way and then the next. She knew she needed to apologise to him for her overreaction. She splashed some cold water over her eyes and applied a bit of mascara.

Donovan was genuinely relieved to see her reappear about an hour later. He stood up as she came into the room.

'Hey,' she said, offering a small smile. Her voice was soft, no hint of confrontation there now.

'Hey,' he said. 'Come on in.' He put his arm out in a welcoming gesture.

'I'm sorry about earlier. I shouldn't have stormed off like that. It was an overreaction.' She looked up at him from under her eyelashes. Jesus, she looked so lovely when she did that. Her vulnerability somehow mixed in with her desirability oozing from her eyes. He was sure he'd forgive her anything at that moment. He tamped down all those desirable thoughts that were attempting to push their way up from inside him.

'It's okay. I understand. Come and sit down.' Donovan motioned to the sofa. Ellen sat down and he sat himself close to her, taking her hand in his. He stroked the back of her hand with his thumb. It was good to feel her hand close around his own. 'Look, you probably see yourself in a no-win situation. Think of it this way, what have you got to lose? You can't tell me anything that I haven't come across at some point in my career. You won't shock me. You won't offend me. I just want to know so that I have peace of mind.' Somewhere at the back of his mind, a little voice added: '*and to protect you*'. Donovan had no idea where that came from. Another thought to drive down. She still didn't look convinced. One last attempt on his part. 'Why don't we go for a walk and chat?'

Neutral ground might make her feel less defensive with other things around them to focus on. Sitting side by side in the living room was perhaps a bit too intense for her.

'What about Izzy?'

He was touched that Izzy was her first concern. 'Don't worry, Carla is still here. I'll ask her if she doesn't mind staying a bit late tonight. She does from time to time.'

He waited, watching Ellen consider the proposition. Her feelings were so transparent at times. She was now in the midst of inner conflict, whether she should accept his offer or not. It was a good sign, thought Donovan. She wasn't dismissing the idea immediately. He allowed her the time to come to a decision.

'Okay, why not?'

Yes. She was agreeing, just as he had hoped.

Chapter Fifteen

'I don't think Carla was too impressed about babysitting,' said Ellen, as they walked through the village towards the local pub.

'She's fine, honestly.'

'For a psychologist, you really have trouble reading the signs sometimes.'

He looked across at her, amusement and irony clearly on her face, despite the darkness of the evening. 'I was trying to make you feel better,' he said.

She laughed at this. No words needed. They both knew Carla was anything but fine. 'I thought maybe she was a bit jealous.'

'Really?'

'Yes, really. Having to share you with someone else, i.e. me.'

Donovan let out a laugh. 'Listen, I do the psychoanalysing around here.'

'Okay, maybe not jealous. What about protective?'

'Let's settle for loyal.'

'Okay. Loyal it is,' said Ellen. ' Although, tonight she was more flustered than anything else. She went off saying something about needing to make a phone call.'

Donovan considered this for a moment. 'Yes, you're right, she did seem agitated, now I think about it.'

'Has she got a partner or husband that she would have to ring about staying late?'

'No. She lives on her own. She's a widow. She's got a brother nearby and her mother.' Donovan paused. There was more to Carla's situation than just that but it wasn't for him to say. Client confidentiality still existed, no matter how long ago the counselling had taken place. However, he was also acutely aware that explaining things in more detail to Ellen might actually help the working relationship between the two women. He decided to expand slightly, without breaking any ethical obligation. 'Carla's had it tough over the years. It's not easy becoming a widow when you've barely been married, especially when you find your soul partner later in life.'

'Oh, that is sad. How did her husband die?'

'A road traffic accident. Carla was driving.' He paused midstride while he considered how much more to reveal. So far he had said nothing that hadn't been widely reported in the local papers at the time. He continued. 'Foreign lorry driver, totally miscalculated the bend. There was absolutely nothing she could do.' He let out a sigh. 'Carla naturally took it badly. I mean, who wouldn't? A widow within ten months of becoming a bride. She felt totally responsible for his death. It's been very difficult for her and continues to be. Anyway, I helped her as much as I could.'

'Counselling? But I expect you can't tell me that. Client confidentiality etc. And she now works for you. Is that you still helping her?'

'She's an excellent PA. I think she helps me more.'

'Very diplomatic.'

'And very true.' He began walking and taking hold of her hand, gave Ellen little option but to follow.

They were now making their way along a very narrow road in the village. It had no footpath and was flanked on either side by high flint walls. Headlights swung round the bend, dazzling them both.

'Jesus!' exclaimed Donovan. The car accelerated, apparently not seeing either of them. He threw himself against Ellen, pushing her hard against the flint wall, shielding her body with his. The car swerved at the last moment but didn't slow down. 'Bloody idiot!' Donovan shouted into the darkness as he moved back from Ellen. He turned to her. 'Are you okay?'

Ellen was rubbing her cheek. 'Yes, I'm fine. I caught my face on the wall.'

'Here, let me see. Donovan placed his hand under her chin and examined her cheek. He couldn't see much without any street light, and took his iPhone from his pocket, switching on the light.

The purr of a car distracted him. He could hear the ticking over of an engine, the vehicle stationary and out of sight, just around the corner behind them. The beam of the headlights crept along the wall, casting a white glow across the road. He looked at Ellen. Her eyes were wide, looking over his shoulder. She'd heard it too.

The engine revved. Once. Twice. Three times. The last time it practically roared, staking its claim as king of the tarmac jungle. Donovan heard the change in the roar of the beast. It had begun stalking its prey. Without wasting a moment more, he grabbed Ellen by the coat sleeve, pushing her forwards, then overtook her, dragging her along. 'Run!'

Donovan looked over his shoulder. Two beams of light illuminated the lane, dazzling him completely. Then the lights went out. He recognised the change in the roar as the clutch was dropped, the lights went onto full beam and the beast burst into life. Donovan heard himself shout to Ellen to run faster. If they could get round this corner…

'Over the wall!' he shouted, as they ran. He was glad Ellen was light on her feet and not stupid enough to stand and question his orders. She hurled herself at the wall and Donovan pushed her backside, rather unceremoniously, tipping her over the low part of the flintwork, straight into a cottage garden. He didn't need to glance back to know that the car was upon them. He threw himself over the wall. Something hit his flailing foot. He didn't know if it was the wall or the car. He didn't care. Landing on top of Ellen was not ideal but they were safe.

He rolled over and jumped up, trying to get a good look at the car. With its lights now switched off, he had no hope of trying to work out what make or model it was. In an instant it was gone. The cottage garden they had landed in was illuminated only by the porch light. There were no signs of life from within. Their encounter had gone unnoticed.

'Are you okay?' he asked, crouching down. Ellen was now in a sitting position. She put her hand on his shoulder and he helped her stand up.

'I think so.' Her voice was shaky at first, then the shakes began to ripple through her body. She was in shock. Donovan drew her to him, squeezing firmly to try and stop the tremors. He rubbed his hand up and down her back and made soothing sounds, not dissimilar to those he'd make to comfort Izzy. It seemed to do the trick and after a minute or two she had regained her composure.

'I'm fine. It shook me up, that's all.' Ellen pulled away from him and wiped a stray tear away with her fingertip. Donovan passed her a tissue from his pocket, one of the benefits of being a single-parent dad. He had learnt to always keep a clean tissue on him.

'Come on, let's get out of this garden, for a start,' he said, guiding her by the elbow towards the little gate. He checked up and down the road, listening carefully. Not a sound. 'Let's go and have a drink at The Fox. I think we both need it.'

They made themselves comfortable in a corner seat of the pub, grateful that for midweek it wasn't too busy. Donovan had his usual whiskey and opted for a strong Bacardi and coke for Ellen. She had stopped shaking but he could see the upset in her eyes. Wait, make that fear. She was frightened.

'Thank you,' she said, taking a small sip of her drink, followed by a larger one. 'I suppose this is where I tell you everything.'

'That's kind of how I thought it would go,' he replied.

Ellen knew there was no getting out of it now. He had saved her life and he deserved an explanation. Especially, as he would now most definitely sack her.

'It's a long story so I'll give you the abridged version,' she said, taking a rather large gulp of her drink. 'Please don't judge me. Or analyse me, for that matter.'

'I won't judge you. Like I said, there's nothing you can say that will shock me. As for analysing, I'll do my best not to.'

She appreciated his smile. 'When you said about running away, you were right. I've run away from my ex-boyfriend. I didn't tell him I was leaving. I hadn't planned when I would do it, yet I had known for some time that I would. It was just a case of timing.' Another gulp of her drink. She realised half of it was gone already. 'I had been with Toby for three years. Lived with him for the past year. Initially, he was great fun to be with. He was the life and soul of the party. Had a good job as a city banker. Lots of friends. Everyone liked him and looked up to him. We did lots of things. Holidays. Parties. Meals out. Weekends away. All that sort of thing.'

'Sounds good,' said Donovan. 'But I'm guessing it didn't stay like that.'

'No, otherwise I wouldn't be here, would I?' Ellen's retort was rather sharper than she'd intended. She checked herself. 'Sorry, that was uncalled for.'

'It's okay.' He smiled again, probably to reassure her, she thought, but she was grateful all the same. Besides, wasn't it part of his job to listen and put people at ease; make them tell him everything while his mind whirled away, analysing, labelling, predicting? Noticing his expectant look, Ellen came back to the story.

'Toby likes everything to be just right. He's a bit of a perfectionist. Doesn't like any surprises or anything that he's not in control of. After a couple of months, I realised that the control issue extended to me. It crept up on me slowly. I even found his, shall we say, proprietorial tendencies, quite flattering. I didn't totally understand him until it was too late. Until he was very much in control, or at least trying to be. One day, I had my hair cut, just a bit shorter and slightly more layered than normal, and he went mad. He didn't like the fact that I had made a decision on my own. I realised then that I wasn't even buying clothes without checking with him first. Everything I did rested upon his approval.'

Ellen stopped and looked down at her glass. Another large gulp. It was practically gone. 'Isn't this the bit where you're supposed to ask me how I felt about that? Or blame it on some childhood issue. Maybe, I was deprived of love by my father and thought that by seeking to please the men in my life I would gain their approval and acceptance.'

Donovan met her gaze. 'You're good. You've seen the TV shows.'

Ellen gave a small laugh. She liked his sense of humour and she liked that he wasn't patronising her, either. Just for that response, he deserved to hear the rest. 'Sometimes he would get irritated if I didn't check with him first on any decision that needed to be taken. He'd suddenly get cross … and … well, he's always been a bit of a hothead when he gets cross, let's just say, he got heavy-handed.'

Ellen was staring back at her glass again. She didn't notice his hand reach across the table but she felt him push up the sleeve of her jumper. His fingertip carried out a dot-to-dot of her scars. She knew what he was asking. The anger and shame churned in her stomach. Not anger with Donovan for asking, but anger with herself for letting it happen. For not getting out sooner. The shame of admitting to someone else what a coward she was. How humiliated Toby had made her feel. A tear brimmed her eye and slid freely down her cheek.

Donovan wiped it away with his thumb, the palm of his hand cupping her face. He left it there for a moment and Ellen felt herself leaning into it, drawing strength from him. As she took a deep breath, his hand moved away, but only as far as her own. He took both her hands in his and held them across the table.

'Didn't anyone say anything? See what he was doing to you?'

'He was very clever. He didn't do anything that could easily be seen. It was always somewhere that I could cover up. The ribs.

The tops of my thighs. My back. Arms.'

'Those marks aren't just from being heavy-handed.'

Ellen closed her eyes in an attempt to hold back more tears that were threatening to race each other down her face. It was a few minutes before she could trust herself to speak.

'The family I was working for at the time had gone to a dinner dance and were late back. The husband gave me a lift home. I didn't think anything of it. It meant I would get back quicker than having to take the bus or try to flag down a taxi. Toby didn't see it like that. He accused me of having an affair with the dad, or at least encouraging him. He decided I needed a permanent reminder not to flirt in future. My arm made a good ashtray. I'm sure he only took up smoking so he could do this.' The tears came now. A cloud burst from her eyes, splashing her cheeks, puddling on the table.

Donovan produced yet another clean tissue from his pocket. 'I'll get some more drinks. Don't go anywhere.'

Ellen was glad of the few minutes reprieve to regain her compose. She was aware that the bartender had thrown a cautious look over in their direction. No doubt he thought they were having a lovers' tiff or something. Having a lovers' tiff … the thought of her and Donovan being lovers made her feel strangely annoyed, yet happy, both at the same time. She shouldn't be even contemplating getting involved with anyone and, if it was anyone other than Donovan, she felt sure the thought wouldn't even be on her radar.

'There you go,' said Donovan, returning with two more drinks and placing them on the table. 'Are you okay?'

'Yes, I'll be fine. Sorry about that. I didn't mean to get upset, but I haven't really spoken to anyone about it. I'm not even sure where all that emotion came from.'

'You've had one hell of a day,' said Donovan. 'It's no wonder you're feeling a bit emotional.' He circled his finger on the table a couple times, before speaking again. 'What about your family? Have you ever spoken to them about what was going on?'

Ellen shook her head. 'I don't have a great relationship with my dad. We speak occasionally, see each other rarely. Christmas and birthdays, his children's birthdays that is. I like to give my half-brother and sisters a little gift. My life wasn't something we talked about in any great depth.'

'Would Toby have tried to contact him to find out where you are?'

Ellen had already considered this. She shook her head again. 'No. He has only met my dad twice and then it wasn't for long. Looking back, I now know that he felt threatened by Dad. He had the potential to be an influence on me. Something out of Toby's control which he didn't like.'

'What about friends? You must have had some friends. Do they know where you are? Have you kept in touch with any of them?'

'Only Kate knows where I am. I've been friends with her for years. She's stood by me even though she can't stand Toby. All my other friends drifted away. He made it difficult for them if they came round to see me and even more difficult for me if I saw them.' She felt so ashamed saying this out loud. 'I used to meet Kate in secret most of the time.'

'Do you think he may have persuaded Kate to tell him where you are?'

'No. She wouldn't. Absolutely not.'

'It's just a thought that's occurred to me as we've been sitting chatting.' Again, there was the placing of hands over hers. 'Do you think it's a plausible idea?'

The warmth of his hands was reassuring. It felt right. She felt comforted. Ellen searched Donovan's face, trying to gauge his true feelings. He didn't look cross with her. And his actions certainly weren't those of a cross man. Was there pity? She didn't want that. No, not pity, maybe empathy. Understanding. Compassion, but not pity. 'A plausible idea? I suppose so. Although I really don't know how he could have found me. Kate wouldn't have told him.'

'Through the agency? Could he have got your address from them?'

'No. He doesn't know I'm working for them.' Ellen felt a little uneasy. This was where she would have to admit her deceit. 'When I realised how controlling he was, I knew I had to escape him but I also knew I couldn't just walk away. He would never have simply let me go. Too much damage to his pride. I planned it months ahead. About a year ago, I told him that I had been offered a new job through another agency. I even went as far as registering with that agency, in case he checked up somehow, but really I stayed with Cherubs. I opened a new bank account without telling him and had my salary paid into that. Then every month I transferred it over to the joint account Toby had insisted we have. I made the payment look like it had come from this other agency so it looked realistic on the bank statements.'

'You went to an awful lot of trouble,' said Donovan.

'It was the only way. I needed to build up some money in my new account and …' Ellen paused. Would he understand the next bit? She wasn't quite sure if she did herself. 'And, somewhere inside of me, I hoped that he would change. That things would get better. I was also frightened. Not only of him but of what the future held. I didn't have the confidence to leave sooner.'

'Low self-esteem. Feelings of insecurity brought on by being constantly told how unworthy you are. A self-fulfilling prophecy.'

'Now you've gone into professional mode,' said Ellen. 'You weren't supposed to do that.'

Donovan leant back and held his hands up. 'Sorry. Guilty as charged.' He smiled at her. 'I do understand and I'm not judging you.'

'But your mind is racing as to Izzy's safety. If Toby has found me and is doing these things, then that makes me a liability.' She might as well say it now. What was the point in pretending that Donovan wanted to know all this simply because he was interested in her welfare? After all, she meant nothing to him, not compared to his daughter. There was no way he'd put Izzy in any danger because an employee, whom he'd known for a short time, was having problems with an ex-boyfriend. Besides, if it was Toby, then she needed to move on. Somewhere else where he couldn't find her. 'It's okay, Donovan. I understand. I'll get my stuff together tonight. If I can say goodbye to Izzy in the morning, I'd appreciate that.'

Chapter Sixteen

Donovan tossed and turned all night. Izzy was, of course, his number-one priority. She always had been and always would be. Fact. Letting Ellen walk out of here to escape from her ex-boyfriend was the most logical thing. But something was tugging at his conscience. Could he really let Ellen walk away when she was clearly in danger? What if something really bad happened to her? He knew from profiling stalkers before, and from counselling them, that most of them were harmless, but Toby, well, Donovan couldn't assess him properly merely on what Ellen had said, but it certainly sounded as though he had narcissistic tendencies. This, coupled with his controlling nature and, ultimately, being rejected by Ellen, all pointed to Toby being dangerous. He was somewhere between the rejected stalker and the predatory stalker. Unless stopped now, things would only get worse for Ellen, no matter where she went. Toby seemed intent upon tracking her down.

Donovan was also aware of the little niggling feeling in his stomach that the thought of Ellen leaving triggered. Reluctantly, he acknowledged this had nothing to do with Ellen being stalked. More to do with the feelings he was surprised he was already developing for her. Maybe, it would be better if she wasn't around. Getting involved with his daughter's nanny was surely a recipe for disaster. No good would come of it. Well, that's the advice he would give to one of his patients. Whether he could take his own advice was another matter.

'Sod it,' he muttered to himself, as he flung the duvet back. He was about to do something he'd probably regret.

This was getting to be lik déjà vu thought Donovan as he stood outside Ellen's bedroom door, waiting for her to answer his knock.

The look on her face when she opened the door told him that she was probably thinking the same.

'Seems we're making a habit of this,' he said, adding a smile to show that he wasn't cross or angry.

'A bit like Groundhog Day,' she said.

'Only not so nice. I'd sooner it was Groundhog Day when something good had happened.'

'Me too.' She looked expectantly at him. Concern settling on her face. 'Is everything all right? Is there something wrong with Izzy?'

Once again, he liked the fact that her first thought was of Izzy and not herself. 'No, it's all right. She's fast asleep.'

The concern didn't move from her face. 'Has something happened? You know … Toby?'

'Everything is fine,' he reassured her. 'Can we talk?'

The concern was replaced by a frown. 'What, now?'

'It's important.'

Ellen opened the door and stood back. 'You'd better come in.'

As Donovan entered the bedroom and closed the door gently behind them, he was fully aware of the warm, cosy feeling to the room, a light scent of Ellen floated around in the air from her bed, the open duvet, the sheet rumpled where she had been lying just a few moments earlier.

'What's so important?' she asked, as she walked over to her bed and folded the duvet down, concealing the intimacy of the room. She turned and stood facing him across the blue rug spread out over the floorboards. A physical divide. You stay your side and I'll stay mine. He read the signals.

'I don't want you to leave in the morning. I wanted to tell you

97

before you got up and spoke to Izzy.'

'What? After the note, the car, the cat and what I told you last night, you want me to stay?' She laughed. 'You should see a shrink. You must be mad.'

He grinned at her comment. 'I've been thinking for hours about it all. You don't know for sure it is Toby. It could be a coincidence.' Why the hell was he saying that? He knew he didn't believe in coincidences. However, Ellen didn't know that, and he wanted more than anything to convince her to stay. 'We should report it to the police. They won't do anything as there's no hard evidence, but it won't hurt to make an official report so it's on record.'

'I'm not making a statement to the police.'

'You sound pretty adamant about that.'

'That's because I am.' She tilted her chin up as if to reaffirm her words. 'I don't want to be connected with Toby in any way, shape or form.'

'It will all be treated confidentially. You really don't have anything to fear.'

'You make a statement if you want but I'm not. Sorry.' Her voice betrayed her words. She wasn't sorry, she was determined.

Donovan assessed the situation for a moment before he spoke.

'In that case, we will have to be on our guard. Take extra care. I'll do the school run with you every day. You be vigilant and we will just see what happens,' he said with rather more confidence than he felt. 'I'll have a word with Ken, you know my friend who's the DCI at the local police station. All off the record so don't worry, I won't mention any names. For my own peace of mind, I want to have at least spoken to Ken about it.' He also had in mind that he'd ask Ken to get an officer to pay a visit to Toby but he'd keep that to himself for now, he didn't want to make Ellen any more anxious.

'Why?'

'Why, what?'

'Why are you willing to put yourselves in danger just for me?'

'Because Izzy really likes you. She's taken to you and she would be upset if you went.' As would he, but he'd keep that to himself as well. 'Also, because I think if there is anything to this, you are putting yourself in more danger. You can't run away from him forever. You need to confront this. To bring it to a head. Deal with it. Sort it. And then you can live the rest of your life freely. You don't want to be looking over your shoulder forever?'

She appeared to reflect on what he said. 'Okay. I'll stay. For Izzy but only if you are sure.'

'Absolutely.' He took a step forward on to the rug but then stopped himself. Much as his desire to find out what was beneath her dressing gown, he knew this was not the time. To take advantage of her when she was vulnerable and afraid would be a bad move. A very bad move.

As if sensing his intentions, Ellen moved towards the window, pulling up the roller blind to let the pinky-red dawn sky fill the room. She spoke without turning. 'Of course, it may not even be Toby.'

'No, this is true,' agreed Donovan, glad for a second that she had moved, but kicking himself for not being able to avert his eyes from her. 'What's your other theory?'

'It could be one of your clients.' She turned and faced him now. 'Or some criminal you helped convict and who is now seeking revenge.'

'A bit TV cop show, but true,' he replied, although he had to admit it was a valid suggestion. 'Another reason for you not to make any rash decisions and leave.'

'It's okay, you've already persuaded me to stay.' She turned and smiled at him. 'You win.'

'Naturally,' he said. He returned the smile before taking his leave.

As Donovan made his way back to his bedroom, he was very aware of the feeling of satisfaction that he had achieved his mission. Ellen wasn't leaving.

He looked furtively over his shoulder, checking he wasn't being followed. Things so far had been easy and low-risk. Now, however, he was moving up a gear. He rapped on the door and waited as he had been instructed to. The back door in the side street opened an inch.

'Yeah?'

It was the sort of greeting he expected. 'I've come to see Danny.'

'Ain't no Danny here.'

'He's expecting me. We've got a business transaction to carry out. I've come to purchase some iron.'

'Who sent you?'

'Micky Thomas.'

The door closed and he listened to numerous chains being set free before he was let in. It was dark inside and smelt of weed. A haze of smoke drifted down the hallway. He followed the door keeper towards the room at the back of the flat. A small orange light filtered across the room. Danny sat on the sofa, a joint in one hand and a beer in the other. His eyes assessed the guest, who shifted uncomfortably on his feet.

'So, you've come for some ironware. Micky said you were good for the deal. Let's see your money.'

'I want to see the merchandise first.'

Danny nodded and reached down over the side of the sofa. He retrieved a shoebox and slid it across the coffee table. 'Untraceable. The serial number's been filed off.'

He pulled the box closer to him, took the lid off and removed the cloth. The handgun was heavy in his hand. Moving the butt to his palm, he closed his hand around it, his forefinger taking position against the trigger.

For a moment he let his mind wander as to what he was going to do with it. A smile seeped across his face.

'Afternoon, mate.' Ken's northern tones greeted Donovan as he answered his mobile.

'All right?' Donovan replaced his coffee cup on his desk.

'Just keeping you in the loop. Stella Harris regained consciousness yesterday.'

'How is she?'

'Groggy. One of my team went to see her this afternoon,' said Ken. 'She can't remember a thing about the attack.'

'Shit.'

'Shit, indeed.' Donovan heard his friend exhale, before continuing. 'Short-term memory loss. Not uncommon with head injuries. There's every possibility she will start to remember bits and pieces as she recovers, but the hospital can't put a timescale on it.'

'Any news on Lampard?'

'I was just coming to him. Yes, he's turned up. Been at his brother's at Petworth. Apparently he lost his phone when they were out mountain-biking. That's why we haven't been able to get hold of him.'

'You've been able to verify all this, I take it.'

'Of course, I haven't made it to DCI without reason. Checked with his brother and with the phone company.'

'Sorry, Ken. Wasn't questioning your thoroughness. Just clarifying for my own benefit.'

'I know.' Ken gave another sigh. 'I also know you're convinced he's behind the attack and I'm inclined to agree, however, we've got no evidence.'

'Something doesn't sit right,' muttered Donovan.

'Hopefully Stella Harris will start to remember a few details,' said Ken.

Donovan didn't think Ken sounded particularly hopeful, the frustration clear in his friend's voice. He ended the call and sat back in his chair, going over their conversation again. The nagging feeling in his gut remained. What the hell was bothering him?

Chapter Seventeen

Ellen found herself beginning to relax a bit more again as the days passed by. The car incident she could pass off as 'one of those things' but the note still bothered her. She had mentioned it again to Donovan but he seemed unconcerned, telling her to forget about it.

Ellen looked at her watch. It was now ten o'clock and Amanda was late. She was supposed to be here an hour earlier. The sound of the doorbell ringing; an insistent and persistent buzz told Ellen that it was probably Amanda now.

Ellen heard a high-pitched trill of a woman's voice calling out Izzy's name.

'Mummy!' Izzy jumped to her feet, a look of excitement and surprise on her little face. She looked at Ellen as if seeking confirmation.

'I think it is,' said Ellen, although she had no idea what Amanda sounded like, she guessed it couldn't be anyone else. She held out her hand and beckoned to Izzy. 'Come on, let's go and find her.' Izzy practically ran out of the room. Fearing she'd stumble on the stairs in her rush to greet her mother, Ellen caught hold of Izzy's hand. 'Mind how you go.'

Izzy took the stairs at almost a run and, leaning over the bannister at the first floor, shrieked with excitement. 'Mummy!

Mummy!' She dragged on Ellen's hand to get down the stairs quicker.

'Darling,' said Amanda holding her arms wide. It took only seconds to get down the stairs but she looked impatiently at Ellen. 'Let the child go. Can't you tell she wants to see me?'

Ellen thought about protesting that she wasn't holding Izzy back for any reason other than her safety, but thought better of it. Why make an enemy out of Amanda? Letting go of Izzy's hand, she slowed her descent so as not to intrude on the mother and daughter reunion.

Ellen stood rather awkwardly at the foot of the stairs. The embrace seemed to be going on for rather a long time, drawn out by Amanda. Izzy attempted to wriggle free from the bear hug she was enveloped in, but her mother clearly had other ideas. Ellen looked over at Carla, who was standing patiently to one side in the hallway. The two women exchanged a look. Carla raised her eyebrows but so subtly that Ellen couldn't decipher their meaning. She looked back at Izzy as she continued to be squeezed, held at arm's length, looked over, kissed and hugged again by her rather enthusiastic mother.

Ellen shifted her weight from one foot to the other, wishing Donovan would hurry up. As if her prayers were answered, the door to the office opened and he appeared in the hall.

'Hello, Amanda,' he said politely, with little warmth. Amanda stopped cuddling her daughter and responded accordingly.

'Hello, Donovan. How are you?'

He ignored the enquiry of his wellbeing. 'Ellen, this is Amanda, Izzy's mother, as I'm sure you've gathered,' he said. There was a coldness in his eyes that Ellen hadn't seen before. 'Amanda, this is Ellen Newman.'

Ellen held out her hand. 'Pleased to meet you.' She didn't really know how to address the woman and thought for a moment that Amanda was going to snub the handshake. She seemed to study Ellen's hand for an uncomfortable few seconds before taking it and shaking it briefly.

'Hello. You're not as young as I thought you might be,' she said.

Ellen wasn't quite sure if this was a good thing or a bad thing, so decided not to comment and smiled banally instead. Amanda continued. 'However, it seems that Donovan likes you and so does Isobel, so that is a good thing. Perhaps we could talk in the living room. Donovan, where are your manners?' She shrugged her peacock-blue coat from her shoulders which Donovan took without being asked, a gesture that had obviously passed between them many a time over their marriage. Donovan hung the long cashmere coat over the hall stand.

Ellen followed Amanda into the living room, glancing at Donovan as he stood back to allow her through the door before him. She bit the corners of her mouth to stop the smile that was trying to break free, as he winked at her; a small private moment between them.

'So, tell me about yourself,' said Amanda, as they sat down on opposite sofas. Donovan sat down on the same one as Ellen. A gesture of solidarity, for which she was grateful. 'Where have you worked before?'

The next hour passed slowly. Amanda was forthright and opinionated, Ellen learnt. However, Ellen stuck to her well-rehearsed story, which Donovan was happy to back up by reassurances that he had spoken with the agency too. Amanda paid a bit too much interest in Ellen's personal life than was necessary but Ellen suspected this might be because she was checking out whether Ellen had any designs on Donovan. A careful line to tread. Even though they were separated and going through a divorce, Ellen didn't want to set Amanda's imagination off and cause any problems for Donovan, or herself, for that matter.

'Well, if that's everything, I suggest we take Izzy out to the park,' said Donovan.

'I'll go and get her ready,' offered Ellen, eager to leave the room. Amanda's mobile phone began to ring. Perfect timing, thought

Ellen as she got up.

'Get your coat as well,' said Amanda, pausing with her mobile in her hand. 'Yes, you, Ellen. I want you to come.'

Donovan followed Ellen out into the hall. 'You don't have to come if you don't want to. I expect Amanda is only saying that so she doesn't have to play with Izzy herself.'

'It's okay. I don't want to upset her. I like playing with Izzy anyway,' Ellen heard herself respond. The last thing she actually wanted to do was to go for a walk with Amanda but she sensed it would probably pay her to keep on the right side of the woman and if it meant playing with Izzy, then it really wasn't a hardship at all.

'Thank you. And don't worry, Amanda won't want to walk very far.'

They walked through the village again. This time, Ellen was aware that Donovan took them the longer way around, bypassing the narrow road where they had nearly been run over. Whether this was a conscious decision or not, she didn't know.

Walking through Coronation Park certainly blew the cobwebs away; the bracing coastal breeze could still be felt, as it whipped their hair around their faces. Izzy found it very funny as she walked along a low wall, keeping her balance from the blustery wind by holding onto Ellen's hand. Donovan and Amanda walked on slightly ahead, apparently in discussion. About what, Ellen didn't know.

'Look at me!' cried Izzy. 'I can hop on the wall too.'

'Oh yes, you are clever,' said Ellen, watching the eight-year-old. She could have sworn there wasn't anybody coming their way, but all of a sudden, Ellen felt herself bang into someone. Her shoulder clashed against the man's shoulder with such force it knocked the air from her lungs. She let out something between a yelp of surprise and a groan of pain. The man was dressed in a black jacket. In the split second that Ellen had time to look at him, she couldn't see his face at all, only the hood, pulled down. 'Oh, I'm sorry ...' she began, thinking she hadn't been looking where

105

she was going. She half expected the man to apologise as well, but suddenly all her senses were prickling like pins and needles, a coldness clutched her windpipe and without warning, the man, still with his head down, raised his right hand and shoved Ellen hard on the shoulder, sending her stumbling backwards.

Ellen tried to let go of Izzy's hand, but Izzy held fast and as Ellen tumbled backwards, the calves of her legs making contact with the low concrete wall, she felt herself lose her balance altogether and fall over the edge. She landed in amongst the winter shrubs and bedding plants of the raised border.

Izzy let out a scream as she, too, ended up in the soil, and by the time Ellen had managed to scramble to her feet, Donovan was stepping over the wall and scooping his daughter up. A little shocked but unhurt, Izzy cried for all of thirty seconds.

'What happened?' demanded Amanda.

Ellen looked back at the man who had pushed her over. His head still bent, he disappeared round the path that threaded its way through the trees and out into the village.

'That man pushed Ellen,' said Izzy.

'What man?' said Donovan, his head whipping from left to right.

'He's gone,' said Ellen. 'Don't worry, it was an accident. He was a bit rude that was all. Neither of us were looking where we were going and bumped into each other.' She forced a smile at the family before her. 'An accident. Come on.'

They began walking, Amanda and Izzy pacified, but Ellen was acutely aware that Donovan was not. He looked at her for a few seconds.

'You sure you're all right?'

'Positive.' Another false smile. She tried to shrug off the uneasy feeling settling around her.

This was so easy, he thought to himself. The whole lot of them were getting jumpy. Exactly what he wanted. At first he thought it would be fun to scare her, but now the others were starting to

106

pick up on it, he was enjoying putting the wind up the lot of them.

It was getting light. Nearly seven in the morning. The household would be stirring soon. He had to wait until now otherwise the foxes or cats might ruin his plans. He wondered if the kid would discover his surprise first. The idea amused him. That would really fuck the shrink up. His daughter distressed and having nightmares – with any luck.

Stealthily he crept across the patio and prepared his surprise for the household. It only took a minute or two. He paused for a moment to admire his handiwork. Made a slight adjustment to it. Yes. It looked good. Just as he had imagined. He pulled the rubber gloves off, careful not to get any of the mess on his hands and stuffed the gloves into a plastic bag.

Scuttling back up the garden, he squeezed himself into the gap between the shed and the fence and crouching down, he pulled the upright wheelbarrow in front of him like a shield. He had made a small hole in the base of the wheelbarrow. A little spyhole from which he could view the back of the house without revealing his position. He could see the back door clearly. He grinned to himself, in anticipation of it being the kid who came out first.

Chapter Eighteen

Ellen clasped her hand over her mouth to muffle the scream. She half succeeded. Her next action was to screen the sight from Izzy. She spun round and bundled the bemused child back into the kitchen.

'What made you scream?' asked Izzy.

Ellen shut the door and forced an exaggerated eye-rolling movement. 'Silly Ellen. There's something on the patio that made me jump.' She shuffled Izzy down the passageway, back towards the kitchen. 'I'll tell you what, Mrs Holloway will sort you out some milk and cookies. Then we'll get you ready. Mummy is coming to take you out today.'

'I thought we were going on the trampoline?'

'We'll go on it when you get back. I promise,' said Ellen. 'Come on, it's home-made chocolate chip cookies.'

Mrs Holloway looked up from the kitchen table she was setting. 'It's a bit early for cookies, I'm not sure your father would approve,' she began, but then catching sight of Ellen shaking her head, must have realised something was up and added, 'but I don't think it will hurt this once.' Mrs Holloway looked questioningly over at Ellen who mouthed 'in a minute' to the older woman. Once Izzy was seated at the breakfast bar with her milk and cookies and the kitchen TV had tuned into a cartoon channel, Ellen and Mrs

Holloway went down the passageway to the back door.

'There are two dead rats on the patio,' said Ellen, pausing with her hand resting on the doorknob. 'With their insides all over the place.'

'Rats?'

'Sssh, I don't want Izzy to come out.'

'Yes, sorry, of course,' muttered Mrs Holloway in a hushed voice. 'What are two dead rats doing on the patio?'

'You tell me.'

The rats were lying side by side on the edge of the outdoor mat. Mrs Holloway drew a sharp intake of breath at first sight of them before making an *eeeww!* noise. They both peered closer at the grey matted fur, the thick pinky-white tails neatly stretched out. The entrails and other internal parts of the body were also neatly laid out beside each carcass.

'Blasted rodents. And they stink. Looks like a bloody cat has been at them too,' said Mrs Holloway. 'I'll have to tell Donovan to get some poison or something. They've probably come in from the house at the back. It's been empty for years. The builders started work on it recently. Although, can't say they've been there much. They probably disturbed the rats. There will be plenty more, that I can tell you. Bloody rats get everywhere…'

She continued to rant on about a television programme she'd seen and there never being more than six metres between a human and a rat. Ellen had stopped listening. The rats had been put there; she had no doubt about that. Was this connected with the note, the cat in the water butt and the car incident? Surely it couldn't be yet another coincidence.

'Morning, ladies. What's so interesting out there today?' Donovan came down the passageway.

He was wearing a pair of jeans and a black t-shirt, his bare feet making a gentle patter on the tiled floor.

'Rats,' said Mrs Holloway. 'A pair of the buggers. There will be more, you mark my words.'

'Rats?' repeated Donovan. He was looking at Ellen for clarification.

'Dead ones. Two of them, right here,' she replied.

'I'll leave you two to admire the lovely creatures,' said Mrs Holloway, shuffling past her employer. 'I've got food to prepare and they are fair near putting me off.'

Donovan came to stand in the doorway with Ellen. 'What the...?'

'Call it a woman's intuition,' said Ellen, 'but I don't think those two just happened along here and died, laying their innards out neatly in that synchronised way rats are famous for.'

'It begs the questions why and when?' Donovan slipped on his deck shoes, which were by the back door. He stepped out on the patio and walked around the two dead rodents. 'I know you don't want the police involved, but I'm going to have to report this.'

Donovan removed his phone from his pocket and took several pictures of the creatures.

'Why are you taking photos?' asked Ellen.

'Evidence. I doubt the police will send SOCO out. I can't see them dusting for prints, taping off the area and conducting a fingertip search, so I thought I'd keep a few photos.'

'Clouseau,' said Ellen, trying to make light of the situation.

'I like to think of myself more as ...'

'Morse?'

'Well, I was going to say Wallander but my ego has been clearly put in its place.' Donovan cast a forlorn look in Ellen's direction. 'Morse, indeed.'

'Okay, what about we settle on Sherlock Holmes?' Ellen grinned at the even-more-indignant look Donovan gave her. 'Sorry, has that bruised your ego further?'

'Thank you Miss Marple,' retorted Donovan, who then laughed at Ellen's mock look of offence. 'On that basis, I think we will call it a draw. I'll get rid of these.' He nodded towards the dead creatures before heading off to the shed. He reappeared a few minutes later with a shovel and a bucket. 'I'll dispose of them properly later.'

Ellen looked away as the stiff bodies landed in the bottom of the bucket with a thud. She shuddered. Disgusting things. The second shudder that rippled through her was at the thought that someone had deliberately put them there. Something drew her gaze down the length of the garden. The feeling of being watched was intense. A strong gust of wind sent a handful of dead leaves fluttering around the grass and Ellen held her hair from her face as she looked on. It was a damp morning and the garden had a particularly unwelcoming feeling. She didn't like it at all and turning away, she hurried indoors.

Rats disposed of and Izzy out with her mother, Ellen took a cup of tea up to the playroom to sip while she tidied up. She wasn't that surprised when a few minutes later Donovan appeared in the doorway.

'Knock, knock,' he said, tapping on the open door before walking in. 'So then, Miss Marple, any suggestions on who could have left us that delightful present this morning?' He picked up a couple of books from Izzy's bed and restored them to the bookcase.

Ellen shrugged. 'Could be anyone, I suppose.'

'Like Toby?'

'Like a client.'

Donovan perched on the end of the bed. 'I've rung the police and spoken to Ken. As I thought, there's nothing they can really do. Send someone out to take a statement and that's about it. For now, he's just going to make a note of it.'

'My offer still stands,' said Ellen softly, turning to face Donovan. His eyes met hers. 'I'll leave if you really think it's to do with Toby.'

Donovan looked at her for a moment before standing up and walking over to her. He placed his hands on her shoulders. 'Running away won't solve it.'

'But what about Izzy? You said you didn't want to put her in danger.'

'At the moment, I don't see that Izzy is in any danger. Nothing

111

has been directed at her. It seems to be one of us.' He held her gaze. 'Besides, if you were to go now, I'd worry about you. Like I said before, you need to face him. If, indeed, it is Toby.'

Ellen was fully aware of his hands on her shoulders. Strong and firm. Reassuring and safe. She hadn't felt safe for a long time. 'Thank you.' Her voice was almost a whisper and when he pulled her in for a brief but comforting hug, anything else she wanted to say was lost in the fabric of his t-shirt.

A cough from the doorway sent Ellen reeling back from Donovan. She looked round and saw Carla standing there, her cold eyes taking on Antarctic temperatures. Ellen knew she had flushed red, but even the heat from her face was no match for the ice in Carla's eyes.

'There's a phone call for you downstairs, Donovan.' The words came out like the fall of an axe. Sharp and swift.

'Thank you, Carla. I'll be right down,' said Donovan. He spoke to Ellen. 'You look tired. Have a rest this afternoon. Izzy won't be back until late.'

Ellen heard his feet make their way down the hallway before stopping and coming back. She looked up as he poked his head around the doorframe. 'If you go out, be careful.'

Donovan knew he was playing with fire but something about Ellen had caught hold of him and his conscience couldn't let her walk away. She needed to resolve this issue with her past. Only by doing that did she really have a future to look forward to. A future without having to look over her shoulder and without having to be scared. Never having to run away again.

Shit. Who was he trying to kid? That was not the reason he didn't want her to go. He dropped the manila client file he had been looking through onto his desk. It was hard to concentrate. He kept revisiting the feel of her body against his as he had held her earlier when they were upstairs. His hands had taken on a life of their own and had roamed up and down Ellen's back. Meant as a reassuring gesture originally, but concluded as a need to satisfy his desire to touch her. He was grateful when Carla had appeared and Ellen had pulled away first. He wasn't quite sure what would have happened next. Would Ellen have rejected him? Or would she have welcomed him? He seemed to have lost his ability to analyse her as he would a client. Maybe because his own feelings and thoughts were settling in his mind like a mist he couldn't see through.

He picked up the folder again and made an effort to refocus. He was going through his old cases, trying to work out if any of them had reason to hold a grudge against him. Did any of them fit the psychological profile he was building up?

Probably nonpsychotic. Possibly with a pre-existing disorder such as delusions or schizophrenia. He was going through his files, matching the diagnosis, reading the notes, trying to work out the probability of each person being the offender. So far this was quite an extensive list. His work with the police, together with the clients referred to him by the local health authority, were giving him countless possibilities.

He picked up his pen and notebook, writing down more categories. If this person was obsessing over himself or Ellen, then it could be influenced by factors such as anger, hostility, denial, jealousy. A rejected stalker; one that wanted to reverse, correct or avenge a rejection, well, Toby, of course, fitted the remit. Rejected Stalker turning into Predatory Stalker where the victim was spied on so an attack could be planned. This did happen. The thought spiked the sliver of fear that was lurking. It wasn't looking good.

Chapter Nineteen

He followed her along the high street. She was totally unaware he was there. Her mobile phone was stuck to her ear like glue, her heels clicking on the pavement, she headed towards the car park, where he knew she had left her car earlier. He'd been following her since she had left the house that morning. This was the chance he'd been looking for. He needed her to get off the blasted phone. She was at her car now, rummaging in her bag for her keys.

He put his hand in his pocket and pulled out some loose change, pretending to sort through the coins. Looking up, he successfully made eye contact and schooling his face into a winning smile, he approached her.

'I must go now. I'll speak to you later.' He heard her finish her call, her eyes on him.

'Sorry to bother you, but do you have any change for the ticket machine?' he said coming to a stop in front of her.

'No, I don't.' A sharp reply with no return of the smile. She looked down at the coins in his hand. 'Besides, you've plenty there.'

He withdrew his hand, letting the money slide back into his pocket. 'You are, of course, right. It was a stupid and naïve ploy to speak to you.'

'Look, I don't know who you are or what you're playing at but if you don't turn around and walk away now, I'm going to scream blue murder.'

He had no doubt she was telling the truth. He'd seen her in action over the past few weeks when he had been monitoring the house.

'Just listen for one moment. Then if you don't like what I say, I promise I will leave you. It's to do with a certain criminal psychologist and a nanny.'

A little flicker of surprise, or maybe interest, made a fleeting appearance on her face, then quickly disappeared. She neither said anything nor screamed. He took this as consent.

'It would seem we have a mutual interest in the aforementioned. Not so much an interest, more of a problem. I'm sure we can work together to redress the balance.'

She narrowed her eyes but he could see the spark of intrigue there. 'Go on,' she said.

'Shall we discuss this over a coffee in town?'

She looked at her car keys and back at him as she weighed up his suggestion. Then seemingly coming to a decision she opened her shoulder bag and dropped the keys inside.

'Lead the way.'

Amanda seemed to have accepted Ellen being Izzy's new nanny. This was a relief to Donovan. Amanda in the past had been troublesome when it came to nannies. Maybe it was because Izzy was so happy with Ellen. The two had certainly forged a strong bond with each other.

It surprised him, therefore, when he received a call from Amanda towards the end of the following week.

'I've had a chance to look into Ellen's background now,' she said, discarding the need for any small talk. Donovan was happy for it to be so. He always preferred direct talk.

'And?'

'And I don't like what I have found out. Tell me, Donovan, exactly what checks did you make on her?'

Donovan didn't like the tone of his wife's voice. He was all too familiar with the vitriol that was lacing her words. She had knowledge he clearly didn't have. She was at an advantage and he didn't like it. 'All her references checked out fine,' he said.

'Something Carla mentioned troubled me,' said Amanda. 'Apparently, there have been a few strange things happening since Ellen arrived.'

Donovan didn't comment. He was irritated that Carla had spoken to Amanda and even more so that she had divulged information he considered didn't have anything to do with his estranged wife.

'Are you there, Donovan?' Amanda's voice pierced his thoughts.

'Yes, I'm still here. You were saying ...'

'Sebastian hired a private investigator to find out more about Ellen. She changed her name from Helen Matthews to Ellen Newman six months ago. She used to live in London with her boyfriend who, apparently, has filed a missing persons report on his girlfriend Helen Matthews. The description is shoulder-length blonde hair. Five feet, seven inches. Slim build. Hazel eyes. The distinguishing feature is a small tattoo of a dragonfly on her left hip.'

'I wouldn't know anything about the dragonfly,' commented Donovan. Although, he had to admit the idea was attractive. He'd like to inspect that tattoo. In detail.

'So you haven't screwed her yet?' said Amanda. Donovan could almost taste the venom in her words. He didn't reply immediately.

It really was an appealing thought. One he'd like to fulfil. He let a smile form briefly across his face before redressing her catty remark. 'Don't judge everyone by your own standards.'

Ouch. That was probably a bit uncalled for but it was a fact of their relationship that Amanda had slept with her personal trainer, Marco. That was before Sebastian had come on the scene. It pissed Donovan off to think about it because at the time of the Marco incident, he and Amanda had not officially separated. They had the following day, though. Donovan had made sure of that.

The feeling of betrayal, albeit of an already-dead marriage, had only been softened by the satisfying knowledge that Marco wasn't the slightest bit interested in Amanda for anything other than the kudos of sleeping with yet another older and wealthy woman. In fact, Marco's rejection of Amanda had almost evoked a feeling of sympathy towards her from Donovan. Almost.

'You're a bastard,' spat back Amanda.

'You are entitled to your opinion,' replied Donovan. 'Now, about Ellen. As I said before, her references check out fine. There's nothing against the law to say that a person can't change their name. You've seen how much Izzy enjoys Ellen's company and how good Ellen is with our daughter. I really don't think you have anything to worry about.'

'She's hiding something. Why would her boyfriend put in a report saying she is missing?'

'Maybe she doesn't want him to find her. Maybe she wants a new start. What is so wrong with that? Anyway, I thought you were pleased Izzy likes Ellen so much?' Donovan tried to deflect the conversation away to another angle.

'I have changed my mind,' said Amanda. 'I don't like Isobel being so close to Ellen. I don't think it is healthy. I don't like it that dead rats are being put in the garden or that the school is getting phone calls. And you had a note.'

So, Amanda knew about the rats. He'd have to speak to Carla. This was most unlike her. He had never known her to be indiscreet. He would have bet his life that she wouldn't divulge anything.

'I promise you. Everything is fine. There is nothing for you to worry about.'

'Well, I am not taking any chances. I want Isobel to live with me. I am going to apply for sole custody as soon as I can. You will be hearing from my solicitors.'

The line went dead. Donovan looked at his phone for a moment. Amanda sounded serious this time. Shit, he'd been hoping her threat of applying for custody was merely that; a threat, nothing more. It seemed he was wrong.

'Carla!' He shouted from his desk. He was aware it had come out as a bellow. He never bellowed at Carla. Checking himself, he got up to go and find her in the usual polite way. However, Carla appeared in front of him, clearly concerned at the way he had shouted.

'Is everything all right, Donovan?'

He took a deep breath to control his feelings. 'Did you tell Amanda anything about the note that came through the door or the rats on the patio?'

'No, not at all. I would never divulge anything like that.' She looked hurt.

'Someone has told her,' snapped Donovan, not quite managing to keep as good a control of his feelings as he wanted.

'It's certainly not me,' said Carla. 'You should know that you can trust me.'

'It can only be Mrs Holloway then.'

'Or maybe Izzy.'

'She doesn't know about the rats.'

'Actually, she does.'

'What?'

'She saw them in the bucket before you got rid of them. Ellen told me. Apparently, they went into the garden to find things for a collage or something they were making and Izzy spotted the bucket. She was going to use it to collect everything in.'

'Oh Christ,' groaned Donovan. 'What did Ellen tell her? Do you know?'

'She just said they were found in the garden. Passed it off, I think, and left it at that. Izzy must have told Amanda herself.'

It sounded plausible. Donovan felt a sense of shame wash over him. 'I'm sorry for shouting at you. I know how loyal you are and I really do appreciate it. Honestly.' He patted the top of her arm and was immediately rewarded by a smile from his PA. Relieved to be forgiven and feeling embarrassed, he skulked back to his desk. He needed to find out more about Helen Matthews. He scrolled through the contact list on his phone. Finding the name he was looking for, he swiped the screen to make the call.

Ellen surveyed her purchases laid out on the kitchen table. A pumpkin, some child-friendly, pumpkin-cutting tools, a tea light for the inside and two witches outfits. One for Izzy and one for herself. Halloween was upon them. Izzy had been so excited when Ellen told them what they were going to do. It wasn't until then Ellen realised Izzy had never done this sort of thing before.

Ellen checked her watch. She had time for a quick cup of tea before she had to leave to pick Izzy up from school. The house was very quiet. Mrs Holloway had already left, Wednesdays being her half days and Donovan was out at a meeting. Recently, if he was around, he had taken to coming on the school run with her; she wondered if she should hang on for him today. She'd ask Carla when he was expected back.

As Ellen neared the office door, she was surprised to hear Carla's voice, raised and clearly annoyed.

'Now, you listen to me. It's my turn to talk. Be quiet for one minute!'

Ellen knew she should turn around and walk away, but she suddenly became conscious of her footsteps on the tiled floor. Now Carla had lowered her voice she'd surely hear Ellen and then, no doubt, accuse her of eavesdropping. Well, technically she *was* eavesdropping, only it was now unintentional. Carla's voice was still agitated.

'I can't do everything on my own. It's difficult for me. I don't want to arouse any suspicion. We have a plan and need to stick to it… Yes, I know. She needs sorting out, I agree… you keep to your side of the deal and I'll keep to mine. You just have to be patient… Yes. I'll meet you later, as agreed. Please don't phone me at work again. Goodbye.'

The clunk of the receiver being slammed back into its cradle made Ellen jump. She heard Carla's chair wheels squeak as they rolled over the carpet and before Ellen had time to react, Carla was yanking open the door.

She looked startled to see Ellen there but was quick to regain her composure.

'Is there something I can help you with, Ellen?' Her voice was the epitome of politeness but her eyes told a different story.

Ellen gulped. 'Do you know what time Donovan will be back?'

Carla appraised her for a moment. 'No, I don't. These networking meetings can run on for some time. Is there something urgent that I can help with?'

'No, it's fine.'

'Good. Now, if you don't mind I've got work to do and I'd rather you didn't lurk outside my office door like some sort of spectre. I know it's Halloween, but still.'

'Let me do the cutting. I don't want you chopping your fingers off,' said Ellen. She turned the pumpkin onto its side and using the large carving knife, cut off the top.

'I want to do something,' said Izzy, a pout forming. She had been itching to carve the pumpkin ever since Ellen had picked her up from school that afternoon.

Ellen smiled brightly. 'You can use that spoon to scoop out the middle of the pumpkin. 'We can make some soup out of it. Mrs Holloway showed me how. That will surprise her when she gets here in the morning.'

'She'll think you're after her job.'

Ellen looked up as Donovan came into the kitchen. He'd been back from his networking meeting for about an hour but until now had been shut away in his office. It was nice to see him again, although annoying Mrs Holloway wasn't such a nice thought. 'Oh, do you think so? Maybe we shouldn't then.' The last thing she wanted to do was tread on Mrs Holloway's toes.

'I was only joking,' said Donovan. He smiled at Ellen. 'She will be delighted she's passed her talents onto you.' He ruffled Izzy's hair. 'You okay, angel?'

'We've bought sweets for when the trick people come,' said Izzy sliding some pumpkin off the spoon into a bowl.

'Trick people?'

'Trick-or-treaters, she means,' said Ellen. 'We're not going out ourselves,' she added sensing an unease from Donovan. 'We're going to wait for them to come here.'

'We are going to put the pumpkin outside and then they know we have sweets,' explained Izzy. 'That's what Ellen said she did used to do.' She looked eagerly at Ellen. 'And we are going to dress up too.'

'Yes, we're going to be witches,' said Ellen. 'We've got our costumes but you can't see them until later.'

'Witches, eh? I don't think there were ever two people less like witches,' said Donovan, placing his hand on Ellen's shoulder. He smiled at her, a soft smile that made Ellen feel warm inside, then he kissed her on the cheek. The effect sent Ellen from warm to a temperature worthy of volcano status. She wanted to kiss him back but was well aware of Izzy standing next to them, watching the exchange.

Donovan didn't move away immediately, he squeezed her shoulder. 'Thank you.' It was almost a whisper. Ellen frowned and shrugged. He nodded in Izzy's direction. 'You know … for this. It means a lot, to both of us.'

Ellen watched him walk over to the bifold doors and look out across the garden. It was getting dark already and dampness hung in the dreary sky. The trees were bare of their leaves and the borders were straggly and unattractive. Winter was definitely snapping at the heels of autumn. The sound of Donovan sighing brought her attention back to him. He appeared troubled. Ellen approached him.

'Is everything okay?' she asked, standing next to him.

He continued to look ahead of him. Another sigh. This time

smaller. 'Can't really talk in front of little ears,' he said under his breath. 'Just you-know-who stirring things up.'

Ellen wasn't entirely sure she knew who he meant but thought it was probably Amanda. She wondered what Izzy's mother had been up to now. 'If you ever want to talk,' she said, 'then I'm a good listener.'

Donovan turned to her and gave a wan smile. 'Thank you.' He kissed her again on the cheek. Then spoke with what Ellen suspected was false cheer. 'Right, I've got work to finish. Carla has shot off for a while but she'll be back later.'

'Problem?' asked Ellen, hoping she sounded casual.

'Not as far as I'm aware. She's gone to the post office or something. Why do you ask?'

'No reason. Just wondered.'

Ellen thought back to the telephone conversation she had overheard earlier. She decided against mentioning it to Donovan. What Carla did outside of work was none of her business. It might simply be a coincidence. Besides, she didn't want to cause trouble needlessly.

'If there's anything I can do to help, just let me know,' she said.

'That's very kind but it's nothing that can't wait. Now, I really must get on. I've got to pop out a bit later. Meeting Ken for a chat, but I'll be back before Izzy goes to bed.' He turned and headed out of the kitchen. 'Catch up with you two lovely ladies later.'

Chapter Twenty

DCI Ken Froames unfolded the piece of paper from his pocket and placed it on the table, turning it around so Donovan could read the handwriting.

The Fox was busy enough for the two men to only attract a passing look of interest, but not so busy that they hadn't been able to secure a table at the back of the pub in relative privacy.

Ken took a swig of his pint of ale. 'Not much, I'm afraid, mate,' he said. 'Toby Hastings, twenty-nine, works for a city bank, earns in a month more than I do in six. Good at his job. Recently promoted. Has had a couple of parking tickets and one speeding fine. No criminal record. Only time he's so much as sniffed the inside of a nick was when he reported his girlfriend missing, back in April.'

'What happened about that?'

'Helen Matthews? Well, turns out she doesn't really want to be found. Local officers in the Met spoke to her friend, Kate Gibson, who said Helen was alive and well, working abroad, just avoiding the boyfriend. Gibson alluded to domestic violence but refused to say any more. The next day, Helen Matthews turned up at a local police station in the south of France to confirm the story.'

'Did the boyfriend ever find out where she was?'

'If he did, it wasn't from us. He was told that his girlfriend wasn't actually missing, but that's about it. It's not an unusual situation. Adults go walkabout and don't want to be found for lots of reasons. In this instance, no crime had been committed and the officer investigating was satisfied Helen Matthews was okay, so that was that. Incidentally, it won't surprise you when I tell you Helen Matthews changed her name by Deed Poll.'

Donovan shook his head. 'No, it won't surprise me at all.' He looked further down the handwritten note with events chronicled in date order. '28 March. Helen Matthews officially changes her name by Deed Poll to Ellen Newman.'

'And in answer to the question I know is coming next,' said Ken, 'nothing on record under either name. Not known to us in any way, shape or form.'

'Thanks Ken, I appreciate your help.'

'Well, you didn't hear this from me. All right?' said Ken, looking at Donovan. 'This is all off the record and simply because I've got my god-daughter's best interest at heart. Speaking of which, how is Izzy?'

They finished their pints, chatting mainly about Izzy. Both men made a conscious effort to avoid shop talk. 'One more for the road?' said Donovan picking up the pint glasses.

A few minutes later, with a freshly pulled pint in each hand, Donovan turned away from the bar only to bump straight into another customer. Lager and ale sloshed out of the glasses onto Donovan's shoes. He looked up, about to offer his apologies but was momentarily lost for words. The customer wasn't, however.

'Oh, sorry Doc. Didn't see you there.' Oscar Lampard's face creased into something resembling a smile.

'What are you doing here?' demanded Donovan.

'Er … having a pint. No law against it. Free country and all that.' Lampard looked over to where Ken was sitting. 'Oh, there's PC Plod. I would join you but I'm a busy man and it wouldn't really do my street cred much good to be seen with the likes of you. Oink, oink piggy. Quack, quack shrink.'

'Why don't you go home and finish evolving?' said Donovan,

moving around Lampard and making his way back to the table. He placed the two pint glasses down.

'What's that toe rag doing here?' said Ken.

'Being exactly that. A toe rag,' replied Donovan, pulling out his chair.

'Look up. Said toe rag heading this way.'

Donovan didn't sit down, instead he turned to face Lampard, who had now reached their table.

'Evening Detective Chief Inspector,' said Lampard, then to Donovan. 'I forgot to ask, Doc. How is that nanny of yours? And your daughter? Hope they are both well.'

Before Lampard could take a breath, Donovan had grabbed him by the lapels of his jacket and hurled him up against the wall.

'What the fuck is that supposed to mean?' Donovan hissed. He could feel a pulse pumping hard in his neck, his hands pulling tightly together, his balled fists pushing against Lampard's throat.

'Steady on, Doc. Was only asking. Making sure they were okay. That no harm had come to them.'

Donovan was aware of Ken at his shoulder, his friend's hand placed firmly over his wrist. 'Come on, mate. Let him go.'

'Yeah, Doc, let me go. Wouldn't want to have you arrested for ABH.'

'Stay away from my family,' said Donovan, his jaw so tense he could barely form the words. With a Trojan-like effort, he forced himself to release the pressure he was applying. Hands still on Lampard's jacket, he threw him to the side.

Lampard bundled into a table and staggered before regaining his balance, courtesy of a bar stool. He looked around at the now-silent pub. 'You saw that,' he said to no one in particular. 'Police brutality. Remember that, won't you?'

'I'm civilian, not police,' said Donovan. 'Besides, no one's interested. Save your breath for your blow-up doll.' A childish comment, Donovan acknowledged. A reaction that annoyed him as much as Lampard himself did.

Lampard straightened his jacket and, mumbling expletives under his breath in Donovan's direction, left the pub. The burble of conversation started up again, customers returning to where they had left off before the interruption.

'Here, sit down and drink your pint,' said Ken, giving Donovan a small nudge. 'You're a bit tetchy aren't you?'

Donovan acceded to his friend's instruction. 'Sorry, it's just that loads of shit is happening all at once.' He took a long swig of his lager and continued. 'I've got Amanda turning up, wanting custody of Izzy. Ellen and the ex-boyfriend, slash, secret past. All this business with weird things happening, coincidences, which I don't believe in. Even Carla's been acting a bit odd. She keeps nipping off for this, that and the other. I have no idea what's going on. My usual house of calm is descending into a chaos. And I don't like it.'

Donovan was conscious of the fact he sounded like a petulant child stamping his foot, but the truth was his customary ordered life was anything but, at the moment. It was making him feel uneasy.

He pushed his unfinished pint to the centre of the table. 'I'm going to get off.'

'Finish your drink. Unwind for a minute,' said Ken. 'I'm sure everything's fine.'

'No, I'd sooner go home, for my own peace of mind.' Donovan stood up and shrugged on his jacket. 'Thanks for the info, Ken. I appreciate it. I'll catch up with you soon.' The gut feeling Donovan so often relied upon was kicking him hard in the ribs. He had an overwhelming desire to get home as a blanket of unease weighed on his shoulders.

'Right, squeeze up and we'll take a picture of ourselves on my phone,' said Ellen, crouching down next to Izzy, their green-painted faces side by side. Ellen adjusted her witch's hat. 'Now pull a really horrible, evil face. Oh, you're good. Hold it. Ready, one, two,

126

three…' They both giggled at the image reflected back from Ellen's iPhone. 'Now, let's do a nice one. Smile this time.'

'There's someone at the door!' squealed Izzy as the doorbell sounded out. She grabbed Ellen's sleeve and tugged her out of the kitchen and down the hallway.

Ellen gave Izzy the plastic orange bucket with the sweets in. 'Okay, ready?' Izzy nodded and Ellen pulled open the door.

In front of them stood two small children, not much older than Izzy, one dressed as a skeleton and the other with a white sheet over them, looking very ghost-like. Ellen looked beyond them at the edge of the driveway, where a woman, who she assumed was their mother, watched over proceedings.

'Trick or treat?' the children chorused.

Izzy took some sweets from her bucket and dropped them into the bag the other children were holding.

'Thank you!' called the mother as the children turned away.

'Do you think anyone else will come?' asked Izzy.

'Oh, I'm sure they will. Come on, let's go and have that Witch's Ghastly Goo drink we made earlier.'

'Chocolate milkshake!' cried Izzy, running down the hallway, her witch's cape flapping behind her.

How sweet they looked dressed up as witches. How appropriate it was Halloween. This was going to be fun. Well, maybe not for them.

Chapter Twenty-One

It all happened too fast for Ellen to compute. A lone figure at the door, dressed as a werewolf. A rubber mask pulled down over their face, a hairy suit covering their body. The build of an adult and not that of a child out on Halloween trick-or-treating.

She saw the container and felt the slimy liquid hit her fully in the face, as the werewolf sloshed the contents over both her and Izzy. They both screamed in surprise and alarm.

As Ellen turned to grab Izzy, pushing the child behind her for protection, she then felt the white powder hit her. It stuck to the goo already sliding down her face, hitting her straight in the mouth, covering her nostrils, engulfing her and making it impossible to draw breath. She spluttered, spat and coughed, frantically wiping her eyes.

Then there was nothing more as she heard the scrunch on the gravel drive of feet running away. Ellen squinted through the muck on her face but couldn't see anything in the dark. She looked down at Izzy, who was crying. Fortunately, most of it had missed her. Ellen inspected the goo and gunk on her hands. Eggs and flour. Stupid bloody trick-or-treater!

'Come on, Izzy,' she picked up the little girl. 'It's okay. Just some eggs and flour. Sometimes older boys get carried away and do silly things like this. Let's get cleaned up.'

As Donovan entered through the front door, the first thing he heard was the sound of raised voices coming from the kitchen. Two women arguing. The first thing he saw was Izzy sitting on the stairs, clearly distressed.

'What the ...?' he muttered, swinging the front door shut and striding straight down the hallway. He paused at the banisters and gave Izzy a little kiss. 'It's okay, angel, daddy will sort it out. Go upstairs, I'll come and see you in a minute.'

He marched down the hallway, pushing the kitchen door open with such force it hit the wall and bounced back. The noise of wood hitting plaster went unnoticed by the two women.

'I don't actually work for you, in case it's escaped your notice.' Ellen's voice was steely.

'But can't you see,' Carla was hissing back. 'Since you've come here there's been nothing but trouble. You should do the decent thing and leave. We never had any of this nonsense before...'

'Right! That's enough. BOTH of you!' Donovan didn't need to hear any more. The two women stopped, both turning to look at him. 'What the hell do you think you're doing, caterwauling like a couple of alley-cats?' Okay, that was probably uncalled for, but judging by the look of indignation on their faces, he had made his point. 'Now, ladies, although I am using the term very liberally, would one of you care to tell me what is going on?'

They both began at once.

'There's been another incident,' said Carla. 'Eggs and flour all over Ellen and Izzy.'

'It was a trick-or-treater,' snapped back Ellen.

'No it wasn't and you know it.'

'Carla thinks I should leave but I was merely making the point that I don't work for her,' said Ellen, fixing her gaze back on her adversary.

Carla returned the icy look. 'And I was merely pointing out, that in the interest of everyone in this house, especially Izzy, that perhaps Ellen should think about others before herself.'

Donovan held up his hand before the argument could progress into a full-blown row again. He let out a deep sigh. 'Carla, I would expect more from you. If you have any concerns about one of my employees, you should voice them to me first. I appreciate you are worried. We all are. But, it's for me to take on board, not you.'

Carla dropped her gaze. 'Sorry, Donovan. It's just so unsettling. Maybe, we can speak in the morning.'

'Good idea,' said Donovan. 'Now, you, Ellen. I don't expect you to get into a catfight with one of your colleagues. If there's a problem, like Carla, you're to come to me.'

Ellen flushed red and Donovan registered a tiny pang of embarrassment for her as she answered him meekly, her shoulders slumping. 'Yes, of course.' She sat down on a kitchen chair. Donovan appreciated this gesture. He could see Carla visibly relaxing now.

'I think we should talk about this tomorrow once we've all had a good sleep. Everyone is tired and emotional. I'm not impressed by you two in the slightest.'

He was relieved when the two women apologised.

'I think I'll go home now,' said Carla. 'Unless there's anything you want me to do, Donovan.'

He shook his head. 'No, nothing to be done tonight, thank you, Carla. Goodnight.'

He let it go that Carla didn't say goodnight to Ellen. They were, after all, grown women and not children. Now wasn't the moment to introduce circle time and insist they make friends.

'Right, you wait there,' he said to Ellen. 'I need to go and settle Izzy.'

'Izzy?'

'Yes, she heard everything. Sitting on the stairs crying because of you two.'

'I'm so sorry,' said Ellen. 'Do you want me to go and see her?'

'No, I'll deal with this.'

It took at least twenty minutes to settle Izzy and convince her that everything was all right. Donovan had ended up half sitting, half lying on her bed, his arm around her and reading one of her favourite stories, Cinderella.

'Ellen is like Cinderella. Pretty and nice,' said Izzy, her voice heavy with tiredness and emotion. 'And Carla is the ugly sister. All mean and horrid.'

'Ahem, that's not a very nice thing to say about Carla,' said Donovan. He was well aware of the bubble of amusement this statement had stirred within him but, in all honestly, it really wasn't very fair on Carla. He decided a gentle reproach was the best way to deal with this. 'Carla is very nice. She's always kind to you and she is also pretty.'

'Not as pretty as Cinderella-Ellen.'

He couldn't really argue with that. 'Cinderella. We could call Ellen, Cinderellen. Do you think she will like that?'

Izzy giggled. 'Cinderellen. Yes, that's what we will call Ellen now.' She snuggled down further into her father's arm. 'And you are the Prince.'

'Why, thank you.' Donovan squeezed her gently.

'That means you have to kiss Ellen and then you have to marry her and live happily ever after.'

'Is that so?' Donovan tossed this idea around in his head, the kissing bit he would happily manage. The marriage bit, well, maybe he shouldn't visit that notion. 'Now, let's finish this story,' he said making a supreme effort to distract himself. 'Where were we…?'

'Carla's right.'

The words greeted Donovan as soon as he walked into the kitchen, having left Izzy fast asleep. He stopped and looked at Ellen, who was sitting at the kitchen table exactly where he had left her some time earlier. Her hands were clasped together, her thumb making a continual circular motion in the palm of her other hand. Anxiety oozed from her, like sticky syrup from a tin. He drove down a sigh. 'What is Carla right about?'

131

'That I should leave. She's right. I'm bringing trouble to you all and I should think of Izzy. Tonight just went to prove it.' Still she didn't look at him.

'For fuck's sake,' groaned Donovan, the sigh breaking free. He was starting to feel exasperated by this conversation. He sat down on the chair next to her, using the time to draw breath and search for his patient voice; the one he used for Izzy when something needed explaining for the umpteenth time. He took her hands in his. 'How many times do we have to have this conversation? I'm sick to death of it. You're not going anywhere. Not if I have anything to do with it.' Okay, his patient Izzy voice wasn't quite coming through but, Christ, was he weary of this.

She didn't move her hands away, which pleased him, but when her eyes finally met his, all he could see was fear, which saddened him. 'It's really not fair of me to stay here. If all this is happening because of me. If it really is Toby, then I can simply leave and start again where he won't find me. If it's not him, then you will be able to take measures to stop it. That way you will know what you're dealing with.'

'Neither is an option, Ellen, and I mean that,' said Donovan. 'You really think running away is going to solve this? I've told you before, it will only follow you. He will find you again and then I dread to think what will happen. And if it's not him, you staying won't actually make any difference. I can't let you disappear. I would be worried sick about you. How could I have that on my conscience?'

'You're not responsible for me,' said Ellen.

'I became responsible for you the moment you walked over that threshold,' he said. 'As your employer I have a duty of care towards you.'

'If I go, you're not my employer and that duty of care ends.'

'But you're also my daughter's friend, which, by default, means I have a duty of care to you.' He paused; knew he shouldn't say what was on the tip of his tongue but also knew he was going to,

132

all the same. 'And you mean something to me so, once again, by default, I care about you.'

'What happened to the duty bit?' Her voice was almost a whisper. He saw her swallow but her eyes held his.

'There's no duty where you are concerned.' Jesus, this was difficult. With the utmost restraint, he remained motionless, fighting every urge to lean forwards to kiss her, yet unable to pull away.

She made the slightest of nodding movements with her head, as if she understood exactly what he was saying, exactly what he was thinking. What she did next would tell him everything. Did she feel the same? Donovan was aware that he was holding his breath. Waiting.

She leaned into him, her head nestling in his shoulder. The answer was yes. A shy, tentative, maybe slightly confused, or even nervous, yes. But a yes, nonetheless.

He held her for a few minutes, stroking her back, twiddling the ends of her hair with his fingers. She looked up at him and he could see exactly what she wanted reflecting back in her eyes.

He leant in to kiss her and without hesitation she kissed him back. A long, deep kiss. His tongue toyed with hers and explored her mouth. Without pausing, she returned the gesture.

Dear Lord, he wanted her in every possible way, however, his need to know the truth about Ellen Newman came to the fore. He had to force himself to stop the physical desire of his body taking over. It took every ounce of resistance he could muster. There were things he needed to know before he could sleep with her. Now wasn't the time to raise those questions.

'I'd better go,' he said standing up. He couldn't fail to see the look of disappointment settle on her features for a moment or two. Then the disquieting look was gone and Ellen was composed. 'This isn't the right time. Not yet. Not tonight.'

'Yes, you're right. The timing is all wrong.'

He gave her one last kiss on the mouth. 'Goodnight. Sweet dreams, Cinderellen.'

Leaving the room, he was well aware he hadn't handled that as graciously as Ellen deserved but he needed physical distance from her tonight. Plenty of it.

Chapter Twenty-Two

Donovan had insisted they have a walk along Felpham seafront again this weekend. The egging of Halloween night had been put behind them. Both Ellen and Donovan had reassured Izzy it was only teenage high jinks, which she seemed to accept. Ellen, too was clinging on to this idea, despite Carla's polar-opposite opinion and Donovan's inclination to agree with his PA.

'If it was someone other than a trick-or-treater, I'm sure they would have done a lot worse,' said Ellen, doggedly refusing to change her mind. 'A few eggs and flour is such a teenage thing to do.'

'Why weren't any of the other houses egged, then?' retorted Carla. 'I checked and no one had any *teenage high jinks* at their houses.' She emphasised the expression in a derogatory way.

'Because, it wouldn't be particularly wise to egg someone's house and then nip next door to do it again.' Ellen huffed out loud. 'It's obvious they would run off, probably to the next street or the one after.'

'All right, let's leave it there,' said Donovan.

'It's just a coincidence,' said Ellen, not being able to hold the words back.

'I don't believe in coincidences,' said Donovan. He muttered something along the lines of some people being ostrich-like and Ellen decided that it really was time to drop the subject. Carla appeared to be of the same opinion too. Thank goodness.

Ellen had forced herself to be civil towards Carla, who herself seemed to have adopted the same attitude. Polite and civil but nothing more and purely for Donovan and Izzy's sake.

Ellen was pleased to get out of the house today, despite the distinctly wintery feel. She was used to the sea air now and actually beginning to enjoy the freshness of the winter wind and salty taste on her lips. Her mask of a city slicker was slipping fast. Perhaps she was a country girl, after all.

Donovan and Ellen held Izzy's hands and were swinging her between them. A couple walking towards them smiled as Izzy squealed in delight. The thought flashed through Ellen's mind that the three of them must look like a little family enjoying a Sunday-afternoon walk. The thought was pleasing. She glanced across at Donovan, who must have sensed her gaze, for he looked up and shared her smile, but the look in his eyes betrayed him. There was something there, a look she didn't recognise.

'Izzy, why don't you throw some stones into the water,' suggested Donovan, slipping his hand from his daughter's. He picked her up and jumped down onto the stony beach. 'Go on. Ellen and I will watch you from here.' He sat on the wall, looking on, as Izzy scrambled down the shallow pebbles to the water's edge. He didn't turn as he spoke to Ellen. 'Come and sit down, Ellen. Or should I say Helen? Helen Matthews.'

The horizon swayed from one side to the other; her legs felt heavy and useless. Quickly, Ellen sat down, afraid she would collapse in a heap if she didn't. Closing her eyes for a moment, she willed her breathing to a steady rate. When she looked again, the horizon was still.

'Helen Matthews doesn't exist any more,' she said, aware that her voice was no more than a mumble. 'Helen Matthews was weak, full of self-doubt. She allowed herself to be manipulated, controlled and …'

'And abused,' Donovan interjected.

'I have as little to do with Helen Matthews as possible,' said Ellen. The wind was making her eyes water. She wiped her face. Watery eyes. Not tears. Who was she trying to kid?

'You should have told me.' His voice was soft. There was no reproach in it but there was also no pity. She was glad. She didn't want to be pitied. But he was right, she should have told him.

'I know and I'm sorry.'

'Please, Ellen, is there anything I need to know? I don't do surprises.' His hand slid along the concrete sea wall, his fingers finding hers.

Ellen looked on as Izzy ran up and down the beach, dodging the incoming waves and throwing stone after stone into the grey water. She looked down at his hand clasped over her own. She relaxed her fingers and allowed Donovan to lace his through hers.

'No more surprises.' She tightened her grip. 'I promise.'

This time it took a little longer for the note to appear on the doormat. This time it was Izzy who found it.

'Look Daddy! Look Ellen! There's a picture of us on the beach.' Izzy's voice rang out down the hallway.

Ellen tore down the hall to reach her, nearly bumping straight into Donovan as he shot out from the living room.

'Give it to me,' they said in unison, both holding their hands out.

Seeing the look of panic on Izzy's face, Ellen dropped her hand immediately and, crouching down in front of the child, she smiled. 'A picture of us? How nice. Why don't you show it to Daddy first?' She put her hand reassuringly on Izzy's back. 'That's a good girl. Give it to Daddy. Excellent. Well done. I can't wait to see it myself.'

'Yes you can,' muttered Donovan. 'That's a great picture, Izzy. I'll keep that in my study and I can look at it when I'm busy working. It will make me feel happy.'

'Okay,' said Izzy, a look of relief sweeping across her face. 'Can I have some hot chocolate now, please? You said I could when

137

we got in.'

'Of course, run along down to the kitchen, I think Mrs Holloway is doing it now.'

Ellen watched as Donovan dropped a kiss on his daughter's head before the eight-year-old skipped down the tiled passageway.

'May I see?' asked Ellen, taking hold of the edge of the paper. For a moment she thought Donovan was going to refuse, but he must have changed his mind. Ellen let out a little gasp as she looked at the image in front of her.

This time it was a photograph of her, Donovan and Izzy, taken this morning walking along the seafront, all holding hands. The words were once again hand-written.

HAPPY FAMILIES

'You're not telling me this is a coincidence, are you?' she said, needlessly.

Donovan pursed his lips, pinching the bottom one between his finger and thumb. He spoke after a moment. 'It's still not clear who this is directed at. You or me?'

'We still don't know if it's from Toby or a client.'

'I'll look into getting CCTV put up.'

'Isn't that a bit late now?' said Ellen. It came out with rather more sarcasm than she intended.

'Not if whoever it is comes back again,' said Donovan, he held Ellen's gaze for a moment. He was taking this seriously and left her in no doubt that he did not welcome her tone.

'Sorry.' Ellen looked down at the ground, to avoid reading the unspoken words.

'I'll be in my office,' he said before heading back to his study, muttering something about security gates. He seemed to be doing a lot of muttering lately. Ellen let out a sigh. This house would be like a fortress. If only there was some way of finding out who was behind it all and why. Surely it couldn't be Toby. What purpose would it all serve? He had probably moved on to a new girlfriend by now. He really wouldn't be interested in her, still.

It was something of a surprise later when Donovan came up to the playroom where Ellen was putting up some new curtains she had bought. They were a lovely pink and green fabric with little flowers. They matched the new bedspread Ellen had ordered, adding some much-needed colour to Izzy's room.

Izzy was practising her violin, a noise that Ellen had become not only accustomed to but, somewhat thankfully, deaf to as well. The sound of *Twinkle, Twinkle, Little Star* being screeched out, like a cat with its tail shut in a door, was rather abusive to the ears.

'Looks nice in here,' said Donovan, above the F sharp impersonation of chalk on a blackboard. 'Izzy. Izzy! Stop a minute, please.'

Ellen looked round as Donovan, smiling at his daughter, gently coaxed the bow away from the strings. 'Sorry, Izzy, hold fire for the moment. I was just admiring your room. It looks lovely in here. Did you decide what colour you want the fireplace wall painted?'

'I want it pink,' declared Izzy. Abandoning the musical instrument, she ran over to her desk and picked up a little pot of tester paint. 'This one. Ellen painted some squares on the wall and said I could choose. This is my favourite.'

Ellen got down from the chair she had been standing on to reach the top of the curtain pole. She watched Donovan go over to the wall and thoroughly inspect each square. He nodded his approval and in a most serious voice spoke to Izzy. 'Yes, I like that one too. Not too dark and not too babyish. Good choice.'

Izzy beamed and Ellen realised she was beaming too. It made her happy to think Donovan was pleased.

'Now, the reason I came up, was this,' he said, sitting on the edge of the bed with Izzy on his lap. 'I've had a phone call from Mummy this afternoon and she wants to take you out for tea as it's Sebastian's birthday. She said you could have a sleepover at her house and she will take you to school tomorrow. How would you like that?'

'Will we have tea at McDonalds?' said Izzy with the innocent enthusiasm of an eight-year-old.

Ellen suppressed a giggle but catching Donovan's eye, who was equally entertained at the idea, she couldn't stop a snort of laughter erupting out.

'I don't think it will be McDonalds. I'm not sure Sebastian would like that for his birthday tea,' said Donovan.

Izzy pulled a face. 'It will probably be with lots of other grown-ups.'

This time, Ellen felt a wave of compassion rush over her. Poor Izzy, she was probably right. It would be a load of stuffy grown-ups. She tried to make it sound better. 'But you get to have a sleepover at Mummy's. And I bet you'll get to have a fantastically huge slice of chocolate cake for pudding. Wish I was going.'

'Can you come too? You can sleep in the same room as me.' Izzy's face lit up. 'Can she, Daddy?'

Ellen pulled an 'eek' sort of face at Donovan. He returned it. 'I'm sorry, angel, but Ellen can't. She's supposed to have time off at weekends, but for some reason she still likes to hang around. So, tonight, seeing as you're not here, Ellen is having the evening off and she's going out.'

Ellen went to correct this. She wasn't going out at all. She never went out. And Donovan knew that but she managed to say nothing. Donovan was just getting her out of a sticky situation.

'Where are you going?' asked Izzy, not sounding entirely convinced.

Donovan spoke first. 'She's going out to dinner. To a very nice restaurant in Chichester. Now, you need to get bathed and ready for when mummy comes, which I'm sure Ellen will help you with and then after that, you, Ellen, need to get bathed and ready for your night out.'

'That sounds like a good plan to me,' said Ellen enthusiastically, going along with her boss.

Donovan got up and lowered Izzy to the floor. 'So, Izzy, you're to be ready for five and Ellen, you're to be ready for seven thirty.'

Ellen gave a mock salute. 'Sir. Yes, Sir!'

Donovan came over to her. 'I am actually being serious. Best frock. I'm taking you out.'

Ellen could only watch open-mouthed as he sauntered out of the playroom, throwing her a cheeky wink as he went through the doorway. Her stomach was doing a crazy tumbling act, like an acrobatic display team on speed. Donovan was taking her out. Eeeek!

Chapter Twenty-Three

Looking out of the upstairs window, watching Izzy head off with Amanda, sent an unexpected pang through Ellen. She had grown very attached to the little girl; she was so easy to love. Much like her father. Ellen had to admit she was growing fonder and fonder of Donovan each day. She enjoyed his company and was happiest whenever he was around. Even when he was locked away in his study, the knowledge that he was in the same house as her gave her a warm, reassuring feeling.

Her thoughts migrated back to what was happening that night. Donovan was taking her out for a meal. She couldn't deny the excitement she felt and, smiling, she gave herself a little hug. Time to get ready.

It wasn't until she came to look at her clothing selection that Ellen realised the term 'posh frock' had never made it to her wardrobe. Not her wardrobe of the last few months anyway. She hadn't needed anything remotely posh whilst working at the French campsite and since living back in the UK in the Donovan household, she hadn't needed anything except jeans and a jumper.

She fanned her hand across the clothing hanging on the rail, like a pianist thumbing over the keys of a baby grand. It made no odds. There was nothing tucked away in there she had forgotten about. She had one pair of black trousers that could probably pass for 'going out' and a blouse. But they were the stuff job interviews were made of.

Reluctantly she showered and dressed; making an extra effort with her hair and make-up to compensate for the rather sensible clothing. Where was your fairy Godmother when you needed her? How come Cinderella got all the luck?

A knock at the door interrupted her thoughts. 'Come in!' she called. It could only be Donovan. No one else was in the house. She stood on the rug in the middle of the room, feeling slightly embarrassed, not only in her appearance, but because it was as though they were having their first formal date. Her first date with anyone in years. The door didn't open. 'Come in!' she called louder this time. Okay, it looked as though she was going to have to open it herself.

Ellen pulled the door open. 'Ta-dah!' The words faded onto the empty landing. There was no one there. She poked her head around the doorway and looked down the hall. Empty. It was then she felt her foot make contact with something. She jumped and looked down at the floor.

A white rectangular box, tied up with pink ribbon fashioned into a bow.

'Donovan?' she called gingerly down the hallway. 'Donovan!'

Her pulse began to throb in her neck and her throat constricted. She looked down at the box.

Ellen slowly stepped over the box and backed along the hallway, before turning and running down the stairs, taking them two at a time. She hit the middle landing with such force that she had to grab the newel post to stop herself slamming into the banister that overlooked the hallway.

Two strong arms embraced her. She let out a yelp.

'Hey! Ellen. It's me. It's okay.' Donovan's concerned voice brought her eyes into focus. 'What's wrong?' He stood back from her holding her at arm's length, studying her face.

Ellen looked around, aware she was probably appearing like

143

some wild woman. 'There's a box. A white box outside my room.'

Donovan nodded. 'Yes,' he said slowly. 'That's right.'

'With pink ribbon around it.'

'Tied in a bow. Yep.'

'You know about it?'

'Don't you like it?' asked Donovan.

'Like what? The box?' Ellen shook her head. 'How do you know about the box?'

'I put it there. It's a present for you.'

'For me?'

'You don't like it?'

'Like what?'

'The dress.'

'What dress?'

'Wait a minute. Stop,' said Donovan. 'Calm down. Let's go back upstairs.'

Ellen held onto his hand as they went up to the top floor. Donovan stopped in front of the box and letting go of Ellen's hand, he bent down and picked it up. Entering in to the room, Donovan placed the object of Ellen's distress on the bed. 'It's a present from me to you. Go on, open it.'

'Oh,' Ellen managed to say. She felt stupid now for overreacting. She untied the ribbon and lifted the lid. Unfolding the tissue paper, she held up the most beautiful of dresses. A midnight-blue, shift dress. Simple but beautiful. 'It's gorgeous.' She held it up to herself.

'I'm glad you like it and I hope you're not offended,' said Donovan in a soft voice. He picked up the card that was in the box and passed it to Ellen. 'See you in five minutes. I'll wait downstairs for you.'

Ellen read the card.

Saw this and thought of you … Hope you like it. D.x

Ellen knew she should feel more comfortable with this gesture than she did. It unsettled her for the right and wrong reasons. How lovely of Donovan to think of her but it also jarred with her feeling of not being in control. This was the sort of thing Toby would have done.

She folded the dress and went to put it back in the box when she noticed another card. She picked it up and read it.

I know you are debating as to whether this is a good idea or not. I promise you, it's nothing more than a gesture of gratitude. No strings attached. No ulterior motive and no control. Just a beautiful dress for a beautiful lady. If it makes you feel better, we can call it uniform and put it through the expenses. D.x

Ellen gave a small laugh. Uniform. She took another look at the dress. Oh, what the heck. It was too nice not to and compared to what her alternative was, well, there was no competition.

Donovan let out a low whistle. 'You look fantastic, Ellen.' He met her at the bottom of the staircase and kissed her on the cheek.

'Don't sound so surprised.' Ellen gave a small laugh. She felt good and was glad she had evoked that sort of reaction from Donovan.

'Hmmmm, gorgeous,' said Donovan, openly admiring her. 'Come on, Cinderellen, we'd better go. I need some fresh cool air. Haven't got time for a cold shower.'

The restaurant was situated north of Chichester city walls, an understated yet sophisticated place. Ellen gave a silent prayer of thanks that Donovan had bought her this dress; her original outfit would have been so out of place.

Ellen thoroughly enjoyed the meal, sitting eating with Donovan was something she had done so many times at his house that this evening wasn't a trial at all. Sometimes food and first dates could be disastrous. She thought back to one of her first meals out with Toby and the fish dish she had ordered, which had come complete with head and tail. She shuddered, not so much at the memory but at Toby's reaction. He had caused quite a fuss in the restaurant, demanding it was returned and then later, fuelled by alcohol, when they arrived at Toby's apartment, he had proceeded to tease Ellen, calling her an uneducated peasant. It had gone on for quite a while, in some sort of half-joking, half-serious manner, until she had got quite cross about it. Toby, at that point, had claimed it was just banter and her reaction exaggerated. Of course, he had been sorry and in his customary charming manner had managed to dispel her concerns. In fact, as early as those first dates, he had been able to convince her she was overreacting and she had even apologised. The irrational part of her still blamed herself for not reading the warning signs correctly at the first. The rational side of her knew she could never have foreseen how things would turn out and, despite what she had once thought, it wasn't her fault. She was not responsible for his actions.

'Everything okay?' asked Donovan. 'You looked miles away then.'

'Sorry, I was thinking back to a time when I ordered fish and it came with its head and tail still on,' she explained, deciding to leave out how Toby had dealt with the situation. Bringing his name up would only ruin the atmosphere of the evening. She didn't want that. She wanted tonight to be special. She moved the subject on to a lighter, safer topic, which Donovan seemed happy to participate in. Maybe he too wanted to stay away from difficult issues.

Sitting in the back of the taxi, snuggled up to Donovan, Ellen was trying to work out why her stomach had decided to launch itself into a frenzy not dissimilar to that of a whirlpool. The evening had been wonderful; she had felt totally at ease in Donovan's company. She smoothed the blue fabric of the dress across her knee.

'Have you had a nice time?' Donovan asked.

Ellen raised her head so she could meet his eyes. 'I've had a wonderful evening. Thank you.' She tipped her face towards him and luxuriated in a deep, welcoming kiss. His hand reached across and pulled her closer to him, before sliding down her side and running the length of her thigh. The whirlpool continued to churn inside her. Her body was way ahead of her mind. The evening was far from over.

The seat belt was doing a marvellous job of preventing Ellen getting any closer to Donovan. She sat back, a warming smile plastered on her face. That kiss was by far the best. Donovan looked across at her and winked.

'Should be home soon,' he said.

'The sooner the better.'

The taxi ride passed in a blur, Ellen not only felt heady from the wine she had consumed but from a burning desire for Donovan. It surprised her but she purposefully made herself relax so she could enjoy this. At the back of her mind she felt apprehension. She was going to sleep with a man for the first time since she had left Toby. She wanted it to be special. She didn't want the past to taint her future. Sex with Toby as opposed to making love with Donovan. There was no competition and she certainly wasn't going to let the two overlap. Donovan deserved her total and complete attention. She deserved it too.

His breath was warm on her neck, his mouth making no contact with her skin, it was almost like a whisper. Ellen let Donovan take her jacket from her, not caring that he allowed it to slip from his fingers on to the floor. His hands slid around her waist and he pulled her into him, his groin tight against her. The reassuring feeling that he wanted her was evident.

Ellen let out an involuntarily whimper. God, she wanted him, just his touch over her clothes was sending star bursts right through her. He kissed her neck, his hands roaming up and down her midriff, running over her breasts, finding their way to the tops of her legs.

She turned round to face him, hungry for his kisses, hungry for his touch. Without ceremony she pulled his jacket from his shoulders and as he wriggled his arms out, Ellen tugged at his tie, their mouths in contact the whole time. Lips and tongues performed an elegant dance that they both knew the routine for without putting a step wrong.

'Let's go upstairs.' Donovan's voice was husky, laced with desire. His hands roamed through her hair as he worked his kisses from her face to her neck and back again. 'Damn it, I can't wait.'

He walked her backwards to the chaise-longue that was in the hallway, gently pushing her back onto it. He began to unbutton his shirt, Ellen looked up at him. She wanted this to last.

Taking hold of his belt she undid the buckle and found the button on his trousers, opening the zipper. His trousers slid down easily. Donovan had already kicked his shoes off and was now stepping out of his clothing. He bent down to kiss her.

Ellen looked up and gently shook her head, holding her hand against him, her palm cushioned by the dark hair on his chest. Not once breaking eye contact, she edged herself to the end of the chaise and her fingertips began exploring his torso. He kept himself in shape, that was certain, his body was lean but solid, no sign of over-indulgence. Splaying her fingers she fanned her hands across his stomach to his sides and down to his hips. His hands clamped over hers and, with the gaze still unbroken, he raised his eyebrows in question. Ellen couldn't help a small mischievous smile breaking free. She was enjoying being in the driving seat. She was setting the pace and the tone. Donovan wasn't trying to rush or dominate her. It was a liberating feeling; one she hadn't experienced before.

'So, what now?' Donovan's voice was a rasp. Ellen watched him wet his lips and swallow hard. His breathing was heavy and the desire in his eyes clear.

'How about this?' Ellen slipped his boxer shorts down and Donovan let out a low moan of anticipation.

'Jesus, Ellen,' he groaned, his hands clasping her head.

Ellen knew he had reached the point of no return. It didn't matter, she wanted to do this for him. She loved making him feel this way. She loved the way it made her feel. God, she wanted him so much. She took everything he offered.

Afterwards, he stood there and for a moment she thought his legs might give way. 'Oh, Ellen.' He moved himself away but Ellen held his hands and drew herself down to him, cradling his head in her lap.

Ellen dropped butterfly kisses on his head, smoothing his hair with her hand, then gentle caresses down the back of his neck and across his shoulders. He felt so good. There wasn't one thing about him she didn't like.

He responded to her touch. Lifting his head, he knelt in front of her, his hands travelling up her nylon-encased legs.

'Upstairs.' His voice gruff but tender. 'This is pay-back time.' The glint in his eye and the smile tipping the corners of his mouth sent a flurry of excitement straight through her. This time it was she who was too eager to take the stairs.

'I can't wait,' she said as her breathing began to represent that of a marathon runner. She wriggled back up the chaise and pulled her tights down, peeling them off one leg at a time. He reached out and stopped her, his hand resting on her hip. His index finger traced the outline of the pale-blue dragonfly tattoo.

'Beautiful. Graceful. Elegant. It matches its owner,' said Donovan in a whisper as he kissed the body art. Then he sat up. 'One second. Don't move.' He reached over to where his jacket had been discarded and rummaged around the inside pocket, retrieved a condom and put it on the backrest. Then he climbed on to the chaise, his knees parting her legs and slid a hand between her thighs, pulling her underwear to one side. She adjusted her position and within seconds she let out a gasp. She'd never felt this close to the edge before, never felt this out of control. A hedonistic feeling that she wanted to totally surrender to.

'Oh, God, Donovan. Do it.' She sounded like she was begging. She realised she probably was. Ellen patted her hand around the backrest of the sofa until she found the foil packet. 'Please, I want you.' It was a tormented whisper from her as she tore open the foil and thrust the latex at him.

Within a few seconds he was pushing himself deep inside her, with no hesitation. No teasing. No reassurances offered or requested. It was heaven. It was what she wanted. She could feel his need for her. It matched her need for him.

Ellen grasped at his back, her hands finding his shoulders and she pushed him back and dragged him forward, helping build the momentum; she didn't want to stop. This was raw, no-holds-barred sex. She had never wanted anyone so badly.

Her body took control and the dizzy, intense and almost unbearable sensation rushed over her as she climaxed – conscious that Donovan had timed his own to perfection. She was aware of a cry, somewhere in the distance, it was her own but she couldn't focus on anything, only the extreme high that possessed her every cell.

The come-down was slower; gentle waves lapping over her body, her breathing levelled, her heart rate dropped and the dizziness subsided. Donovan was spent, exhausted and lying half on her and half on the chaise. He kissed her cheek and brushed a strand of hair from her face.

'Much as I love this chaise, it wasn't built for two,' he said.

'Where do you suggest instead?' asked Ellen making sure the kiss she gave left him in no doubt what she had in mind.

'It's king-sized,' he said between kisses.

'I know that.' She grinned. 'Now, show me what size your bed is.'

Chapter Twenty-Four

Ellen woke early. Donovan was still sleeping soundly. They had entwined themselves around each other like vines last night and seemingly stayed that way. She didn't want to move and break the feel of him next to her, the sensation of being held safe in loving arms. It was good. She hadn't felt like this in a long, long time. She couldn't deny her feelings for Donovan were shifting. She had been aware of this, somewhere in the recesses of her mind, somewhere she hadn't wanted to rummage around in too deeply. Now, however, there was no turning her back on her emotions.

How did that happen in such a short space of time?

She had promised herself time off from any relationship. After Toby, the last thing she wanted was to get involved with anyone. Her head was telling her this was too soon, yet her heart had other ideas. It was times like this that she really missed Kate. Her friend always had wise words for her, it was just a shame Ellen hadn't paid attention to them sooner where Toby was concerned. Maybe she should email Kate.

Reluctant to leave Donovan's embrace, Ellen resolved to contact Kate later. She hadn't been in touch with her for a while, which although wasn't a problem, Ellen didn't want things to slide. Changing her mind, perhaps now while Donovan was sleeping, she should do it. She'd be busy with Izzy later.

However, as Ellen began to move, Donovan stirred. His arm tightening around her.

He rolled over so he was facing her. 'It wasn't a dream, then? You really are here.'

She smiled and kissed him. 'Oh, yes.' She could feel him against her. All thoughts of Kate dismissed.

Ellen opened the email sitting in the draft folder.

Hello lovely
Thanks for your email. I'm quickly sending you a reply now, as I'm about to head off to work. In answer to your question about Toby – no, he hasn't been in contact since that time he brought the present round. As I said, at the time, he seemed worried about you, like he was actually missing you.
What made you ask about him anyway?
xx

Ellen deleted the email from the draft folder and composed a new one.

Hiya!
Hope work was okay.
Re Toby – I was just checking, that's all. Nothing to worry about.
I'll be in touch soon – we need to sort out a date for meeting up. Somewhere different, not London or here. Maybe Brighton – that's easy for us both to get to.
Have a think.
Xx

Okay, that wasn't strictly true about Toby, but Ellen had wanted to see if he'd been in touch again. She wasn't sure if his silence was a good thing or not.

Shutting down the laptop, Ellen checked her watch. It would

soon be time to get Izzy from school. Enough time for a cup of tea first. She also needed to remind Donovan about Izzy's music concert later in the week.

Ellen trotted lightly down the stairs and met Mrs Holloway coming out of the kitchen with a tray laden with a coffee pot, cream and sugar.

'Do me a favour, Ellen,' she said, the frown lifting slightly from her pink face. 'Take this into the living room. Donovan's got an unexpected visitor and I've got to get off early today. Getting me bunions looked at. My feet are so sore, these shoes are killing me.' She thrust the tray into Ellen's hand and disappeared back into the kitchen.

Ellen gave a small laugh to herself. Mrs Holloway was such a character. Smiling she headed back down the hall to the living room. The door was slightly ajar.

'Knock, knock,' she called out, whilst backing in through the doorway, giving the door a small kick with her heel.

'Come in. Oh, Ellen, I was expecting Mrs Holloway,' said Donovan, a note of concern in his voice.

Ellen turned, concentrating on not spilling the coffee pot, she glanced up. 'Mrs Holloway was …' the words died on her lips as she looked at Donovan and then at his guest. She felt herself sway as the ice-cold spikes of fear ravaged their way down her spine.

Donovan closed the distance between himself and Ellen in a few strides and deftly took the tray from her, placing it on the coffee table. Ellen's eyes remained fixed upon his guest. Unable to form any words, she was aware of Donovan back at her side, his hand on her elbow. 'Come and sit down.' Although his touch was gentle, she found herself shrinking back, resisting his nudge of encouragement.

The guest spoke. 'Hello, Helen.'

She shook her head slightly and closed her eyes. This was not happening.

She opened them. Wrong. It *was* happening. Toby was sitting

153

in Donovan's living room.

'Are you okay, Ellen?' said Donovan. His voice held no emotion. No trace of what he was thinking or feeling. She searched his face for any clue. There was none. Impassive. Observing. Steely.

'How are you?' said Toby, standing up. 'I've been worried about you. I was just telling Donovan here, how concerned I've been.'

Ellen forced herself to answer. It was on the second attempt she managed a semblance of a sentence. 'I'm fine. Why wouldn't I be?'

'Are you feeling better now?' asked Toby.

'What? Better?' Her voice was stronger this time.

'You know, Helen...' he paused. 'Erm, I wonder, Donovan, would you give us a minute alone?'

'No!' She hadn't meant to shout. She gripped Donovan's arm. 'Please stay. I don't want you to go.'

She watched while Donovan took a long hard look at both her and Toby. Pursing his lips, he nodded. 'Okay, I'll stay. Come and sit with me on the sofa.' He took her hand in his. 'Toby, why don't you sit yourself back down in the chair. Come on, Ellen.' This time she didn't resist and her feet took her to the three-seater.

Donovan placed himself on the side of the sofa nearest to Toby, Ellen was grateful for the subtle protection. Toby sat in his chair, his elbows resting on his knees, his hands together.

'Don't look so frightened, sweetheart,' said Toby. 'Like I keep saying, I wanted to make sure you were okay, that's all.'

'Well, as you can see, I am,' replied Ellen, feeling more composed.

'Are you? How shall I put this?' Toby looked at Donovan apologetically and then back to Ellen. 'Are you remembering to take your medication?'

'Medication! What are you talking about?'

Donovan squeezed her hand. 'It's okay,' he said.

She snatched her hand away. 'No, it's not okay. I have no idea what Toby is trying to imply.'

'See, this is what I was worried about,' said Toby to Donovan. 'I said she was prone to outbursts and can be delusional at times.

The doctor said it's like a denial thing.'

'That's not true! You're making this up. Donovan, he's a liar. I don't take medication for anything.' She was aware of the panic in her voice. He had to believe her. 'The eyes, Donovan, it's in the eyes.' Dear Lord, she sounded like some mad woman. Donovan was looking at her, studying her. 'It's not true. I promise. It's not true.' She was willing him to believe her. Was that a small nod of acknowledgement? She couldn't tell.

'Helen,' Toby was addressing her again. Determined to make his point. Some things never changed. 'Helen, remember what your therapist told you. You know, your coping strategies to stay calm. The breathing exercises, you remember, don't you?'

'Stop it!' She could feel the tears gathering in her eyes. Her hands were shaking. She wanted him to stop but she knew he wouldn't. It was just like before. He'd send her into a fit of such anxiety, he would then have to take control. Use his methods to calm her down. Oh God, the 'methods.' Not here, he couldn't do anything to her here. 'Make him go, please Donovan, make him go.' Her voice was reaching that high-pitched nervous level, loud enough to be heard over Toby's drone of lying concern.

'Perhaps you should go back to the doctor, Helen,' he was saying. 'I don't think you've been taking your medication properly.'

'That's enough.' Donovan stood up. 'I think you should go. You're upsetting Ellen.'

'Helen. It's Helen,' said Toby, his eyes fixing firmly on her.

'Here she's Ellen and you're upsetting her.' Donovan gestured towards the door with his hand. 'I'll show you out.'

'Fair enough,' said Toby. He went to move towards Ellen, but Donovan was blocking his path. 'Right, okay. Have it your way. I was only concerned about her mental state. I thought you should know the full picture about her.'

'Thank you.' Donovan's reply was professional, as usual, his thoughts loyally retained behind a poker face.

'Bye, Helen,' said Toby, 'and please, go and see your doctor.'

'That's enough,' said Donovan. 'This way, thank you.' His outstretched hand leaving Toby in no doubt of the exit route. Toby obliged.

Donovan showed Toby to the front door but before opening it he paused and turned to his unexpected visitor. 'Thanks for coming by,' he said. 'I appreciate it.'

'No problem,' said Toby. 'I've been worried about her. She's not had one of these, how shall we say? *Episodes*, for a while.'

'These episodes, how frequent have they been in the past?' asked Donovan, his voice low. 'Do they always manifest themselves in the same way? Has she actually been diagnosed with a delusional disorder?'

Donovan observed Toby as he considered the questions.

'It's when she's under pressure, she escapes into a world of her own.' He glanced back over his shoulder. 'Can we step outside a moment?'

The winter air cut into Donovan as he stood on the driveway with Toby. The dull grey dusk of the evening was already trying to make its presence known. He waited for Toby to speak.

'Helen, or Ellen as she seems to have begun calling herself, last time it was Eleanor. I think she goes for names that are similar to her own so she doesn't get caught out so easily. Anyway, Helen, she's a bit of an attention-seeker and basically when things get a bit tough she blows them out of all proportion. That's when the stories get more and more elaborate. The more attention she gets, the more it feeds her desire for even more attention.'

'Did something trigger this latest episode off?' probed Donovan, an uneasy feeling weaving itself through him.

'You probably won't want to hear this.' Toby paused, looking away and then back to Donovan again. 'She was working for a family and basically couldn't cope with the two young children. She would come home very stressed out. She confessed to me that she had smacked one of them in a fit of frustration. Of course, the parents didn't know and the child was too young to tell.'

Donovan winced inwardly but did not let his professional mask slip, merely nodding in acknowledgement.

'She panicked and did a runner. Thought she was going to get into trouble. Next thing I knew she was making up all sorts of stories about why she had to leave.' Toby pulled the collar up on his jacket and shivered. 'Look, I've taken up enough of your time. I really just wanted to make sure Helen was okay and now I've told you everything, I feel I can leave with a clear conscience.' He held out his hand to Donovan. 'What you do now is up to you.'

Donovan accepted the gesture. 'Thanks for coming by,' he said. 'It's certainly explains a lot of things.'

Donovan turned the recent events and implications over in his mind as he watched Toby walk away down the road.

Going back indoors, Ellen met him in the hallway. Anxiety emitting from every part of her being. She said nothing as she laced and unlaced her fingers.

They faced each over across the tiled hallway.

'I need some time to think everything over,' said Donovan, purposefully keeping any emotion out of his voice. He needed to distance himself from his feelings for Ellen. If he could approach this in the same way he approached his private clients or his police work, then he was sure he'd see things for what they were. See people for who they were. Who they really were. He looked away as he walked down the hall. He couldn't bear to see the hurt on her face. 'I'll be in my office.'

'I'll go and get Izzy,' she said.

Donovan stopped abruptly. He turned and this time did look at her. 'I'll collect Izzy today. You have the rest of the day off.' She looked drained and on edge. Not in the right state to be driving, he told himself. He ignored the voice at the back of his mind that said not in the right state to be looking after a child either. He scooped his car keys up from the hall table and his jacket from the coat stand. 'Get some rest.'

'The eyes, Donovan.' It was almost a whisper. 'The eyes don't lie.'

He closed the door behind him. The eyes most definitely didn't lie.

Chapter Twenty-Five

Ellen stared at the closed front door that Donovan had exited. She had absolutely no idea whether he believed her or not. Toby turning up, acting concerned; was she the only one who could see through him? The thought made her shiver, as if her blood had turned to ice, freezing her insides.

She thought of her wash bag and the bottle of pills. An automatic response to a tense situation. Did she really need one? Wouldn't she just be supporting Toby's accusation? She considered her emotions and physical reaction to the latest incident. She wasn't as strung-out as she thought she might once have been. This was good. Ellen Newman was strong. She believed in herself and her ability to stay calm without the need of artificial help. All she had to hope now was that Donovan believed in her too.

Carla, coming out of the office into the hallway, made Ellen jump. She appeared equally surprised to see Ellen and stopped in her tracks.

Carla frowned as she looked at her watch. 'Shouldn't you be picking up Izzy?'

'No, Donovan is doing it.'

'Donovan? Why has he gone? He never said he was collecting Izzy today.'

'I'm not feeling well. He offered.' Okay, that was a slight bend of the truth but Ellen wasn't going to tell Carla anything.

'Right, well, I've got to go out for a few minutes,' said Carla, adjusting the belt on her navy woollen coat. 'Do you think you could listen out for the telephone and take any messages? Or are you too ill?'

Ellen rose to the challenge in Carla's voice. 'No, I can do that. So long as it is only a few minutes.'

'Ten minutes maximum. I've just had a call from Amanda to say she's coming over.' Carla pulled on her gloves. 'I know we've run out of the decaf coffee she insists on. I was going to ask Mrs Holloway to nip and get some, but then I remembered her saying she had an appointment about her feet.'

'That's right. Would you like me to get the coffee for you?'

'I thought you were unwell.'

'Yes, but maybe some fresh air would do me good.'

'No, I'll go. You stay here.' She hesitated. 'Thank you anyway.'

A terse thank you, but a thank you all the same. Ellen would take that. 'Okay, it's up to you. See you in ten minutes.'

He stood under the oak tree in Coronation Park, where the path turned to the right and out of sight from the road. His collar pulled up, he hunkered down inside his jacket, his hands in his pockets. He felt his mobile in his hand. She had returned his text message, saying she was coming but that she didn't have long. That worked fine with him. He didn't have long either. He couldn't afford to be spotted hanging around. He needed to see her to check a few details. Things needed attending to and he couldn't do it without certain information.

He scuffed his feet impatiently, mulching up the dead leaves in the process. His feet were beginning to feel the cold now. She'd better not take ages.

A figure hurrying up the path caught his eye. It was hard to make out in the diminishing light but the blueness of her coat stood out against the greyness of the road and houses behind her.

'About bloody time,' he said as she came to a halt in front of him.

'It's not that easy, coming at the drop of a hat. I am very busy you know.' Her snarky response irritated him. If it wasn't for the fact that he needed her, he'd fuck her right off this very minute. Snotty bitch, who had nothing to be snotty about. She would come unstuck one day. He momentarily flirted with the idea of what that unstuck would involve before dismissing it. He'd save the thought for later. Now he needed to find a few things out and he needed her to be co-operative and on his side for the purpose.

Ellen sat herself down at Carla's desk and surveyed the organised and tidy area in front of her. Like Carla, nothing appeared out of place. Three blue pens, all identical, were laid out in a line alongside some sticky notes and to the side of that a writing pad. The notes in the pad were all very neat, definitely not the sort of scribble Ellen would expect to see from a busy secretary.

She picked up the central pen and turned it around to face in the opposite direction, idly wondering how annoying Carla would find that. Chiding herself for being immature, Ellen turned the pen back. The shrill of the landline ring cutting through the silence made her jump. Oh God, she'd have to answer it.

'Hello?' That seemed totally insufficient. She realised she had no idea how Carla greeted clients calling on the office line. 'Er ... Donovan's not here right now, can I take a message?'

She hoped that was sufficient.

'That's not Carla, is it? Who am I speaking to, please?'

Ellen recognised that voice immediately. 'Hello, Amanda. It's Ellen. I'm afraid Carla's had to pop out.'

'Oh, it's you.' The tone was derisory. 'If there's no one else there, then you will have to do, I suppose.' She didn't wait for Ellen to respond and continued in her customary off-hand manner. 'Let Carla know I've had a change of plan and I'm not calling in now after all. Something has come up that I need to deal with. Don't mention it to Isobel, will you? I don't want her disappointed. She wasn't expecting me so there's no need to tell her. Got that?'

Ellen was fully aware of the feeling of relief sweeping over her at this information. 'Yes, of course. I'll let Carla know.'

Replacing the receiver Ellen couldn't help wonder what had caused Amanda to change her apparently impromptu plan to visit in such a short space of time. Carla probably wouldn't be very impressed having to go out in that cold weather to buy decaf coffee, which wouldn't be needed now.

When the telephone rang once more a few minutes later, Ellen half expected it to be Amanda saying she'd changed her mind again, such was the unpredictability of the woman. However, the male voice at the other end put paid to that notion.

'Could I speak to Ms Grosvenor?' enquired the man.

'I'm sorry but she's not here, can I take a message?' Ellen picked up a pen and pulled the notebook towards her.

'Could you tell her Meadowlands Care Home called. It's about her mother.'

'Oh, nothing serious, I hope,' said Ellen.

'No, no. Nothing like that. Mrs Grosvenor isn't actually a resident yet. It's just some details I need to check with Ms Grosvenor in advance of her mother coming to reside with us.'

Ellen wrote the phone number down and assured the caller she would pass the message on.

She didn't have to wait long for Carla to return, the clipping of heels down the hallway announcing her arrival.

'Everything okay?' Carla asked unbuttoning her coat and hanging it on the hook behind the office door.

Ellen got up from the desk. 'Amanda rang to say she wasn't coming any more. A change of plan.'

Carla let out an impatient huff. 'That woman is so fickle.'

Ellen was inclined to agree. Amanda was consistently inconsistent. 'There was another message too,' she said moving out of Carla's way so the PA could take her seat at the desk. Ellen pointed to the sticky note she had left on the computer screen.

'Meadowlands Care Home want you to call them about the paper-work for your mother.'

This time the impatient huff was even louder. 'That bloody home!' It was an unguarded reaction that Ellen hadn't been expecting at all. Carla rested her forehead on her fingertips, closing her eyes for a second or two.

'Are you okay?' ventured Ellen. She hadn't seen this side of Carla before. Donovan's secretary didn't respond. Ellen placed a hand on the other woman's shoulder. 'Carla?'

A droplet of water puddled on the desk top. Carla quickly grappled with the tissue box, eventually extracting one before dabbing at her eyes.

'I'm sorry. I'm fine,' she said after a moment. She looked up at Ellen and for the first time, Ellen saw vulnerability in Carla's eyes. 'It's Mother. She's doesn't want to go into the care home and is being a bit difficult about it all.'

'That's tough for you,' said Ellen.

'She's … well … she's too much for me to cope with any more. She has spates of lucidity but mostly she hasn't really a clue what's going on. Who I am. Where she is. You know, that sort of thing.'

'I am sorry to hear that, Carla.'

'God, you sound like I've told you she's died.' Carla held up her hand to quell Ellen's further apologies. 'Forget it. To be honest, sometimes it is like she's died. The mother I've had all these years has been replaced by some mother that is a total stranger.'

'Do you have any family to help you with her?'

'One useless brother who is counting the days until Mother is six feet under so he can then count his inheritance.' Carla screwed the tissue up and dropped it into the bin. 'I'm fine. Just a bit exasperated by it all.'

'I can imagine.'

'You can't. Not until you've been there yourself.' The reply indicated that the old Carla was back in control. Ellen had been allowed a momentary glance at what went on in Carla's personal life. But it was merely a glimmer. Normal service now resumed. 'Anyway, enough of all this. I must get on with some work.'

'Yes, of course. I'll see you later.'

'Ellen,' said Carla. She looked up over the computer screen. 'Don't pay much attention to me, I'm just a grumpy old bag at times. I'm sure Donovan's told you that.'

Was that a small smile she threw Ellen's way? Maybe she had misjudged Carla. Maybe she and Carla had something in common after all. They both had things going on in their personal life that they didn't want to share with anyone else. A small feeling of empathy for her colleague began to nudge its way into Ellen's consciousness.

Donovan stood outside Ellen's bedroom door. He had seen to Izzy that evening, bathing her and putting her to bed himself. He hadn't seen Ellen at all, although Carla assured him she was up in her room resting.

He had hoped Ellen would come down, but it seemed she was keeping well out of his way.

He tapped on the door and waited.

The door opened slowly, Ellen looking uneasy as she shrugged on her cardigan over her t-shirt and pulled it around her in a protective way.

'Can I come in?' he asked.

She stepped back into the room and he followed, closing the door behind him.

His eyes toured the room and came to rest on the dressing table. Perfume. Nail varnish. Hair brush. Hairdryer. A packet of tissues. What he was looking for wasn't there. He looked at Ellen, who folded her arms and tilted her chin slightly, defiance emanating from every part of her body, except for the eyes. The unnecessary blinking and wide pupils gave her away.

Without saying a word he strode over to the en-suite. Opening the door, he paused briefly to take another look at Ellen. Her shoulders took a subtle dip and he saw her swallow, but the game of brinkmanship continued. Donovan went into the small shower room and opened the mirrored door to the bathroom cabinet. He looked at the contents. Nothing remarkable and nothing in there that shouldn't be. He closed the door.

Was that relief he felt? The one thing he had been looking for, he hadn't found. That was good, right? It was then he noticed the wash bag and the relief waned. As much as he didn't want to check there, he knew he had to.

His stomach lurched as he found the plastic bottle of pills. He turned the container over in his hand, looking for the printed prescription label. There wasn't one. Instead the label simply read *Calms Remedy*. He opened the lid and shook several pills out into his hand.

'You can buy them over the counter.' Her voice called out. 'A natural herbal remedy for stressful situations. Non-addictive. Totally legal.'

Donovan returned the pills to the bottle and after replacing the lid, he put it back in the wash bag. The relief was back but this time accompanied by a sense of shame. He couldn't help but feel a complete shit. He'd had no right to march in here and go through her belongings as though she was some criminal. She deserved to be treated better.

He returned to the bedroom. Ellen was still standing in the middle of the room.

'Do you believe me now?' she said.

'I'm sorry,' said Donovan. It was wholly inadequate. Sorry didn't even begin to cover it.

'You only had to ask.'

He nodded. 'I know.' He stood in front of her, closer than was necessary. He knew he was invading her personal space but he wanted to be near her. He wanted to hold her, feel her against him, trace a line over her shoulders with his hands. Hold her. Kiss her. Explore her. He held those thoughts at bay. There was more he needed to know.

'I've got to ask you a couple of things. I'm only going to ask once and I want you to give me an honest answer. Promise?' His voice was low, his forehead almost resting on the top of her head. He could feel the warmth of her breath against the hollow of his neck.

Looking up at him from under her eyelashes, she looked so beautiful. There was a vulnerability but also depth. 'I promise.' The strength in her voice dared him to ask her, challenging him to beat her. He liked her spirit. She was a fighter, that was for sure.

'Have you ever slapped a child?'

She drew breath sharply and the look of surprise on her face told him she wasn't expecting that. The look of indignation that swiftly followed told him the answer before she even spoke a word.

'No. Categorically and emphatically no. Never.' She took a step back as if the mere suggestion was too distasteful to be near.

It was the response he wanted. His hopes rose a level. Now for the next question.

'Is there a shred of truth in what Toby suggested earlier.'

This one she had obviously been expecting. She looked him straight in the eye. Her hands moved to her sides and her shoulders tipped back.

'Not. A. Single. Shred.'

Again it was the response he hoped for. It was the truth. That he was sure about.

'Thank you,' he said softly.

'You believe me?'

'Without a doubt.'

She crumpled. He caught her in his arms. She cried. He held her tight.

A tsunami of emotion flooded from her. Most of all he sensed the relief. He continued to hold her until the wave of feeling receded and the sobs had died to a sniffle.

'Oh, Donovan. I was so worried you would think I had mental health problems. That you would believe him.'

'He was good, but not that good.' He cupped her face and kissed her tear-streaked skin. 'Like you said, it's in the eyes.'

He felt her hands draw across his back and his own made their way down her neck, over her shoulders, pulling her tightly to him, their bodies melding together.

God, he wanted her. His kisses travelled to her mouth and she responded eagerly. Her hands now at the waist band of his trousers. He groaned as she slipped her hand inside his boxer shorts.

Discarding her clothing like a quick-change artist, Ellen positioned herself on the bed, propped on one elbow, running her fingers tips over her thigh as she watched him undress.

He forced himself to take his time as he climbed onto the bed, rolling her onto her back, his hands either side of her head as she opened her legs so his knees were in between hers.

'Wait, I need to ask you one thing?' she said.

'What? Now?' He kissed her and smiled. 'Is it important?'

'Yes. Your name. What's your name? It doesn't seem very romantic calling you by your surname all the time.'

He let out a laugh. 'Believe me, my surname is the better option and if I told you now it would kill the moment. It is neither exciting nor romantic.'

He kissed her again, this time not breaking contact, so she couldn't say anything. She made a small whimper of a noise, turned her head away and mumbled. 'Okay, you win. For now.'

He closed his mouth on hers and let her guide him into her. Soft, warm and welcoming. She clearly wanted him as much as he wanted her.

Donovan paused to enjoy the sensation of being inside her, not moving, just taking a moment to commit this feeling to memory. Her gaze met his. Intense and sincere. His own feelings reflecting right back at him.

'It's always in the eyes,' he said.

She nodded. 'Always.'

Chapter Twenty-Six

When Ellen arrived downstairs the following morning with Izzy for breakfast, she was surprised to see Donovan sitting at the kitchen table with a man she had never seen before. He looked to be in his mid-thirties, his hair was cut quite short, rather like someone who was in the military. He was wearing a suit and Ellen assumed he must be a business colleague of Donovan's, here for a breakfast meeting. This idea was supported by the fact that Carla was there too. Mrs Holloway was busy making a fresh pot of tea. She turned and smiled at Ellen, indicating that she should sit down at the table. A proper welcoming committee, if ever there was one. Perhaps they weren't having a breakfast meeting, after all. Ellen ushered Izzy into her seat.

'I didn't expect to see you this morning, Donovan,' said Ellen, buttering Izzy a slice of toast. 'I thought you were away in London for a few days. Profiling for the Met.'

'I'm going up there a bit later. I wanted to introduce you to Ben.' Donovan nodded towards the man.

'Hello,' said Ellen, still not sure what this was about. Was she supposed to know who Ben was? Had Donovan mentioned him? She didn't think so.

'Good morning, Ellen. Hello, Izzy,' Ben said. He smiled at them both.

'Ben is going to be with us for a while. He'll be able to drive you around, do the school run, after-school clubs, shopping, that sort of thing. He'll even go to the park with you,' said Donovan. The over-casual tone to his voice, told Ellen everything in a heartbeat. Ben was, in effect, going to be some sort of bodyguard. Donovan was obviously spooked enough about the latest incidents. Ellen wasn't quite sure how she felt. In some respects, having Ben there would be reassuring but on the flipside, his presence would just reinforce the idea that she was in danger.

'You are going to be our driver?' asked Izzy.

'That's right,' said Ben. 'I'm here to help out your dad, especially while he is away.'

'Okay.' It was a simple acceptance. Izzy appeared unperturbed by it. Maybe Ellen should simply accept it like Izzy had. She could tell by Donovan's tense body language that there really was no choice in the matter.

'I have to leave now,' said Donovan, standing up and taking one last mouthful of his tea. He put the cup back down on the table and, walking round to Izzy, kissed her on top of the head. 'Now be a good girl for Ellen and I'll be back in a few days.'

'Are you coming back for the music show?' asked Izzy.

'Of course, I wouldn't miss your show. I'm looking forward to it.' Donovan half-grinned, half-grimaced across the table at Ellen. She suppressed a giggle. Hearing Izzy play *Twinkle Twinkle Little Star* on the violin for the past few weeks had been painful enough, but the thought of hearing a quartet of eight-year-olds doing the same was terrifying.

'Daddy is really looking forward to hearing you all play together,' said Ellen, smiling at Izzy whilst trying not to laugh.

'I most certainly am,' said Donovan. 'I tell you what. Why don't we bring Ellen along too? I'm sure she'd love to listen to you.'

Ellen was about to protest when she saw the look of excitement on Izzy's face. 'Will you come, Ellen? Please.'

How was Ellen supposed to say no? 'I'd love to. What a good

169

idea.'

'Excellent. That's that sorted,' said Donovan. He grinned at Ellen and then had the effrontery to throw her a cheeky wink. 'I really must go. Have a good week everyone and I'll see you soon.'

Ellen realised that she was still grinning as she poured herself another cup of tea. She looked up. Carla was looking at her. Only this time, instead of a frosty glare, Ellen was certain there was almost a warmth behind the PA's eyes. That would be a first. As if confirming Ellen's thoughts, Carla smiled at her. Another first. Ellen smiled back, the previous feeling of empathy morphing into camaraderie. It felt good.

The next few days felt like a week. The time dragged while Izzy was at school and three-fifteen became Ellen's highlight of the day. Ben proved to be a good companion for the few days Donovan was away. It was nice to have someone who she could relax with and just chat about everyday things. Donovan was due back the following day and Ben was helping Ellen put the finishing touches to the paintwork in Izzy's bedroom.

'That looks great. Thanks for all your help,' said Ellen.

'No problem. I quite enjoyed it.'

'Is there no end to your talents?'

'Probably. Just haven't found it yet,' said Ben.

She had tried to probe him about his background but he had been particularly vague. She had managed to glean dribs and drabs from conversations that he had, indeed, been in the military once upon a time, but now worked in the private sector. He used the term 'driver' but Ellen knew as well as he did that he was far more than merely a driver. She had to admit that despite the thought slightly unsettling her, it was outweighed by the comfort this knowledge brought. She liked the feeling of security he offered. It was the same feeling she got when Donovan was around. Having Ben there kept that sense of security in place.

Ellen was also pleased with the new direction her relation-ship with Carla had taken. Although they hadn't yet reached the cosy-sit-down-and-have-a-chat-over-coffee level, things were definitely improving between the two of them, which had a positive knock-on effect to the whole house – the atmosphere was definitely much lighter.

After dropping Izzy at school, Ellen now found herself with time on her hands. She flicked on her laptop and fired off an email to Kate.

Hi

Hope you are well. How's that lovely little brother of yours – turned into a miserable teenager yet?

I had a bit of a shock the other day. Toby turned up at the house. I have no idea how he found me. It was awful. I'll have to tell you about it properly when I see you but, basically, he spoke to Donovan and was trying to convince him I had mental health issues – that I was crazy. Fortunately, Donovan didn't believe him.

There's been a lot of weird things going on around here lately. I'd say come down and visit but it's probably best to leave it until all this stuff has died down. Don't worry about anything, though, I'll keep you up to date. Just be on your guard with Toby. I wouldn't put anything past him, as you well know.

Love and hugs, as ever.

Xx

By the time Thursday afternoon arrived, Ellen wasn't sure who was most excited at the prospect of Donovan coming home. Her or Izzy.

The whoop of delight and being swept up into his arms in a big hug was, however, strictly reserved for Izzy, much as Ellen felt she wanted to do pretty much the same. She had missed him being around the house this week.

'Wasn't sure I was going to make it; the traffic has been dreadful,' said Donovan, putting Izzy down and closing the front door behind him. To Ellen's surprise and, she had to admit, delight, he then proceeded to give her a kiss on the mouth and wrapping his arm around her held her for a moment. 'That feels good.' He didn't seem the least bit bothered if anyone saw. He continued to talk as if it was the most natural thing in the world. 'How's everything been? All quiet on the Western Front?'

'Nothing to report,' said Ellen, trying to maintain a calm exterior, despite the happiness she felt inside that he was home. 'Everything is fine.'

'That's good. Oh, hello Carla,' he said, looking beyond Ellen's shoulder. 'I'll be with you shortly.'

'Hello, Donovan. I'll make you a coffee.' She returned to the office.

Donovan looked at Ellen. 'Is everything okay?'

'She's got a lot on her mind at the moment?' said Ellen. 'I'll tell you about it later.'

Donovan raised his eyebrows, a look of curiosity on his face.

'Later,' insisted Ellen, stealing another kiss. 'Come on, we need to get ready for Izzy's music concert.'

'Now you're using the word *music* very liberally,' said Donovan.

'All the right notes, just in the wrong order,' said Ellen through a smile. She flicked him lightly on the arm. 'Now get moving.'

Donovan and Ellen sat next to each other on blue plastic chairs, squashed in the hall, with about one hundred other proud parents, all there to watch the annual music evening. There was barely any room to move, especially as it was a cold wintry evening and most people were wrapped in bulky coats. Ellen found herself squeezed right up against Donovan, their shoulders touching. It was a nice feeling, one which Donovan appeared to share in, for instead of moving his end seat further out into the aisle, he chose to stay where he was. Throughout the event, they exchanged small smiles of amusement as they watched and listened to the children file on stage with their various instruments, play a well-rehearsed tune and then totter off again. Some had rather more musical prowess than others.

'Here we go, Izzy's turn,' whispered Donovan, leaning even closer to Ellen. 'Have I got the earplugs or have you?'

Ellen got through the performance without wincing too much. She swapped sideways looks with Donovan every now and then when a note wasn't quite achieved. Fortunately, this particular rendition of *Twinkle Twinkle Little Star* was only one verse and one chorus long. At the end they both applauded loudly, Donovan clearly sharing in Ellen's relief that it was over. Bless Izzy, she did look so proud of herself and, despite the torture his ears had endured, Donovan too, looked extremely proud of his daughter. Father and daughter waved and smiled at each other, which Ellen found touching.

The scramble to leave the hall at the end of the concert was second only to the January sales in Oxford Street, thought Ellen, as avoiding elbow nudges and impatient feet clipping the back of their heels, they were swept along in a throng of parents.

Out in the playground, where they had to wait at the classroom doors to collect their children, the parents gathered in the rain. The poor weather had started off earlier as a gentle drizzle but had now developed into a steadier downpour. Ellen wished she had thought to bring an umbrella.

'We're going to get soaked getting to the car,' she said, remembering that Ben had needed to park outside the school grounds. The school car park was only small and had been full when they arrived. The driveway of the school swept round to the main entrance, providing a one-way system for drop off and pick up. 'Shall I go and find Ben and get him to bring the car round here?'

'I'd rather you didn't go off on your own,' began Donovan, before he was interrupted by a tap on his shoulder from another parent.

'Hello, it's Isobel's father, isn't it? Plenty of room under here for you,' said a mother, raising her umbrella to cover Donovan's head.

Ellen didn't relish the thought of either trying to squeeze, uninvited, under the umbrella, or standing in the rain while the two parents chatted. 'Be back in a minute,' she said quickly, before breaking into a small run and heading out to find Ben and the car. She heard Donovan call after her but chose to ignore him. All she wanted to do right now was to get in the dry.

Oakdale School was in a truly lovely setting, thought Ellen; a small Sussex village nestled in the South Downs. On a winter's evening like tonight, however, with the persistent rain, the wind whipping up, and to make matters worse, hardly any street lighting, the appeal just wasn't there.

Ellen peered up the road, her eyes scanning the row of cars parked along the grass verge. She thought she'd be able to see the black Range Rover above the other vehicles, but only now she remembered that a large four by four was a popular choice amongst the parents. The lack of lighting wasn't helping, and the fact that all the vehicles were empty, their owners no doubt waiting, like Donovan, for the children to be let out. Ellen made her way along the narrow footpath. She could see a big black four-wheel-drive at the end which looked as though it could be Donovan's.

The slamming of something or someone into her shoulder was so unexpected that, at first, Ellen didn't even register the pain. Her brain didn't have time to make sense of what was happening as she collided with the high brick wall that surrounded the school grounds.

She felt a hand grab her shoulder. To stop her falling, she thought. Funny how you can think things in a nanosecond. Ellen wondered if she was thinking quickly or if events were happening slowly. She turned her head to see who had come to her rescue, but instead of seeing a friendly face, she saw the silver of a watch strap and the hand at the end, clenched in a fist coming her way. In that moment, the sudden realisation that she was being attacked registered. Instinctively, she threw her head to the right to try and avoid the blow. Hard-boned knuckles connecting with her left cheekbone, sending a ripple of pins and needles surging out across her skin. Her right eyebrow made contact with the brick wall but the adrenalin tearing through her body smothered the pain, much the same way as her attacker's hand smothered her mouth, eliminating any sound.

Ellen heard a stifled groan and realised it had come from her. She clawed at the hand over her mouth but the grip was tight, squeezing the sides of her face so firmly into her mouth, she thought her skin would tear.

She knew she was panicking. She needed to think straight. Her survival instinct kicked in. She brought her knee up swiftly, using all the strength she had in her, making contact with his groin. Simultaneously, she forced her mouth to open wider, the top of his hand slipped between her teeth. She bit down on the flesh. He let out a yell of pain and instantly released his hold on her.

She heard herself shouting. 'Help! Donovan! Ben! Help! Someone!'

She realised she couldn't wait for someone to come to her rescue. She had to keep trying to physically fight back.

With a gargantuan effort, finding strength where she thought all had left her, Ellen thrust her hands at his chest, shoving him backwards. She didn't wait to see where he stumbled. She was running like she'd never run before. She had no idea where, but she knew she needed to put distance between her and the man.

All of a sudden she was caught in the arms of someone. She screamed. How had he got in front of her? She thrashed her arms wildly but he held her tight. She could hear herself almost sobbing hysterically. This couldn't be happening to her.

'Ellen! Ellen!' He knew her name. How? How did he know her name? 'Ellen. It's all right. It's me. Donovan.'

She struggled some more. Her brain acknowledged it was Donovan, however her body had taken on a life of its own. For a few moments she fought wildly but her strength began to sap. Her arms had no force to back up the flailing and her shoulders were weak as they attempted to shrug his hands off. Then she was all spent. No energy. No adrenalin to keep her fighting. Her body slumped. He held her tight, enveloping her in his arms. She felt her knees soften and thought she would slip right through his embrace. He held her tighter, making soothing noises. The relief was overwhelming. He had her. She was safe.

'Oh God, Donovan. Someone's just attacked me,' she was crying, holding tightly onto his neck.

'I told you not to go off on your own. What were you thinking of? And where the fuck is Ben?' snapped Donovan. She shuddered at the harshness in his voice and then he spoke more gently. 'I'm sorry I didn't mean to shout.'

As if waiting for his cue, Ben came skidding to a halt beside them. He was panting hard.

'What's happened?' He swivelled round, looking up and down the road.

'Someone attacked Ellen,' said Donovan. 'Where were you? Did you see anything?'

'Shit,' muttered Ben. 'I've been in the car. I didn't see a thing?'

Ellen pulled back from Donovan to look at Ben. 'Nothing? Nothing at all?'

Ben shook his head apologetically. 'Sorry, Ellen.'

'How could you not have seen anything?'

'It's dark. The car's back up there a bit. The first thing I knew was when I heard you shouting,' said Ben.

'I'm not making this up.' Ellen could hear the desperate tone in her voice. They had to believe her.

'It's okay, Ellen. Stay calm,' said Donovan.

He was talking to her as though she was a child; the same way he way he spoke to Izzy to pacify her. Then another wave of panic engulfed her. 'Izzy! Where's Izzy?'

'Oh, shit!' Donovan released Ellen and was running back towards the school as he called out to them. 'Get the car! Meet me at the front of the school.'

Chapter Twenty-Seven

Soaking wet, Donovan sat in the Range Rover next to Ben, with Ellen and Izzy in the back. He listened patiently as his daughter recounted the music evening as if he had never been there.

As Izzy's chatter moved on to the new Barbie doll her friend Daisy had brought with her, Donovan's mind slipped back to the events of the evening. He had practically steamrolled into the classroom, pushing past other parents, to make sure Izzy was still there. A very surprised and disgruntled Miss Armstrong had assured him that Izzy was perfectly fine and would never have been allowed to go with anyone else. He knew he'd appeared to be overreacting but he also knew he had good reason.

He smiled at Izzy and she continued to chatter about this and that. Then he looked at Ellen, huddled in the corner, her face bruised. She had refused to go to the hospital and, likewise, hadn't wanted to call the police.

Donovan hadn't quite made up his mind for her reasoning behind this and he wanted to get to the bottom of why she didn't want to go. He knew she was scared but what exactly was she scared of? Doubt stalked his thoughts. Doubt in the form of Toby and what he had said when he had visited the house, that Ellen was delusional.

He side-stepped the thought. He had dealt with this already.

Dismissed it and believed Ellen. Believed her because he could make the facts fit with her version of events, or because he had wanted to believe her? Another doubt that had snipered his belief.

Izzy skipped her way through the open front door, telling Carla all about the evening, while the three adults trudged their way in. Donovan noticed the look of alarm on Carla's face as she saw the state Ellen was in. He shook his head and nodded towards Izzy. He didn't want attention drawn to it.

'I'm going to have a shower,' said Ellen, keeping her head down.

'First let me look at your face properly,' said Donovan. He shepherded her in the direction of the living room, away from the others who were making their way down to the kitchen. 'I'll be with you in a minute.'

Once satisfied that she wasn't going to protest, Donovan went down to the kitchen to get some cotton wool and warm water to bathe Ellen's wounds. He also needed to make a discreet phone call to the station.

A few minutes later he was in the living room with Ellen. He perched on the coffee table in front of her.

'I'll be all right,' protested Ellen.

'I'll be the judge of that.' He dipped the cotton wool into the small bowl of water and, squeezing out the excess liquid, he tipped her face up towards him. He winced as he saw the graze on her right temple and grimaced further, when he saw the red swelling on her left cheek. Fortunately the skin hadn't been broken. 'You have to report this, Ellen. You do know that.'

She looked down. 'Maybe it was a random attack.'

He dropped the cotton wool onto the tray beside his mini first-aid kit and spoke in a soft voice. 'Maybe. Maybe not. It still needs reporting. I've already rung Ken.'

He leaned forwards and kissed her. A small kiss that tasted so sweet, he stayed for more. He stroked her sodden hair and kissed her again. He felt the wetness of a tear run between their lips and he pulled away but swathed her in his arms and held her close to him as she cried from the shock of the evening.

He wanted to protect her, to make things better. To take away her pain. He didn't know how, so he simply held her even tighter as she clung onto him, the tears turning to sobs and eventually subsiding. Spent of emotion, she was still clinging to him.

Eventually, the quietness of the room was broken by a knock and Carla entered. Ellen pulled away and rummaged in her pocket for a tissue.

'Sorry to interrupt but DCI Froames is here.' She glanced over at Ellen and then back to Donovan. 'Would you like me to settle Izzy tonight?'

'Thank you, Carla, that would be great,' said Donovan. 'I'll just say goodnight to her.'

He got up and followed Carla into the hall where Ken and a female police officer were waiting. 'Give me a minute, Ken, and I'll be with you.'

Izzy's protest at not having either her father or Ellen put her to bed was short-lived, exhaustion and excitement from the concert getting the better of her. With the promise of an extra story from Carla, Izzy went on her way, much to Donovan's relief. There had been enough drama for one night.

Donovan took Ken and the police officer into the living room, where Ellen was patiently waiting. He sat quietly while Ellen answered the questions put to her in a calm and collected, almost matter-of-fact, manner. As far as he was aware, she hadn't taken one of those calming pills. He still felt guilty for challenging her about Toby's insinuation that she was on medication. He should have known better. Known her better. He couldn't help but admire how composed Ellen was. It made him think that maybe she was used to detaching herself from events, being brave, being strong. Maybe her past experiences with Toby had made her like this. It saddened him. It also angered him. However, now wasn't the time to turn on the alpha male. Ellen needed his love and support.

Love?

Shit.

Where the hell did that come from? A feeling he wasn't expecting. A feeling he had long since relegated to the depths of his heart. He dismissed the notion and focused on what Ken was asking Ellen.

'Is there anything about the attacker that stands out? Anything you can remember?' Ken's voice was soft; it reminded Donovan of how the big detective spoke to Izzy. Encouraging, warm and reassuring.

Ellen looked troubled. 'I can't really think of anything,' she said after a while.

'Don't rush. Give yourself time,' said the police officer.

'No. Sorry,' said Ellen finally.

'I think that's enough for one evening,' said Donovan. Ellen looked exhausted. He winced inwardly as he studied her grazed face. *He* should have gone for the car and left her to wait for Izzy.

Donovan walked to the front door with Ken.

The DCI spoke to the female police officer. 'Wait in the car for me. I won't be long.'

'Yes, sir.'

Donovan waited until the police officer was in the car. 'What do you reckon, Ken? Any chance you'll get the bloke? Do you think it could be the ex-boyfriend?'

Ken gave a wry smile. 'You're the criminal psychologist. What do *you* reckon?'

Donovan pinched the bridge of his nose, exhaling the sigh that he had wanted to let out no end of times but had refrained from doing so in front of Ellen. 'A simple answer. Yes. It could well be the ex-boyfriend. It's worrying that if it is him, he's turned from passive stalking to aggressive attack.'

'It could, of course, have nothing to do with the ex-boyfriend and be someone else.'

'So Ellen keeps telling me.' Another sigh broke free. 'What

happens now?'

'Procedural process. We log the attack. I can send SOCO down to have a look at the area tomorrow. No good doing it now in the dark.'

'You're not going to find anything after all this rain. Besides,' Donovan hated what he was going to say next, 'there might not be anything to find in the first place.'

Ken raised his eyebrows. 'You think she's making it up? What about the bruising and the cut on her face? She's hardly likely to have done that to herself.'

'Not likely but not impossible either.' Donovan closed his eyes. He despised himself for even thinking it, let alone saying it out loud but his emotions were swinging wildly from belief to suspicion.

'Take it from me, mate,' said Ken. 'Ellen doesn't strike me as some sort of psycho who would go to those extreme lengths. She seems genuinely shaken up by the whole thing. Taking all my years of policing into account, I'd stake my salary on her telling the truth.'

It was a reassuring testament, from which Donovan took heart. 'I know, it's just the seed of doubt, that's all.'

'I'll tell you what I'll do. Just between us, we don't have to let Ellen know. I'll send someone to check out what the ex-boyfriend has been up to tonight. See if he has an alibi. How does that sound?'

'Thanks, Ken. I would appreciate that,' said Donovan. 'While they are at it, get them to check out Lampard too, will you?'

Donovan went back inside and after gentle persuasion, he convinced Ellen to go to bed.

'You should get some sleep. It's been a shock for you,' he said.

'I don't know if I can sleep,' replied Ellen, standing up and resting her head against his chest.

Donovan held her for a moment. 'Try and relax. I can sit with you for a while if you like.'

She looked up at him. 'To make sure I don't take one of my pills?' There was a challenging tone to her voice.

'No, that's not what I was implying at all,' he said.

'I'm sorry, I didn't mean to snap at you.' She ran the lapel of his jacket between her finger and thumb. 'I've stopped taking those pills.'

'You don't have to explain yourself to me,' he said, although Donovan couldn't deny that this was good news. Despite knowing they were only a herbal remedy and non-addictive, he didn't like the idea of Ellen depending on them. It also confirmed his thoughts that she was a strong woman, probably stronger than she herself appreciated.

She wrapped her arms around his neck and kissed him before burying her face in his shoulder. 'I'd like it very much if you stayed for a while.'

'Of course, angel.' He'd stay all night if she wanted him to, his earlier doubts sinking as his gut feeling of believing in her resurfaced.

He hadn't planned to rough her up earlier but he certainly had no regrets. It hadn't even been on his agenda to come into any contact with her. He had followed them up there with a mind to causing some damage to the car; a bit of paint-spraying and slashing of tyres. Something that would inconvenience them. Ruffle the feathers some more. Not only the adults, but the kid as well. As it happened, he was quite pleased with the way things had turned out.

The minder they now had with them didn't get out of the car as he thought would happen. He scoffed at the suggestion of the name. The *minder* hadn't exactly fulfilled his job description. And as for Donovan, well, he was just as bad. They had both let her go off on her own. It had been an opportunist moment.

He could have done without the knee in the balls or the bite to his hand, though, that was for sure. He rubbed the skin between his thumb and finger where she'd bitten him. Bitch. Still, she'd pay for that – he'd make sure of it.

It only took a matter of days before Donovan received a phone call from Ken.

'Lampard has an alibi for the incident with Ellen at the school', said Ken. 'He was in Cornwall taking part in a 10k run. His brother can back this up. We've seen confirmation that he took part. No denying it, he was there all right.'

'Long-distance running and mountain-biking. He really is quite the action guy, isn't he?' said Donovan. 'He was definitely there?'

'Yep. Each entrant has an electronic tagging device so their timings are accurate. Lampard went through the start at 10.03 and at 10.56 he went through the finish line.'

'So there's absolutely no way he could have been anywhere else?'

'No.'

'What about if someone took his tag through with them as well as their own?'

'Already checked that out. No one had the exact same time. It would be pretty near impossible for one person to take two separate electronic tags over at different times.' Ken was adamant. 'We checked his Facebook account and he's been tagged in several pictures that same afternoon, enjoying a pint at the local pub in Cornwall. There's no way he could have got back to Sussex in time to be around when the concert was on.'

'So it definitely wasn't Lampard then.'

'Definitely not Lampard,' said Ken, pausing for a moment.

'There's something else?'

'Yes, you're not going to like this much.'

'Why did I have a feeling you were going to say that?'

'Because you know me too well, perhaps?' said Ken. 'Now, about Toby Hastings. I sent someone round to speak to him but I'm sorry, Donovan, he wasn't there.'

Donovan cursed silently to himself before he spoke. 'Has anyone seen him? What about work? Has he been to work?'

'Hang on, who's the detective around here?'

'Sorry. I guess I've been hanging around the police station for far too long.'

'In answer to your questions. Yes he has still been going into work. We've left a message on the number Ellen gave, and asked him to make contact. Any developments and I'll let you know. How is Ellen today?'

'She's okay. A tough cookie, that one,' replied Donovan.

'I get the feeling that young lady has been through quite a bit before now,' said Froames.

'You're not wrong there.'

After finishing his conversation with the DCI, Donovan went back into the kitchen. Mrs Holloway had phoned in sick, so Ellen was busy preparing breakfast. He had offered to do it himself but Carla had already delegated the duty.

'Where's Izzy?' he asked as he came into the kitchen.

'She's out in the garden, on the trampoline,' replied Ellen, nodding towards the window. 'Don't worry, Ben's with her.'

'That was Ken on the phone.' Donovan took some side plates out of the cupboard and began laying the table. 'They haven't been able to speak to Toby yet but as soon as they do, he's going to call me.' He looked for some sort of reaction, but Ellen carried on filling the kettle, a mere nod to acknowledge what he'd said. 'About Toby,' he continued, 'do you know much about him? What he was like before you were with him? Old girlfriends, have they ever said anything about him?'

Ellen let out a laugh. 'Oh, Donovan, you really do sound like a psychologist now. Next you will be asking me if he had a troubled childhood or telling me it's all to do with his mother making him wear pink jumpers.'

'Did she?'

'How would I know?' Ellen laughed again. 'That's such a cliché.'

'Hey, don't knock it, it's a valid theory. Why do you think clichés exist? Because they are often based on fact.' He smiled. He did that a lot when Ellen was about. Anyone else making a similar remark may well have irked him, but Ellen just made him laugh.

He moved towards the cutlery drawer at the same time as Ellen moved to the cupboard above it to get the cups.

Without time to consider what he was doing, Donovan found himself putting his arms around her and drawing her towards him. There was no hesitation on her part when his mouth found hers. He felt her arms slide up his shoulders, pausing momentarily as they clasped his neck, before joining together across his back. He could feel the warmth of her hands through his shirt and the curves of her body against his. Every nerve ending in his body, and he meant every single one, felt as if it were on fire. Jesus, all he wanted to do was take her to bed, in fact, he wasn't even fussy if they didn't make it to the bedroom. This was bad. He groaned and pulled away.

'Sorry.' Ellen dropped her hands and took a step back, embarrassment flushing her face red.

He caught her hands and kissed each one. 'Don't be sorry. It's not that I don't want to but I think here on the kitchen table may well put Carla off her breakfast.'

The red flush remained but was accompanied by a smile and a look of relief. 'Oh, in that case then, I'm not sorry. But maybe I should be. Actually, I wanted to talk to you about Carla.'

Donovan felt the good mood slipping. 'What's up? Problems?'

'Yes, but not in the way you're probably thinking.' She kept her arms around him. 'Carla's got a lot on her plate at home. Her mother needs full-time care in a nursing home and Carla's been left to sort everything out. Her brother hasn't been much help and I think she's finding it difficult. Not only the pressure of organising everything, but the emotional pressure too.'

'I had no idea,' said Donovan, genuinely shocked. 'I knew Carla called on her mother several times a week to make sure everything was okay. I hadn't realised it had got to this stage.'

'Maybe you could give her some more time off or something. I know I'm not exactly up to Carla's PA standards, but I can answer the phone for you and do a bit of office work while Izzy is at school.'

185

'You are such a kind and considerate person, always putting others first,' said Donovan. 'Even though you and Carla aren't the best of friends, you're still thinking how you can help her.'

Ellen grinned at him. 'Carla's okay. We seem to have reached an understanding with each other.'

'That's good to hear. I always said her bark was worse than her bite. Thank you for being so understanding of her. I think that's one of the qualities I love most about you.'

At that moment, Carla walked in. He smiled at her and reluctantly disentangled himself from Ellen. 'Morning, Carla.'

'Good morning, Donovan. Ellen.'

'Morning,' replied Ellen, as she opened the fridge. 'Oh, we've no milk. I'll nip round to the shop and get some. Mrs Holloway usually picks it up on her way in.'

'I'll go,' said Donovan. He didn't want Ellen going out on her own. 'Or I'll ask Ben.'

'No, it's all right. It's only around the corner,' said Ellen, already heading out of the kitchen.

'You can't go,' said Carla to Donovan. 'You have a telephone consultation in half an hour and you wanted time to prepare for it. Remember?'

Donovan swore silently to himself. He'd forgotten about the consultation and Ellen was already halfway out the door. He strode to the hallway and called down to her. 'Wait while I get Ben to go with you.'

She turned round and, smiling, pulled her mobile from her pocket and waved it in the air at him. 'Stop worrying, I'll be fine.'

Chapter Twenty-Eight

The leaves were soggy underfoot as Ellen made her way down the road towards the village shops, picking her way around the puddles left from the rain the previous night. However, the sun was shining, albeit low in the sky and she squinted against the dazzle of the light.

Felpham wasn't exactly the busy hub of the south coast, but today the road was particularly quiet and deserted. Passing the trees, the sun now put in a full appearance, blinding Ellen momentarily, she put her hand above her eyes to shield the sun from her face.

She could make out the silhouette of someone walking towards her. A tall well-built figure of a man, but with the sun behind him. An unexpected little trickle of fear pooled in the small of her back, as her senses hit full alert. She stepped out into the road, heading for the other side.

The blast of a car horn behind her made Ellen jump violently and she let out a startled yelp. The black vehicle swerved to avoid her and came to a dead stop only metres away.

The door opened and out jumped the driver.

'Ellen! Are you okay?'

It was Ben. Ellen recognised his voice first, her eyes adjusting from the glare of the winter sun. 'You frightened the life out of me,' she gasped.

'You're lucky you've any life left to frighten – stepping out into the road like that,' said Ben, taking her by the arm and steering her towards the passenger door. 'Donovan sent me to find you. He didn't like you coming out on your own.'

As she climbed in the car, Ellen looked ahead. The man who had been walking towards her, was nowhere to be seen. She swivelled in her seat, craning her neck to look behind her in case he had walked by without her noticing. Not there either. He had vanished.

'What's up?' said Ben getting in to the car and starting the engine.

'Nothing,' said Ellen, dispelling the uneasy feeling the figure had brought to her.

'Sure?'

'Yes, perfectly sure.' The last thing she wanted was to give Ben or Donovan any more reason to worry, or to doubt her for that matter. She didn't want them to think she was imagining things or worse, making things up. 'Come on, let's get that milk.'

A knock at the door accompanied by the simultaneous ring of his phone meant only one thing to Donovan. Amanda. This was the way she always announced her arrival. Great, it was just what he needed for her to turn up early. She wasn't supposed to be here until after lunch to take Izzy out.

Walking out into the hallway, he could see the distinctive peacock blue of her coat through the obscured glass. He cut the call, not bothering to answer it and opened the front door.

'Good morning, Amanda,' he said, letting her in. He wanted to avoid her seeing Ellen in the state she was in. He could really do without Amanda asking any awkward questions. 'Come into the living room. Would you like a cup of coffee?'

'It always makes me laugh the way you invite me into my own house and ask me politely if I would like coffee. As if I'm merely a guest.'

'To be honest, Amanda, it's not your house. It's mine. And if we're going to get petty because you are obviously in one of your pissy moods, then, yes, you are a guest. A guest who is here early. Any particular reason?'

'Do I need a reason to see my daughter?' She placed her handbag on the sofa and unbuttoned her coat, turning her back to Donovan in anticipation of him taking it from her.

Donovan shrugged. 'No, but it would be nice to know in advance. That is the arrangement, after all. I need to make sure Ellen knows so she can have Izzy ready.'

'Speaking of Ellen, where is she?' said Amanda, looking over her shoulder, as Donovan took her coat, which he then draped across the back of the sofa.

All Donovan's instincts were on high alert. 'In the kitchen. Why?'

'Oh, dear Donovan, if I didn't know you better, I'd say you were starting to get very protective of Ms Newman.' She didn't give him time to answer before she spoke again. 'Actually, there is something I wanted to talk to you about first.'

Amanda fished in her bag and pulled out a packet of cigarettes. Donovan went to protest but caught the defiant look in his wife's eye. He could do without an argument. Instead he walked over to the French doors and opened them wide onto the side garden.

'So, what is it you wanted to say?' he asked, as she seated herself on the sofa. The look of smug aloofness wasn't fooling him. He was pretty damn sure he wasn't going to like what was coming next.

'About Ellen ...'

His feeling was right. Immediately, he felt himself prickle. 'Yes? Get to the point for God's sake.'

'Are you sure you know everything about her?'

'Of course. Why do you ask?'

'I'm concerned about her being around Isobel, that's all.'

'You've nothing to worry about on that score, I can assure you.' He fixed his gaze on his estranged wife.

'Tell me, then,' said Amanda, drawing deeply on her cigarette and then blowing the smoke out into the room. 'When I spoke to Isobel on the phone, why did she say a bad man had pushed Ellen and that Ellen had a sore face?'

Donovan drove down the exasperated sigh that was threatening to escape. He hadn't anticipated Izzy mentioning the graze on Ellen's face. He had simply told her that Ellen had slipped. Izzy must have overheard them speaking about it.

'It's nothing for you to worry about. I told you that already.'

Amanda stood up, ignoring the ash that dropped onto the rug. 'Well, what exactly happened then?'

'Amanda, it was just a random incident. Someone bumped into Ellen in the dark and she fell against the wall. Izzy wasn't with her at the time.' It was the truth, although he appreciated not the whole truth, but he really didn't need Amanda going into one of her rants about it. He didn't want to give her any ammunition in the divorce courts.

'I'm not entirely convinced,' she said. She stood up and took a step towards him. Her voice low and sinister. 'If I so much as think there has been another incident, then I'll be putting in for sole custody of my daughter. Do you understand? I am not even letting you have joint custody if anything might endanger her. And that includes Ms Newman.'

With that, Amanda strode out of the living room, calling for Izzy. Donovan looked on through the doorway. Fortunately she appeared almost straight away, coat on, ready for her mother. Ellen was with her. Not that it really mattered, now. Amanda knew what happened at the school.

Ellen turned her head to meet his gaze. Standing in the light that streamed through the picture window, she had an angelic glow around her. By contrast, his wife stood in the shadow, looking the polar opposite. He sighed. Amanda had always had a ruthless streak, but in the early days of their relationship, the softer side of her had far outweighed it. The avarice, the hunger for materialistic possessions and the dependency upon alcohol had gradually become stronger and stronger. And now, it was the sum total of what she was.

Ellen, on the other hand, was the opposite. Money wasn't enough to keep her in a bad relationship or guide her into another one, it would seem. She had an inner strength that she was too humble to even acknowledge in herself. She thought running away from Toby was a weakness when, in fact, it was possibly the strongest thing she had ever done. She had left all the material trappings behind to save what was left of her. Donovan admired the strength she showed in doing this.

'So, now you're free for the rest of the weekend, how about I take you out for dinner this evening?' said Donovan as he closed the front door after waving goodbye to Amanda and Izzy.

'That would be nice,' replied Ellen. 'Just the two of us? '

Donovan walked over to her and kissed her on her forehead. 'Carla, of course, has the weekend off, I think she's sorting out her mother's belongings.' He kissed the tip of her nose. 'And before you ask. Ben's …'

'Let me guess,' interrupted Ellen. 'He's not working this weekend, either.'

'You've got it. He's going to hang around for a couple of hours while I attend to some work.' This time he kissed her mouth before pulling away and smiling at her. 'I've got to go down to the police station this afternoon. Nothing to do with you, it's okay, don't look so alarmed. I have a meeting with one of the detectives from CID. Odd day, I know, but I have to fit in with the shift patterns and, unfortunately, this sometimes falls on a weekend.'

'Okay, I'll probably curl up with a good book,' replied Ellen.

'Be ready by seven.' He kissed her on the mouth again, this time longer and definitely with more meaning. Ellen stifled a moan that was threatening to escape. She would much rather be curled up with him than with a book but, hey, she could be patient.

Toby waited on Kate's doorstep. He rang the bell again rather impatiently. He knew she was in there, he had seen her arrive home from work. A few moments passed and he was pleased to hear the sound of the lock being turned. Kate's face peered through the gap afforded by the safety chain.

'Toby. I wasn't expecting you.'

'I would have rung but I needed to speak to you in person,' he said. She didn't look as though she was going to open the door. 'Can I come in? It's about Helen.' The sincere smile he tagged on the end did the trick and Kate closed the door, slid back the chain and let him in.

'I've just got in from work. Do you want a coffee?'

'No thanks. I'll get straight to the point,' he said sitting himself down on the sofa, not waiting to be invited. 'I've been to see Helen.'

Kate nodded but she didn't seem surprised. Clearly, she was already privy to this information. 'How did that go?' she asked.

'It was difficult, as you can imagine.' He squeezed his bottom lip between his finger and thumb. 'I spoke to her boss. He seems a decent sort of bloke.'

'Yes, Helen speaks very well of …'. Kate's words died out. There, he knew he had been right all along. Kate was in regular contact with Helen. Kate looked embarrassed.

'It's okay, don't worry. I know you and Helen keep in touch.' He patted her arm reassuringly. He didn't want her to clam up now. In fact, he wanted quite the opposite. He needed to enlist Kate's help. He carried on. 'I didn't really get much of a chance to speak to Helen herself, though. I think she felt a bit awkward in front of her boss. I explained to him about her medication and everything but I don't think Helen had told him. I may have dropped her in it.'

'Her medication? What do you mean by that?' Kate didn't sound totally surprised by this and Toby wondered if Helen had already mentioned this too. He wouldn't say anything, though, he'd go along with her for now.

Toby shook his head and let out a small groan. 'Don't tell me you didn't know about that either? Of all the people, I would have put money on Helen confiding in you. She told you everything.'

'She never once mentioned any medication to me.'

'Are you sure?'

'Of course I'm sure. What was the medication for?'

Toby looked down at his feet and then back to Kate. 'She had little episodes of delusion. Sometimes, she'd make stuff up and actually convince herself it was real.'

Kate got to her feet. 'Toby, I have no idea what you're talking about. Helen wasn't like that. I'd have known.'

'Kate, please sit down. I'm sorry to break the news to you, it's obviously a shock. I assumed you would know.' He coaxed Kate back down onto the sofa next to him. He placed his arm gently around her shoulders. 'It's something that developed over the last twelve months or so. The doctor says it was triggered by stress. If things got on top of her, she'd retreat into herself and her way of coping was to invent her own version of events. A bit like some sort of parallel life. One that she felt she was in control of.'

Kate still didn't look convinced. 'I'm finding this very hard to take in and believe,' she said. 'I'm sure I would have noticed if something like this was going on.'

'Maybe it was there in front of you, but you never saw it because you didn't know what to look for?' he suggested. 'Helen found it difficult to admit herself. I encouraged her to go to the doctor's and even after she was diagnosed, she was in denial for quite some time. It wasn't until the medication kicked in that she started to acknowledge her problem.'

'I can't believe she didn't say anything,' said Kate, her voice heavy with sadness. 'I could have helped her.'

'I know she often came to you when we had rowed or had a disagreement,' said Toby. 'I'm guessing she probably told you things. You know, things about us. Things that, at the time, she was convinced had happened but maybe didn't really.'

'You mean she lied to me?'

'Don't see it as a lie. She wasn't conscious of telling any lies. The doctor said that she would have been utterly convinced and believed totally in what she was saying, but really it was just her mind trying to block out what was really upsetting her and replacing it with a different thought.'

'I feel awful that I didn't know this. Why didn't you tell me before?'

'I'm sorry, I know now I should have done but I was trying to protect Helen.' Toby sat back in the sofa and closed his eyes. 'She would have been devastated if anyone knew. I was only trying to protect her. Protect her from herself.'

Toby sat quietly while he waited for Kate to take in what he had told her. He knew it wouldn't be an easy thing for her to believe but right now he really needed her to.

After a few minutes' silence, Kate spoke. 'So, what now? Did you tell her boss this? Is she still suffering or is she better?'

'I spoke to her boss but I didn't get a chance to speak to Helen on her own. If we had been able to speak in private, she may well have opened up to me. I could have found out if she was still taking her medication. I mean, that's the biggest worry for me.'

'Why's that?'

'Because if she's not taking her medication she could be a danger to herself, or someone else. What with her looking after children … I'm not saying she'd do anything to that kid she's minding, but you never know.'

'Maybe I should speak to her?' Kate seemed to believe he was telling the truth. This was a good moment to put his proposal to her.

Chapter Twenty-Nine

Something about Ken's call earlier had been bugging Donovan. His gut instinct was bringing him back time and time again to their conversation about Lampard and his alibi, but he couldn't pin anything down.

Arriving at the police station in plenty of time, he sought out Ken.

'Can I have a look at all the stuff you've got on Lampard so far?' he said.

'What's up?' asked Ken.

'I don't know. Something is bothering me but I don't know what. I thought maybe going over the case notes again might bring whatever it is to light.' It was a long shot but Donovan couldn't ignore the feeling that he was missing something. 'Any news on Stella Harris?'

'No. One of my officers went down there yesterday to have another chat with her. We thought we might be making a break-through. Stella Harris was starting to get small flashbacks. Anyway, it got a bit much for her, the stress brought on a flippin' asthma attack. The doctors have said we've got to lay off her for a bit longer.'

Donovan looked at the detective. His mind was whirring. 'Wait a minute.' He put his hand up to halt Ken from continuing. 'Stella Harris is asthmatic?'

'Yes, that's right. What of it?'

'She uses an inhaler, right?'

'I guess so.'

'Presumably she used her inhaler at the hospital when she was being questioned.'

'Presumably ….'

'What colour was the inhaler?' Donovan could feel the anticipation building up inside him. This is what had been bothering him. 'Where's the police officer who interviewed her at the hospital? Get hold of them. Ask what colour the inhaler was.'

'What's this all about, Donovan?'

'Humour me for a minute,' said Donovan. 'Get hold of Lampard's GP. Find out if he is asthmatic or has ever been prescribed an inhaler.'

'But it's the weekend,' protested Ken.

'That's never got in the way before, has it?'

'All right, I'll do it, although I have no idea where all this is leading.' Ken turned and picked up the telephone. 'While I get on with this, haven't you got a meeting with CID?' He nodded towards the door. Donovan took the hint, although he knew it would take all his powers of concentration to get through the meeting without his mind wandering back to the results of Ken's enquiries.

Toby sat in his car watching the skate park. He scanned the kids on their skateboards, BMXes and scooters racing up and down the ramps, attempting turns and spins, with varying degrees of success. He was looking for one lad in particular. Patrick, Kate's younger brother.

He was certain that in the past Helen had said how Patrick loved to take his scooter on the ramps. He hoped the boy was still as mad about it as ever.

His hunch paid off when he caught sight of a dark-haired lad with distinctive curls scoot down a ramp, gaining enough speed to take him to the top of the opposite ramp, whereupon he gave a fancy little turn in mid-air, before mistiming his landing and taking the down slide on his backside.

Toby checked his watch. He still had enough time to convince Kate to go along with his plan. It was a shame she had refused earlier, just when he thought he was getting somewhere with her. He had been sure she had believed him about Helen's state of mind but at the last minute she'd had second thoughts. It was annoying and frustrating all at the same time. However, it was a good job he had plan B. It would be getting dark soon and Patrick would, no doubt, head home.

His patience was recompensed about twenty minutes later when he watched Patrick complete one last attempt at the taller ramp, only to fail again. Clearly having had enough, judging by the way he kicked his scooter, Patrick bumped fists with his friends and scooted out of the park.

He darted out through the gates and headed along the pathway, weaving in and out of pedestrians. The street lights had come on a few minutes ago and Toby was able to track Patrick's progress from his car. As the lad turned the corner out of sight, Toby started his engine and drove off after him.

Toby knew that Patrick would have to cross the road at King's Street and being a teenager, guessed he probably wouldn't use the zebra crossing. That would be far too nerdy for a cool skate-ramp kid.

Aware that he was driving slower than the traffic required, Toby pulled over and let a few cars pass him. He couldn't have planned it better. The lull in the flow of cars gave him the opportunity to pull back out onto the road. He could see Patrick through the glass of the parked cars, turning and looking over his shoulder. He too was seeking out a break in the vehicles. Toby slowed right down. Patrick darted out of sight between two parked cars. Toby accelerated.

He had to congratulate himself on his driving skills. Any faster and he would surely have had the boy on his bonnet, any slower and

Patrick would have scooted off, oblivious. Instead, Toby slammed on the brakes and screeched to a halt centimetres away from Patrick's right leg.

Patrick's look of fear and frozen body had Toby leaping out of the car and running around to the boy.

'Bloody hell! What are you trying to do? Get yourself killed?' A car was stopping on the other side of the road. The driver wound down his window. Toby called over. 'It's okay, mate. All good. No damage. Just this little shit scooting out between parked cars.'

He waved his thanks to the driver, who continued his journey.

Toby turned his attention back to Patrick.

'Now, lad,' he paused. 'Wait a minute, I know you. You're Patrick Gibson, aren't you? Kate Gibson's brother.'

Patrick nodded. 'Yeah.' He was beginning to regain a bit of colour to his ashen face.

'You remember me?' continued Toby. 'I'm Helen's old boyfriend. Toby. You know, Helen Matthews, best friends with your sister?'

A look of recognition swept over Patrick's face. 'Oh yeah. Toby. Yes, I remember.'

'Good lad. You are okay, aren't you?'

'I think so. Sorry about that.'

'No problem. Look, I tell you what. Why don't I give you a lift home? I need to speak with Kate anyway.' Toby took Patrick's arm and eased him off the scooter. 'Come on, sit in the front and I'll show you how fast she goes. Bit quicker than your scooter.'

Driving the long way home to impress the lad was actually quite enjoyable, thought Toby as twenty minutes later he pulled up outside Kate's house. Now, he just had to hope she was in.

'Go on then, in you go,' he said to Patrick, passing him the scooter from the boot of the TT. 'Tell Kate I'm outside.'

He watched Patrick scoot up the path and disappear around the back. A few minutes later Kate was at the front door. She looked over and stood there looking at him for a moment before coming to the pavement.

'What are you doing bringing Patrick back?' Her voice was guarded.

Toby shrugged and gave her his best innocent smile. 'Nothing. I saw him down on King's Street. Nearly ran him over, actually. You should be thanking me for getting him home safely.'

'He's quite capable of getting home himself. He's not supposed to get in the car with strangers.'

'Come on, I'm not exactly a stranger.'

'Still, he's been told about accepting lifts,' said Kate, her brow furrowing.

'Fair enough. I apologise,' said Toby. 'Look, I wanted to catch up with you anyway.'

'What for?'

'I wanted to chat to you about helping me find Helen.'

'We've been through this before,' said Kate. 'I can't help you.'

'Can't or won't?' He started the engine and spoke again. 'You know, the roads are really dangerous. You should tell Patrick to be more careful. Wouldn't want anything like that happening again. The next car might not be able to stop in time. I'll be in touch about Helen later.'

Putting the Audi into first gear he held the clutch down, hit the throttle and revved twice before releasing the left pedal and speeding off down the road. He checked his rear-view mirror and was pleased to see a distressed-looking Kate standing at the end of her path watching him go.

The house felt eerily quiet. Ellen was grateful that Ben was still about. She wasn't keen on being in the house on her own. She knew it was foolish but, all the same, it was nice to know he was there. The sound of the doorbell made her jump.

Going downstairs, Ellen saw Ben was already opening the door. In breezed Amanda with Izzy.

'I've brought Isobel back,' said Amanda, giving her daughter a gentle nudge in Ellen's direction who, by now, was at the foot of the stairs. 'Something's come up and she can't stay with me overnight any more. Right, Izzy, give mummy a kiss.' Ellen watched as Amanda knelt down and offered her cheek to her daughter. Izzy stood still, not moving or speaking. 'Isobel. Give Mummy a kiss,' repeated Amanda.

Izzy looked back over her shoulder at Ellen.

Ellen nodded silently, trying to look as encouraging as possible. With obvious reluctance, Izzy gave her mother a small peck on the cheek.

Amanda stood up. 'Be a good girl now. Next time I'll make sure nothing gets in the way and you can spend the whole weekend with me. Bye, bye, darling.'

Ellen exchanged a look with Ben as the door shut behind Amanda. No words needed. Ben's expression clearly matched her own thoughts on Amanda's parenting skills. Ellen skipped over to Izzy and took her by the hand. 'Come on, why don't we do some painting or something?' she suggested. She received a grateful look from Izzy. 'And you, Ben. You can join in as well.'

'I'm not sure painting is really my thing,' said Ben.

'Oh, I don't know. You made a good job of Izzy's bedroom walls. Didn't he Izzy?'

'Yeah, but that was different,' said Ben.

'Nonsense. Come on. Do as you're told. You might actually enjoy it.'

'Okay, you were right. This sort of painting isn't so bad after all,' said Ben as he sat back and admired the picture of a tank he had been creating for the last twenty minutes.

Ellen smiled. 'It's very therapeutic.' She dropped her brush into the murky glass of water. 'What do you think to my vase of flowers, Izzy?'

'Very pretty,' said Izzy. 'I don't like Ben's tank.'

'No, I think Ben should have painted it pink, don't you? Brown is a bit boring.' Ellen laughed at the mock look of disappointment on Ben's face. Izzy giggled too.

'Yucky boy's colour,' she said.

'Tanks can't be pink!' exclaimed Ben.

Ellen's phone rang out and made her jump. She looked at the screen. '*Kate calling*'. A little butterfly of fear flapped in her stomach. They had agreed to only ring in an emergency. Ellen hit the accept button.

'Hello. Kate? You okay?'

'Listen carefully. I need to meet you. Today.' Her voice was full of anxiety; she sounded as though she had been crying. The butterfly flutter in Ellen's stomach morphed into a flock of squawking seagulls. Something was clearly wrong.

'Kate, what's the matter?' Ellen was now standing. Alert and anxious.

'I can't tell you over the phone,' replied Kate. A sob was muffled. She spoke again. 'I'm in a taxi on my way over to Felpham. Meet me at the duck pond at the top of Sea Lane.'

'You're here in West Sussex?' Not only was Ellen surprised but she was alarmed too. 'Kate, please tell me what's going on. You're scaring me.'

'I'll tell you when I see you. Meet me in ten minutes.'

The line went dead. Ellen looked at her phone as if it was going to give her some sort of explanation all by itself.

'Problem?' asked Ben. Ellen looked up at him. He had slipped back into professional mode. His eyes alert, his body tense.

'I'm not sure. I've got to meet my friend. Something's happened. I don't know what.' Ellen looked at Izzy and smiled at her. 'You stay here with Ben, I've got to pop out for a minute.' She dropped a kiss onto the child's head and hurried out of the kitchen.

Ben followed her. 'Ellen. Wait. You can't go on your own.' He stood in front of her. 'I can't let you go rushing off like this.'

Ellen sidestepped the ex-soldier. 'I've got to. My friend needs me. Something's wrong.'

This time Ben put his hand over the front-door handle. 'I'm

under orders from Donovan. Why don't you ring your friend back and tell her to come here?'

Ellen sighed. She quickly called Kate's number. It went straight to voicemail. She tried again. And again. 'She's not answering. I'll have to go and meet her. Look, I'll bring her straight back here. How about that?'

Ben shook his head. 'Sorry, Ellen. No can do.'

'You can't hold me hostage, you know,' said Ellen, trying to keep her voice down. Ben said nothing, merely raising his eyebrows. He probably could keep her here against her will, she thought. 'Okay, plan B. You drive me down there to meet her and we all come back to the house?'

'That's more like it.' Ben smiled. 'Go and get Izzy, I'll get the car started.'

Something about the phone call was bothering Ellen. It wasn't just that Kate was in some sort of trouble or had bad news. It wasn't that she was in West Sussex. It was something else. She pushed the niggle to the back of her mind as they approached the duck pond at the end of Sea Lane.

'She's not here yet,' said Ellen, scanning the area. 'Why don't you park up round the corner on the main road, where there are some parking bays. I'll get out and wait by the pond.'

For a minute, she thought Ben was going to be as stubborn about this as he was about letting her come, but then he relented. 'Okay. But I tell you what, me and Izzy will wait by the pond so that we're near you. We can feed the ducks.' He pulled a sandwich bag from his pocket which held a couple of slices of bread.

Ellen raised her eyebrows and smiled. 'You're such a Boy Scout. Always prepared.'

'Dib-dib. Dob-dob,' said Ben.

Donovan took the steps two at a time as he made his way up to Ken's office. The meeting with CID had gone on for longer than he would have liked but his professional integrity hadn't let him cut any corners, despite wishing he could. Happy that he had everything he needed to begin profiling a suspect, he was eager to hear what Ken had found out.

He knocked and without waiting to be invited in, opened the door and stepped into Ken's office.

'So? What did you find out?'

'Ah, come on in Donovan, don't stand on ceremony,' said Ken with a wry smile. 'Let's cut to the chase, no preamble.'

'Sorry, Ken,' said Donovan sitting down in the chair. He waited patiently for the DCI to speak.

'Right then. The most commonly used inhaler is the blue one. Ventolin …'

'Used to dilate the airways to aid breathing,' interrupted Donovan, trying to reign in his impatience.

'Yes, exactly,' said Ken. 'Now, Stella Harris uses …'

'A brown inhaler. Steroid-based,' finished Donovan, his impatience galloping away. 'What about Lampard – is he asthmatic?'

Ken Froames shook his head. 'Nope. Not according to his GP. Never has been. In fact, he hasn't visited his GP in over eighteen months.'

'So, we have Lampard, into his mountain-biking and long-distance running, hasn't been to his doctor in ages; an apparently fit and healthy man. Agreed?'

Ken nodded. 'Agreed.'

'Yet, he has an inhaler. A brown one. The sort of one Stella Harris would have.'

Ken looked confused. 'I'm not following you. When did Lampard have this inhaler?'

'When I first interviewed him. Here at the police station. He was fiddling around with it.'

'You think it belonged to Stella Harris?'

'I'm certain it belonged to Stella Harris. No one would have realised it was missing because no one was looking for it.' Donovan sat forwards in his seat. 'Lampard took that as a trophy. And my bet is he still has it, somewhere in his flat I would imagine. Somewhere where he can look at it and admire it – a trophy prolongs the crime, nourishes the fantasy. It's a symbol of power and conquest. That's Lampard's prize. He's gets a kick out of just looking at it. It empowers him. Find that inhaler and that will link him to the attack. He would have no reason to have it, other than as a trophy for what he did.'

Ken was already reaching for the phone. 'I'll get a warrant to search his flat arranged right now.'

Chapter Thirty

Ellen positioned herself against the flint wall at the top of Sea Lane. Here she had a clear view down Middleton Road. She glanced back over her shoulder at Ben and Izzy by the pond. Ben was watching her. Ever the professional, he wasn't really duck-feeding but keeping an eye on his charges.

'Any sign of her?' Ben called over.

'No, not yet.'

Ben walked across to her. 'Has she been here before?'

'No, never. That's why it must be important.'

'And she suggested that you meet here?'

'Yes, that's right. I suppose it's because she wants to talk to me in private. She probably didn't want to turn up at the house in case I wasn't alone. Especially if she's upset.'

'When she suggested you meet here, what exactly did she say?'

Ellen frowned. 'To meet her at the duck pond at the top of Sea Lane. And that's what we're doing. What's wrong with that?'

'You're missing the point,' said Ben. He looked serious. 'If she's never been here before, how does she know about the duck pond?'

A feeling of unease crawled across Ellen's skin. Her voice was bleak. 'She wouldn't have known about the duck pond, not unless someone had told her.'

'Someone who has been here before,' said Ben. 'Someone who

knows her. Someone who also knows you. Someone like Toby.'

Ellen felt physically sick but before she could say anything, the tooting of a car made her turn away from Ben and look back across the road. A BMW had pulled over. From the passenger side emerged the blonde head of Kate, looking extremely distressed. Their eyes met across the roof of the car. There was such sadness in Kate's eyes, it almost broke Ellen's heart there and then.

Ellen pushed herself away from the wall. Kate's face was so sad. A mark, maybe a bruise, sat under her eye; it was hard to see clearly from across the road. Her bottom lip looked swollen. What on earth had happened? Ellen attempted a smile. Kate looked back. Her eyes bore into Ellen's as if they were trying to tell her something.

It was then Ellen noticed someone else getting out of the driver's side and walking round to Kate.

Dear God. No.

She felt her stomach turn and for a moment she thought she was going to be sick. Standing next to Kate, sneering in her direction was Toby. Ellen looked at Kate. Distress oozed from her friend. Ellen could see that Toby had his hand firmly around the top of Kate's arm.

The slight shake of the head by Kate and mouthing of the word 'sorry' from across the road at her said all that needed to be said. Kate wasn't here of her own free will.

'Stay here,' said Ben. 'That's him, isn't it?'

'I've got to go to her,' said Ellen.

She felt Ben's hand tug her arm. 'Wait! You'll get yourself run over.' He nodded at the bus heading their way.

Kate and Toby stood at the edge of the pavement; Kate's eyes still on Ellen, Toby's on the bus. Kate began to struggle, trying to wriggle her arm free of his grip. Toby looked across at Ellen. The sneer was of evil proportions as he held firmly onto Kate's arm. The bus was only metres away. Toby curled his lip in a primeval way.

In a split second, Ellen knew without doubt what Toby was about to do. She opened her mouth to shout … to shout what? A warning to Kate? A plea to Toby? A command to Ben? Whatever, no sound came out. Ellen watched in total despair as Toby released Kate from his grip and propelled her out into the road.

The scream that followed was inhuman. The thud sickening. Tyres screeched. Gasps sounded out. Ellen felt Ben pull her face to his chest, shielding her eyes. She felt small hands grapple around her legs. Izzy. Please don't let Izzy have witnessed that.

The smell of hot brakes on rubber flooded the air. Ellen fought her way from Ben. She needed to get to her friend. She must help her. Kate. Darling Kate. Her friend for so many years.

'Ellen! Stop!' Ben was in full command. He pulled her back against the flint wall. 'There's nothing you can do. Nothing. I'm sorry.'

Ellen looked beyond him at the scene of panic playing out on the other side of the road. The bus had stopped but, of course, not in time. People were rushing to the scene. One woman was crying, people were shouting, the bus driver was in a serious state of distress. Through the legs of the rapidly gathering crowd, she caught a glimpse of a shoe. A black ballet pump; the sort Kate always wore. Pandemonium reigned before her. All she could think of was Kate's face as she had mouthed *sorry*.

The next sob she recognised as her own. The one after belonged to Izzy.

'Oh, darling,' said Ellen, scooping Izzy into her arms. The poor love must have seen it all. How awful.

'Ellen!' cried Izzy, pulling back from the embrace and wildly hitting Ellen on the shoulder.

With Izzy still in her arms, Ellen turned just in time to see Toby, now on their side of the road, swinging something black in his hand towards Ben's head.

Ben was already turning but wasn't quick enough to throw up a defence. The full force of Toby's fist and whatever he was holding hit Ben on the temple. It must have knocked him out immediately. Ben fell to the ground, limp and lifeless. Toby knelt down beside him and rummaged in his pocket, pulling out his mobile phone. He looked up at Ellen. His eyes narrowed as his mouth set a firm line across his face. A second later he was on his feet and striding towards her.

Ellen screamed. She had to get away from Toby. Holding Izzy close to her body, Ellen began to run towards the duck pond. How she thought she was going to outrun him, she didn't know, not on her own, nor while she was carrying Izzy. Even if she put Izzy down, the little girl wasn't going to be able to run fast enough. Not even Ellen could. It was pointless running, yet the instinct to flee took over.

She had only made it a few metres before she felt his hand clasp the back of her neck and yank her backwards.

'Don't be silly, Helen,' came Toby's voice. Moving his hand to her arm, he turned her around. Ellen gulped. There in his other hand was a small handgun. No wonder Ben had dropped like a stone. Ellen pulled Izzy closer into her. 'I wasn't bargaining on you having company. My fault. I didn't make sure Kate told you to come alone.'

'You…' hissed Ellen, stopping herself from swearing in front of Izzy.

'Tut, tut, Helen. Not in front of the children.' Holding tightly on to her arm, he poked the muzzle of the gun into Ellen's ribs. 'Shall we go for a ride, darling? My car is parked over there.'

Ellen put Izzy down and held the child's hand. 'This is my friend, Toby. We're just going to go for a nice ride in his car.' She wondered whether she would be able to break free once they got nearer to the car or possibly attract someone's attention. There was quite a crowd gathered now.

The look on Izzy's face told Ellen that her acting skills were far from Oscar standard. 'I don't want to,' said Izzy, coming to a standstill. 'I want to go home. What about Ben?'

'Ben will be okay. Come on, Izzy. Be good for me, please.' Ellen ran her hand over Izzy's head and down through the dark hair which was tied back in bunches.

'That's it, Izzy, be a good girl. We're going to have lots of fun.' Toby smiled at Ellen. 'Oh and so you don't try and do anything clever, like call Donovan, I'll have your phone.' He held his hand out. 'Come on, pass it over.'

Reluctantly Ellen took her phone from her handbag and gave it to Toby. She wanted to cry. It was the only way she thought she'd be able to let someone know where she was and what had happened to her. 'Please, Toby. Let's not do this,' she said. Maybe if she tried to reason with him, she could get him to see sense. He clearly wasn't in his right mind. Even by his own overbearing, controlling standards, kidnap, was way off the radar.

As they approached his car, Ellen didn't dare try calling out to anyone. Toby dug the gun further into her ribs as a reminder. She desperately tried to make eye contact with someone, but they were all too preoccupied with the accident. Ellen retched as she thought of Kate and what had happened.

'I think I'm going to be sick,' she said.

'Shut up and get in the car.' He shoved her in the back.

'Can't you leave Izzy here?' Ellen knew she had a pleading tone in her voice. Petrified as she was, she knew that Izzy didn't deserve to witness whatever it was that Toby had in mind. 'She's only eight, please, let her go.'

Toby laughed. 'Don't think your whining and pleading is going to make a difference. If you'd only done as you were told in the first place and come alone, then we wouldn't be in this position, would we? Whatever happens now is your fault. Remember that, won't you?'

Fear rippled through her but Ellen drove down the nerves. She needed to stay calm for Izzy. Again, she gently ran her hand over the child's hair. This time, she managed to free the red ribbon from the band and she let it flutter to the ground.

Chapter Thirty-One

Donovan didn't like it one bit. Not only was Ellen's phone going straight to voicemail, but Ben's was doing the exact same thing. He had even tried the house phone but that had just rung out to answerphone. He toyed with the idea of contacting Amanda and Izzy to see if they knew anything but quickly dismissed that notion. It would only give Amanda something else to hold against him at a future date.

As he pulled into the drive of his house, he was even more alarmed to see that the little Fiesta was not in its usual place.

Donovan tried to ignore the voice at the back of his mind telling him that the very fact the car was gone and neither Ben nor Ellen were answering their phones meant that something most definitely wasn't right.

Maybe Ellen was sleeping and Ben had gone out in the car. It had, after all, been a stressful week. But then again, he'd left strict instructions that Ben wasn't to leave Ellen alone. Dumping the flowers he had bought for her on the hall table, he took the stairs two at a time up to the second floor. He tapped on Ellen's door and when he got no answer, called out her name.

Pushing the door open, he knew he shouldn't be surprised to see she wasn't there. A sense of dread embedded itself in his bones.

'Donovan!' A voice called out from downstairs. 'You here,

Donovan? It's Ken.'

Donovan yelled out an acknowledgement and tore down the stairs. The look on his friend's face told him it wasn't a social call. 'Ken?'

'You left the door open. Not like you.'

Donovan looked distractedly at the door and then back to the DCI. 'Is it Izzy?' He didn't need soft talking. He liked things straightforward. 'She's with her mother. Has something happened to her?'

Ken gestured to the living room. 'A drink?'

'Just tell me, Ken. What's this about?' Donovan stood his ground. Fuck the drink. He needed to know what was going on.

Ken drew a deep breath in. 'Ben was found up by the duck pond with a nasty blow to his head. He's alive but unconscious. At this stage, we've no idea what happened. The Fiesta was parked up on Middleton Road.'

'And Ellen?'

'That's what I was coming round for. To make sure she was all right?'

'She's not here.' Donovan was aware of the dryness invading his throat. 'I left her here with Ben.'

'Is it possible she would have gone off on her own somewhere?'

Donovan pulled his hands down his face. 'It's possible, I suppose.' He began pacing backwards and forwards. 'Didn't anyone see what happened to Ben? Have you asked? Maybe they saw Ellen with him.'

'It seems that at around the same time there was another incident. A young lady was hit by a car. It wasn't Ellen, that much I do know, so dismiss that thought straight away. She's not a local, apparently. Holiday-maker they think. Everyone's attention was on that. Brought the village to a standstill, as you can imagine. It wasn't until afterwards that someone spotted Ben.'

'Jesus Christ.' Suddenly a drink sounded like a good idea.

'You don't know what Ben was doing there or if Ellen would

have been with him, do you?' asked Ken taking the tumbler of whiskey offered by Donovan.

'No idea whatsoever. I can't get hold of her on the phone. I don't like the sound of this, Ken.'

'She hasn't left you a note or anything? Perhaps saying where she has gone.'

Donovan scanned the living room for any sign of a note. If anywhere, Ellen would have left it in the kitchen. He hurried down the hallway. The sight of paint pots, brushes and paintings turned his throat even drier.

'What's up?' asked Ken, coming to stand beside him.

'Izzy went out with her mother this morning. She was staying overnight.'

'And?'

'She didn't do any painting before she went. She must have been back.' Donovan walked over to the table and picked up a picture of a tank. 'Looks like Ben was here too.'

Ken dabbed his finger on one of the paintings. 'The paint's pretty much dry. I'd say they were all sat together painting.' He dabbed a couple more pieces of paper. 'Whatever took Ben up to the village, my guess is, took Ellen and Izzy too.'

'So where the hell are they?' Donovan pushed his hands back through his hair. Now wasn't the time to go into headless-chicken mode. He needed to stay calm and focused. With as much control as he could muster, he began sifting through the paintings, looking for any kind of note. Nothing.

'I'll get on to the station and report them missing. We'll get a search party out. Any ideas where they might have gone?'

'Toby must have something to do with this. Ellen wouldn't have just gone off. She knows how worried I'd be. She would have got a message to me.' Donovan could feel his heart beginning to pump faster.

'We'll send someone round to find Toby,' replied Ken, taking out his phone. 'Keep calm, mate. We'll do everything we can to find them and bring them back safely.'

Donovan was conscious of the fact that Ken was making no promises. It hung in the air like a guillotine.

'You thought you were clever, didn't you?' snarled Toby. He pulled the rope tightly around Ellen's wrists. 'Changing your name. Getting a new bank account. Having all your post sent to Kate. Even getting a new job organised.'

Ellen winced as he gave the ropes a tug. Already they were pinching her skin. 'Please, you don't need to tie Izzy up,' she said. 'She's terrified. Please, Toby. Don't.'

Toby gave a small laugh. 'And leave her free to escape and get help? You really do take me for a mug.' He prised Izzy's hands away from Ellen and, clasping them together behind her back, began wrapping the rope around the child's wrists. Izzy began to cry.

'It's all right, darling. Please don't cry. It will be okay. Daddy will be here soon,' said Ellen.

'Do you really think Donovan is going to rescue you?' Toby let out another laugh. 'You are such a fool, Helen, you really are.' He inspected his handiwork and then roughly pushed Izzy into Ellen. 'You think you've been clever planning everything but you haven't been clever enough and neither was Kate. You should have picked your ally better.'

'You pushed her, didn't you?' Ellen's voice trembled as she spoke. Tears trickled down her face as she thought of her friend.

'It was her fault. She was trying to run away.' There was a patronising tone to his voice that made Ellen shudder. In the past this had so often been the prelude to his violence. Toby continued. 'If she hadn't wriggled, she wouldn't have fallen into the road. Mind you, she was getting a bit tiresome. It took me quite a long time to convince her to make the trip down here and to arrange to meet up with you.'

Ellen thought back to the bruising on Kate's face. She knew only too well how he must have convinced her friend. The bastard.

213

Complete and utter bastard. Her fear was rapidly turning to anger. How dare he do this?

'Do you really think you can get away with everything you've done?' She almost spat the words at him. 'What are you actually trying to achieve out of all of this?'

Ellen flinched as Toby raised his hand. When he gently caressed her cheek, she wondered what frightened her more. The violence, she knew how to deal with, but this faux tenderness was scary.

'Don't be worrying about details,' he spoke softly. He checked his watch and sat back, studying her and Izzy as if he was working out his next step.

Ellen wanted to delay any change. At the moment they weren't in any immediate danger, albeit they were tied up in one of the old beach huts at Old Point. They were so close to Donovan, yet there was no way of letting him know. Surely they would be looking for her and Izzy by now? Someone would have found Ben and raised the alarm. She thought of Ben lying on the path, blood seeping from his wound. She hoped to God he was okay. Right now, though, she needed to concentrate on stalling for time.

'What are you hoping to achieve by all this, Toby?'

'You. That's what I'm going to achieve.' He shuffled forwards to her and rested the palm of his hand against her cheek. 'You're with me until I say it's time to go.'

Ellen held her nerve. Now was not the time to become flaky. His touch repulsed her but she tamped down the reaction to shy away. 'You only had to ask.' Her voice was soft and betrayed her emotions. She needed to be clever; to get him on her side. If she could make him believe she wanted the same thing, then she might stand half a chance of getting herself and Izzy out of this unscathed. 'You didn't need to bring us here. In fact, you didn't need to bring Izzy at all.'

'She wasn't supposed to be with you. I didn't want to bring her but I had no choice. You should have come alone.' His hand cupped her chin and she felt the pressure increase. 'You've been away too long. I couldn't trust you just to come at my request. Don't take me for a fool. I know you will need time to realise that I know what is best for you.'

'That's okay. I understand,' she lied, 'but please let Izzy go home to her father.'

'All in good time, sweetheart.' He gave her face a squeeze. 'Remember, I'm in charge. Not you.'

A feeling of hopelessness coiled itself around her. Toby's mental stability was on shaky ground. She didn't want him to contemplate her and Izzy's fate; this might force him into taking some sort of drastic action. She needed to deflect the conversation away. 'How did you find me?' she asked.

'That was easy. If anyone was going to know where you were, it was Kate.' He released his hold on her and settled himself on the floor, his delight apparent now that he literally had a captive audience to whom he could boast about his detection skills. 'I called round there several times. Credit to her, she stuck to the story that she had no idea where you were. I was even beginning to believe her myself. But then I called round there unannounced, just to see if I could catch her out.' He grinned, his eyes wide open. 'And I did. It was an envelope on the table, addressed to Ellen Newman. Now, I may not have paid that much attention to it, but you see, dear Kate tried very discreetly to move it. I knew then, it had to be important and what was the one thing Kate wouldn't want me to see? Of course, anything to do with you. Despite the different name, I knew it was you. I mean, Paul Newman was one of your Hollywood idols. And what with the message on the back of the postcard. It didn't take a genius to work it out. It all tied in nicely with the name on the letter Kate had tried to hide. Oh, don't look so crestfallen, Helen. Your friend didn't give you up straight away.'

A look of amusement and self-satisfaction matured on his face. Ellen had to ask, 'How did you get her to tell you?'

'She thought she was so fucking clever. Told me she believed me when I played the nutter card. You know, the one that I played

215

on Donovan? About your delusions – your mental illness.'

'She would never have believed you. She knew the truth. She saw what you did to me.'

'I underestimated her. My mistake. At first I thought she had fallen for it but then she tried to be clever, didn't she?'

'What did she do?' Ellen needed to know. Her best friend hadn't given her up. Dear Kate had paid the ultimate price for her loyalty and belief in her.

'She prepared an email to you saying she wanted to meet you, that it was important.'

'I never got that.'

'No, you wouldn't have done. I didn't let her send it. She used the names Helen and Katherine. She didn't bank on me noticing. The thing was, I had looked at an email sitting in the draft box, once she had prepared for you, but you hadn't yet opened. You two didn't call each other Helen and Katherine in the email. In fact, you didn't even use your names, so for her to put the name in, I knew then she was playing silly buggers and trying to be clever. Trying to alert you by changing the format.'

Ellen felt herself shiver at the obvious pride in his voice, the patronising way he used to speak to her just before things would turn nasty. 'So, what did you do? How did you get her to make that call to me?'

'Patrick,' replied Toby. 'I knew she wouldn't have wanted any harm to come to her younger brother. Again, she wasn't entirely convinced I meant what I said. At one point she threatened to go to the police if I didn't leave her alone. Changed her mind when I dropped Patrick home to her. I explained to her how dangerous it could be for a thirteen-year-old lad to be scooting around. You know what the roads are like, very dangerous with all this traffic. As it seems Kate herself has found out.'

Ellen shook her head slowly. Toby was evil. Even more evil than she had ever imagined. She thought back to the time a pigeon had flown into the patio doors of Toby's apartment. It had flapped around on the floor - stunned. Toby had picked it up and, stating that it needed putting out of its misery, had wrung its neck, right there and then. No remorse, but definitely a flicker of pleasure on his face as he did so.

Ellen began to cry as she thought of Kate. Her loyal, dependable friend. Darling Kate. Ellen was more sorry than she ever felt possible. She should never have brought Kate into this whole mess.

Her tears snapped Toby out of his reflective account. He stood up abruptly and brushed his trousers down. From the table at the end of the beach hut, he took a piece of cloth and a small bottle with clear liquid in it. He unscrewed the lid and, placing the cloth over the bottle, upturned it.

'A few drops are all we need.'

He grinned and raised his eyebrows at Ellen.

'Don't!' cried Ellen. She tried to move between him and Izzy but with her hands tied she had no way of pushing him off. Toby simply backhanded her across the face, sending her sprawling to the ground. Izzy was screaming and shouting out for Ellen before Toby smothered her mouth and nose with the cloth. Almost instantly, Izzy passed out.

'Oh my God,' sobbed Ellen. 'What have you done?' That sickly-sweet smell of the liquid; she had smelt it before. The memory crashed to the front of her mind. The cat in the water butt. The collar she'd picked up in the garden and the smell on the tag and her fingers. It was the same smell. Chloroform.

'Don't worry, she's only having a little nap. She'll be okay. I've got to go out and I don't want either of you screaming and shouting, drawing attention to where we are.' He picked up the bottle again and this time upturned it twice. 'Need a bit more for you.'

Ellen fought and screamed as much as she could but again his sheer strength was too much. Within a few seconds the blackness was closing in around her.

Chapter Thirty-Two

Donovan felt totally and utterly helpless. He didn't like this feeling. He wasn't used to it. He paced towards the living-room window for the umpteenth time, looking out onto the private estate, which was normally quiet and refined. But today it was littered with police vehicles, police officers and dogs. All desperately trying to find Ellen and his daughter.

Carla had come over as soon as he had phoned. The police had wanted to talk to her to see if she could shed any light on the situation; whether she had noticed anything out of the ordinary. Apart from the obvious strange goings-on, as she had put it, she knew nothing that could help them find Ellen and Izzy. She had insisted on staying in the absence of Mrs Holloway and was busy making coffee. Coffee that Donovan had no stomach to drink.

He picked up his phone and dialled Amanda's number again. It was just ringing out to voicemail. He'd left a message earlier for her to call back. Told her it was urgent, but so far, no response. For some reason he was yet to discover, she had brought Izzy back early. If she hadn't, then Izzy wouldn't be caught up in all this.

A knock on the living-room door turned his attention away from his hostile thoughts towards his wife.

Ken came into the room. 'A bit of a breakthrough. We've got a clearer idea of what we're dealing with.'

'And that is…?' Donovan tried to hide his impatience.

'Ben has come round and been able to answer a couple of questions. Not great news, I'm afraid.' Ken paused. Donovan wished he'd get on with it. 'It seems Ellen had a call from her friend, Kate, to meet her at the duck pond. Said it was urgent. Kate turned up with Toby. They parked on the other side of the road, where the woman got knocked down by the bus.'

Ken paused while Donovan filled in the gaps. 'The woman … that was Ellen's friend, wasn't it?' Ken nodded. 'Jesus Christ,' groaned Donovan. 'She didn't step out by accident in front of the bus, did she?' This time the confirmation was a shake of the head.

'It was Toby who whacked Ben on the head. Ben's pretty certain it was with the butt of a handgun.'

'A gun? Jesus, Ken, what the hell is happening? Does anyone know where he is? And what about Ellen and Izzy?' Donovan didn't know what to do with himself. He could hear the panic and frustration in his voice. He felt totally powerless.

'Keep it together, Donovan. We're trying to find them now. Ben was able to give a description of the car. We've got everyone looking for it. I've got an armed response team on standby and the dog unit is already here.' Ken paused and cleared his throat before continuing. 'There is one thing.' He pulled out a red ribbon from his pocket, laying it across the palm of his hand. 'Recognise this?'

Donovan swallowed what felt like a golf ball in his throat. He moved to Ken and took the ribbon from his friend's hand. It had a loose knot halfway along. He acknowledged the rational thought that it probably belonged to his daughter. 'Izzy's ribbon. Where …?' The dryness was in his throat again, strangling his words.

'Middleton Road, opposite the duck pond.'

'Izzy is definitely with Ellen and Toby, then.' It was a statement not a question.

'It looks that way.'

'If you find Toby, you find Ellen and Izzy,' stated Donovan.

'Let's hope so.'

Once again, Donovan noted the lack of reassurance from his friend. Ken was not in the business of making promises he couldn't keep. For once, Donovan wished he could be ignorant to the inference of the DCI's reply.

The cold seeped up from beneath her into every pore and advanced into her muscles. Ellen went to move and for a moment couldn't understand why her hands were stuck together. The pain in her shoulder ripped into her as she adjusted her position. Opening her eyes, she took a few moments to attune to the darkness. A grey shaft of light was drifting through a gap in the curtains; blue-checked curtains covering a small pane of glass. Then she remembered. The abandoned beach huts at Old Point. Toby. Kate. Ben. It all came flooding back with clarity.

Ellen managed to get herself into a sitting position and shuffled over to Izzy, who was lying in the far corner. Ellen tried to wriggle her hands free of the rope but it simply caused even more pain to the burns on her wrists. Putting her face close to the child's, Ellen listened for breathing. It was slight and shallow but it was definitely there. Ellen thought about trying to wake her, but decided against it. It was better Izzy stayed asleep, at least that way she was oblivious to what was going on.

If only there was some way Ellen could get out of here, she could go and get help. Standing up, she manoeuvred herself to the door and tried to turn the knob. It was locked. No surprise there. She pulled on the handle, trying to force it. No joy.

If she could see outside, she might be able to spot a passer-by. Taking a piece of the curtain between her teeth, Ellen tugged it to the left. It moved about one centimetre before jamming. It tasted disgusting too. Ellen tried again but it wasn't going any further. Through the slightly bigger gap she had made, Ellen was able to see that it was getting dark outside. She couldn't see her watch and her head felt too fuzzy for her to even guess how long she had been unconscious for. A wave of nausea made her feel faint.

She could still taste and smell the chloroform Toby had used. She couldn't get over how dangerous this was, especially giving it to a child as young as Izzy.

Her thoughts turned to Toby and what he planned to do with herself and Izzy. God, this was awful. She had never felt so desperate. Surely he wouldn't do anything to hurt Izzy! A small nagging voice at the back of her mind was telling her otherwise.

She couldn't just sit there and do nothing. Giving into him, letting him have his own way, with hardly any protest. No, she couldn't do that. She had Izzy to think of.

A small groan and a whimper emitted from the corner of the beach hut. Izzy shifted position. Ellen shuffled over to her. Izzy wasn't fully conscious and Ellen hoped she would stay that way for as long as possible. Sitting with her back to her, Ellen was able to stroke the child's head. Poor little love. What must Donovan be thinking? Surely they were trying to find them by now.

Ellen must have dozed off for a while as the next thing she was aware of was Izzy crying. She was now fully awake.

'Don't cry, darling,' said Ellen. 'It's all right. I'm here. Daddy will come and find us soon.'

'Can you ring him?' said Izzy, her head on Ellen's lap.

'I'm sorry darling, but I don't have my phone.'

'Use my phone,' said Izzy.

Ellen looked at her. 'Oh, Izzy, that's a good idea but your one won't work. I need a real one.' If only a pink Barbie flip phone would really do the job.

'It is a real one,' said Izzy.

'No, I mean a proper one, like I've got or like Daddy has.'

Izzy pulled herself up into a sitting position, her voice this time quite insistent. 'It is a proper one. Mummy gave it to me.'

'Mummy gave you a real phone?'

Izzy glanced across to her small red satchel that had been thrown in the corner by Toby. She then looked guiltily back at Ellen and nodded. Ellen gave a reassuring smile. Her heart was beginning

221

to hammer inside her with excitement. 'It's okay Izzy, you're not in trouble. Mummy gave you a real phone and it's in your bag?'

'Yes. She said it was for her to call me on if she wanted to speak to me. She said it was a secret.' The worry returned to Izzy's face.

'It's okay. Really.' Ellen shuffled over to the satchel and after a bit of fumbling managed to undo the buckle and retrieve the phone. A small pink flip phone with a Barbie sticker on it. Amanda was crafty, thought Ellen, but in this situation, a genius. 'Hold the phone still for me. I'm going to ring the police.'

With her thumb, Ellen depressed the number nine button three times, then lying down so that her ear was to the receiver, she waited as her call was picked up.

She was about to respond to the operator when she heard the key turning the lock from the outside. It could only be Toby. She just managed to get into a sitting position as he came in.

'You're awake then. I brought you some water,' he said as he came in and shut the door behind him. He placed two bottles of water on the small work surface, which ran along one side of the beach hut.

As discreetly as possible, Ellen padded her hands around on the floor behind her trying to locate the phone. 'You can't keep us locked up in this beach hut forever,' she said louder than was necessary. Her only hope was that the emergency operator was still on the other end of the line. 'We are only at Old Point, the police are bound to look for us here. What then?' More patting the tiled floor in search of the phone, but to no avail. Where was the bloody thing?

Toby put the bottle back on the side and looked at her without saying a word, his eyes homing in on the floor behind her. 'What the fuck are you doing down there?'

Grabbing Ellen roughly by the arm, Toby pulled her forwards. Ellen held her breath. When he grunted and shoved her back next to Izzy, she slowly let out air from her lungs. How he hadn't seen the phone, she didn't know.

Toby turned his attention back to the water bottles. 'Lift your head up and open your mouth.' He instructed Ellen and tipped the bottle. The water came out too quickly, spilling down her chin and running down her neck. Izzy refused the water despite encouragement from Ellen.

'Spoilt brat,' muttered Toby. He tossed the bottle at Ellen's feet. 'You will have to sort her out.'

'How can I with my hands tied up?'

Toby shrugged. Ellen continued. 'Just untie us for a little while, please. It's really bad for the circulation and Izzy must have some water. It's not like we can go anywhere with you standing in the doorway.' Toby appeared to consider this before giving another shrug and, relenting, he untied the ropes on both Ellen and Izzy. 'No fucking funny business. You hear? I don't want to have to get cross with you.' He squeezed the sides of Ellen's face between his finger and thumb.

With her wrists now unbound, Ellen could feel the blood rush to her fingertips sending tingling sensations through her hands. She rubbed Izzy's hands in between her own, as Izzy cried out.

'My hands hurt.'

'It's okay, it's pins and needles. The tingling will stop in a minute.' Ellen smiled. 'Have some water now. That's it. And a bit more.'

Ellen looked at Izzy, whose gaze kept falling down behind her and then back to Ellen. Putting her arms around the little girl, Ellen hugged her whilst, at the same time, discreetly looking over her shoulder. There, in the dim light cast by the moon, Ellen could make out the silver sparkly Barbie sticker. The phone. Izzy had hidden it from Toby. What a clever girl! However, her delight was soon crushed. The phone was shut. Izzy must have closed it, thus ending the call to the emergency services. Ellen felt her heart plummet to somewhere near her shoes.

As carefully as she could, she reached round and slowly picked up the phone and slid it into Izzy's coat pocket. She prayed that Toby wouldn't for one moment think that there was another phone.

223

Amanda stormed into the living room and without breaking stride, marched straight up to Donovan and slapped him hard across the face.

'Liar!' She shoved him in the chest. 'You told me Isobel would be safe. That nothing would happen to her. Liar!'

Donovan let her scream and shout. He couldn't deny her accusations. After another push and a barrage of abusive nouns, Amanda finally sat down on the sofa, her shoulders dropping.

'We will find her, Amanda. The police are out there looking for her now.' God he sounded feeble. What a clichéd reassurance. Amanda wasn't buying it. Her eyes narrowed and she rose from the sofa.

'Once she is found I am having sole custody of her. Do you hear me? You are not capable of looking after her. No court in the country will give you custody after this … this debacle.'

'Now's not the time to get into an argument over custody,' said Donovan, despite the idea alarming him.

'I'm simply telling you, for the record, how it's going to be. Isobel will be living with me from now on. Get used to the idea.'

'Tell me something else, for the record,' retorted Donovan, his anger bubbling near to the surface. 'Why did you bring Izzy back? If you had kept her with you, like you were supposed to, then she would be safe.'

Amanda's phone began to ring. Donovan waited whilst she slipped it out of her bag and looked at the screen. She glanced at him before dropping it back unanswered. 'That is irrelevant now. What matters is that my daughter comes back safe and well. And comes back to me. And you can make plans to sack that useless nanny as well. I won't be employing her, that's for sure.'

'Don't start blaming Ellen. This isn't the time for recriminations,' retorted Donovan. He had never in his life felt so desperate. Waiting at the house for news was like having an axe swaying over his head, held only by a cotton thread. Any minute now there would be bad news and the thread would break.

'Why aren't you out there looking for her?' said Amanda. 'What sort of father are you? Can't look after your daughter and now you can't even go and find her.'

The urge to return the favour of the slap was tempting. If Amanda had been a bloke she would be sprawled flat out on the floor by now. 'I have to stay here in case there's a phone call. The police work better without the public getting in the way.' He opened the French doors as Amanda lit up a cigarette and ignored the cold blast of sea air. It couldn't make the atmosphere any icier than it already was. 'Just so we are clear on one thing, I'll fight you for Izzy. You're not taking her off to France with that dickhead Sebastian.'

Amanda looked as though she was about to reply when once again her phone started ringing. 'I need to take this call in private,' she said, leaving the room. She pulled the door behind her.

It seemed a bit childish, eavesdropping on his wife, but something about her tonight was unsettling Donovan. Despite all his studying, training and practice as a psychologist, she was the one person who could throw him off-kilter. She could leave him wondering about her, such was her enigmatic and complex way.

Amanda was speaking in low tones but Donovan could still just about hear what she was saying.

'You were only supposed to be looking at the one painting.' Her voice was business-like but low and Donovan had to strain to hear. 'The smaller of the portraits is the one I'm interested in.' It sounded like one of her employees had cocked up at the auctions. God help them, he thought. He remembered how she always got a kick out of reprimanding her staff. She liked to reinforce her position as boss. 'You weren't actually supposed to buy either of them. The bigger one is your problem, not mine. Do what you like with it but don't involve me and don't ring me again. I will contact you. Understand? Good.'

Yep, she was pissed off all right.

225

Chapter Thirty-Three

Silhouetted by the rising moon and against the backdrop of the grey sea, Toby's shadowy outline flicked back and forth across the open doorway to the beach hut, his mobile pressed to his ear. He had retied Ellen and Izzy's hands but, seemingly distracted, he had bound them together in front rather than behind their backs. He was agitated now and his voice rose.

'I couldn't help it. What was I to do? She would have blabbed if I hadn't.' A shudder rippled through Ellen. Toby clearly wasn't working this alone. Someone out there knew exactly what he was doing. They were pulling his strings by the sounds of it. Toby, for once, wasn't in control as he usually was. This frightened her even more. 'Leave it with me. It will be my pleasure. Yes. Yes! Understood.'

Ellen didn't like the sound of it at all. Things weren't looking good. She couldn't understand why the police hadn't found them yet. Surely they were scouring the beach and the local area with sniffer dogs. Someone must have seen Toby leading them away. Or had they? Everyone had been preoccupied with the accident. The memory of Kate falling in front of the traffic came rushing back. Bile rose in Ellen's throat and she shook her head, trying to stop the incident replaying in her mind.

Think. She had to think of something. And quick.

She whispered to Izzy and then called out to Toby as he finished his call. 'Both of us need to go the toilet.'

'Can't you wait?'

'Wait until when? And actually, no, we can't. Especially Izzy.'

'This is so typical of you. Here, I'll get you a bucket.' Toby began rummaging around the beach hut, looking on the shelf and in the cupboard. 'I can't find anything.'

'We still need to go,' said Ellen, barely containing her relief that there wasn't anything suitable in the hut. She needed to get them outside. 'We will go round the corner of the beach huts.'

'What and run off. Do you really think I'm that stupid?'

'No, I'll sing or whistle all the time, so you can still hear us.' Ellen sent a silent prayer up that he would agree to this.

'Okay, but I want to hear both of you.'

She sent another prayer of thanks. 'You will have to untie my hands, though. I can't get my trousers down otherwise.'

Toby pulled her by the rope around her wrists to a standing position. 'I'm warning you, Helen,' he said. 'No funny business.'

'I promise,' she said, mustering as much sincerity in her voice as she could.

'I tell you what. Instead of behind the beach huts where I can't see you, I want you to go behind that upturned boat over there.' He nodded towards the edge of the grassed area where a couple of small dinghies and an old wooden boat lay. 'And I want one of you standing in the open while the other one's doing ... well, you know.'

'I'll have to help Izzy,' said Ellen. She needed to be with Izzy just for a moment out of Toby's eyesight. 'She can't do her clothes herself.'

'Well make it quick.'

Snatching a couple of tissues from her bag, Ellen hurried Izzy over to the boat. 'Let's get you sorted first.' Seeing that Izzy was about to protest, Ellen called loudly over her shoulder to drown out Izzy's voice. 'Can you hear us, Toby? Is this loud enough?'

Safely behind the boat, Ellen grabbed the phone from Izzy's pocket, flipped it open. There was only Amanda's number in the contact list.

'I can't hear you!' bellowed Toby.

Ellen began singing a nursery rhyme, encouraging Izzy to join in. 'Sing louder, Izzy.' Ellen pressed dial. The mobile made the connection and began ringing Amanda's phone. Holding it close to her ear, she heard the click as it was answered. No one spoke at the other end.

'Amanda? Is that you?' she hissed. 'Can you hear me? We're at the disused beach huts at Old Point ... Toby has us held hostage. Get help, get ...' She stopped. The line had gone dead.

'You've gone quiet and I can't see you.' Toby sounded like he was getting nearer.

'We're still here. I'm just pulling Izzy's trousers up. Won't be a minute and then she'll be standing where you can see her.' Frantically, Ellen dialled Amanda's number again. It went straight to voicemail. She turned to Izzy. 'Okay, darling, you go and stand over there where Toby can see you.'

She took Izzy to the edge of the boat and looked over at Toby. He had stopped to answer his phone. Going back behind the boat, Ellen closed her eyes for a moment. She needed to get hold of Donovan. She didn't have time to go through emergency services and try to explain everything. She had no idea of his mobile number but tried to recall the home phone number she had put down on a school form for Izzy the previous day. What was it, now? At the time, Ellen had thought it was an easy number to remember. Five-eight-five ... Oh God, what was it? She tapped in the first three digits. Five-eight-five ... seven-five-eight. That was it!

It was answered within a few rings. Ellen could have cried to hear Donovan's voice.

'Donovan, it's me, Ellen.'

'Ellen! Jesus Christ! Thank God. Are you okay? What about Izzy?'

'We're fine. Listen. We're at the beach huts. The ones that are going to be demolished at Old Point.'

The shot rang out loud in the night air. Ellen and Izzy screamed simultaneously. Ellen looked up over the boat. Toby was pointing the gun directly at her, his arm fully outstretched. He began walking purposefully towards her. He fired another shot and Ellen automatically ducked down. She could hear Donovan shouting down the phone at her.

Izzy ran straight into Ellen's arms and the two of them cowered behind the boat. Ellen looked behind her. There was a drop of about ten feet from the seafront down onto the shingle beach. But where would she run? It was too difficult to run on the stones. Too noisy. He'd pick them out easily.

And then he was upon them. Waving the gun from side to side as if making up his mind who to shoot first. Instinctively, Ellen hugged Izzy to her body, shielding the child's eyes from the sight before them.

'Please, Toby, not Izzy. Please don't hurt her. She's only a child.' She heard the click of the safety clip being released. Tears sprang to her eyes and streaked their way down her cheeks. Dear God, he really was going to shoot them. 'I'm begging you…'

A small smile crept its way across his face. 'Begging me. I like that. Go on, Helen, beg some more.'

The bastard. He was enjoying this. She didn't have any choice. Perhaps if she could stall him long enough for the police to arrive. 'I beg you, Toby. Please let Izzy go.'

'You know what, Helen? You keep that up and I might just do that.'

'Ellen!' Donovan was screaming down the phone. He could hear shots. He could hear crying. He was sure he could hear Izzy. What the fuck was going on?

'What is it? Donovan, tell me!' Amanda was tugging at his sleeve.

'Ken!' shouted Donovan, pushing his wife away. Ken was in the

229

room in seconds having been in the hallway taking a phone call. 'Ken, that was Ellen. They're at the abandoned beach huts. There were shots. Ken, get a team down there!'

'We're already on it,' said Ken. 'The car has been discovered at Old Point, at the back of the disused car park. The sniffer dogs and the armed response team are practically there already. I was just coming in to tell you.'

Amanda was pulling on Donovan's arm again.

'Has he shot them? Tell me, Donovan, what's happened?' She was crying when Donovan turned to look at her. She was mumbling half to herself. 'He wasn't supposed to harm her. I told him not to.'

Donovan grabbed her by her shoulders. 'You bitch,' he hissed. 'You were behind this.' It was a statement, not a question. Suddenly it was all falling into place. The phone call about the artwork. There were no paintings. No portraits. It had been Izzy and Ellen she had been referring to. He pushed her to the sofa. She was poisonous. 'What sort of mother are you? You set your own daughter up to be kidnapped?'

'It wasn't like that.' Amanda's eyes were wild and pleading. 'He wasn't supposed to take Izzy. He wanted Ellen. He wanted her back. And I wanted to get rid of her.'

'You used her as bait. You wanted to use it against me. All the things that happened to Ellen, you and he planned it together. He, so he could get revenge and you, so you could get custody of Izzy. You wanted the courts to think it was too dangerous for her to be with me.'

'I'm sorry. It wasn't meant to end like this. He wasn't meant to get Izzy.'

'But taking Ellen was all right?'

'He said he merely wanted to frighten her a bit. I didn't think he was going to do her any real harm.'

'*Merely*,' he scoffed at the word. 'How the hell did you two come to this arrangement?'

'He found me, actually. Followed me after I had been visiting here. Asked me if I knew what sort of nanny I had.' Amanda's face crumpled. 'I didn't think it would get this bad ... I'll never forgive myself if something happens to Izzy.'

'You'd better pray nothing does or I swear to God I won't be responsible for my actions.' The tug on his arm this time was from Ken.

'Come on, Donovan. That's enough for now.' He looked up at the sound of a knock at the door. A female police officer came into the room.

'Sir. We've just had this information come in.' She held out a piece of paper, which Ken took and read before turning to Donovan.

'Well, it seems there was an emergency 999 drop call earlier, from a mobile phone registered to a Mrs Amanda Donovan.'

Donovan sucked air through tightly gritted teeth. He had to turn away. He couldn't bear to look at Amanda. How could she be so deceitful? So self-centred.

'I'm sorry.' Her pitiful voice was strangled by a sob.

'Crocodile fucking tears,' muttered Donovan.

Ken motioned to his officer.

'Sit with Mrs Donovan. Don't let her go anywhere.' He tapped Donovan on the shoulder. 'Come on. I dare say the first person both Ellen and Izzy will want to see is you. Let's go and get them.'

This time Donovan felt reassured by the DCI's positive words.

Donovan's heart leapt and fell at the same time. The sight of his daughter running out of the darkness and being swept up by a fully kitted-out member of the armed response team brought a tidal wave of relief crashing over him.

Taking her from the police officer, he held her tightly. So very tightly. Kissed her, and kissed her again. She was unharmed. She was safe. The paramedics were there and reluctantly he passed her over to them so they could check her over. He pulled the blanket around her.

'Okay, angel. Everything's going to be all right. I promise.' He kissed her again on the forehead. 'These nice ambulance people are going to keep you warm and safe. They're going to make sure you're okay.'

'What about Ellen?' Izzy voice was full of concern.

'I'm going to wait for her here and then we're both going to come into the ambulance with you.' He squeezed her hand. 'See you in a minute, darling.'

As Donovan watched the paramedics take Izzy away, the relief that she was safe was immediately replaced by fear for Ellen. The fear was of epic proportions as he looked on at the scene playing out before him. Once the police had arrived, Toby had apparently discarded Izzy, his focus now on Ellen.

A helicopter circled above, the light shining down onto Toby and Ellen. Toby had his arm around Ellen's shoulders, pinning her back to him, using her as a human shield against the armed officers now spread out around the beach-hut area. In his right hand he held the gun against Ellen's temple.

'Put the gun down.' Ken's voice sounded out over the megaphone. 'Let Ellen go. It's over now. Come on, lad.'

'Fuck the lot of you!' shouted back Toby.

'Take him out, for God's sake, Ken, give the order!' Donovan realised it was his own voice shouting out.

Ken waved his hand at Donovan. 'Keep it together, Donovan, or get out of here. You won't help Ellen getting all wound up like that. Go and sit with your daughter in the ambulance.'

'I'm not going anywhere without Ellen,' said Donovan. 'Just get her out of there, Ken.'

'That's what I fully intend to do,' said Ken. He held the megaphone to his mouth again. 'Toby, we can end this now without anyone getting hurt. Think about it. This can all be over in a matter of minutes. Release Ellen.'

'How can I trust you? You'll shoot me as soon as I do what you want.'

Without thinking, Donovan jumped up. He shouted out, 'Look Toby, you can trust me. Let Ellen go and I'll come to you.' He held his arms outstretched, he could hear Ken ordering him to get back. Donovan ignored him. 'Toby, take me instead.'

'You think I can trust you?' shouted back Toby. 'How do I know you're not as bad as your wife? She told me she wanted Helen out of it then starts ranting at me because the kid got involved. That wasn't my fault, you know. I never planned to take her. She was there. That was Amanda's fault. She shouldn't have brought her back to the house. Stupid, fucking bitch.'

'I'm not like Amanda,' said Donovan. He took three more steps. 'That's why we're separated. Amanda and I are nothing like each other. You can trust me. I give you my word.' Donovan began walking again, slowly but without stopping this time. 'We can talk about this. I can help you. I can vouch for Amanda being involved. She confessed to me earlier.'

Toby's arm relaxed slightly and he lowered the gun as far as Ellen's shoulder. 'Why would you stand up for me when I've kidnapped your daughter?'

Play it cool. Play it cool. Donovan took a deep breath. He was only a few metres away from Toby now. 'Because I believe you when you say it was Amanda's idea.' He didn't actually know what to believe at the moment but if it meant winning Toby's confidence and saving Ellen, then Donovan was prepared to say anything. He would lie through his back teeth. 'Come on, Toby. You can trust me. You don't want to take all the blame.'

A movement in the shadows to Donovan's right caused him to hesitate and turn. Shit! Some bloody over-zealous officer was moving in. Pandemonium broke out. Toby began shouting at Donovan.

'You liar! You're just like the rest of them!'

He lifted the gun to Ellen's temple.

'Don't shoot! Don't shoot!' Donovan wasn't sure who he was shouting at the most, Toby or the armed officer.

Ellen let out a scream and thrashed wildly at Toby's arm. They stumbled backwards. A shot went off, then another. Donovan watched in horror as both Ellen and Toby fell backwards over the edge of the sea wall. There was a thud and a crunch as their bodies landed on the pebbles ten feet below.

Immediately there was running and shouting as the armed officer tore towards the drop. Donovan willed his legs to move. They felt heavy and sluggish but, somehow, he got to the edge first and, without thinking, hurled himself down onto the stones. Two bodies lay perfectly still. The helicopter hovered lower, the sound of the rotor blades drowning out the crashing waves of the incoming tide; the draught from the machine whipping up Donovan's hair and jacket. He looked at Toby lying there staring straight up into the sky. No sign of life. The angle of his neck told its own story. Donovan pulled at Ellen. Sliding his arm under her back, he cradled her head in the crook of his arm.

'Ellen! Ellen!' She wasn't responding. He rubbed his hand up and down her to try and invigorate her into life. He realised his hand was wet. Wet with blood. A bright-red stain was spreading out across her shoulder. He looked wildly around him and shouted over his shoulder. 'Someone get a paramedic! NOW!'

Chapter Thirty-Four

Donovan didn't know how long he had been sitting beside the trolley in the crash room at St Richard's Hospital. Holding her hand, willing life into her. The nurses had tried to persuade him to leave but he couldn't leave her there alone. They were going to move her soon, that much he did know.

'Mr Donovan.' The touch of the nurse's hand on his shoulder made him jump. 'We need to take Ellen down to theatre now.' He looked up at the dark-haired nurse as she spoke. 'DCI Froames is here. Why don't you go with him?'

Donovan stood up, still holding Ellen's hand. He couldn't bring himself to let go. The nurse gently took his hand away while the porters released the brake on the trolley and began wheeling Ellen away.

'What time is it? I need to call Carla, make sure Izzy's okay.'

'It's nearly midnight. I've spoken to Carla. Everything is fine. I promise. Carla will ring if there's any problem. Come on, mate. Let's get a coffee.' Ken steered Donovan out to the waiting area. 'It's going to be a good few hours before we know anything more about Ellen.'

Donovan watched the trolley with Ellen on it disappear behind the closing doors of the lift. A unexpected feeling of nausea bubbled up from his stomach. He had never known what it was like to be sick with worry before. He now had a pretty clear understanding of the phrase.

'If she doesn't make it, I don't think I'll be able to bear it,' he said.

'Think positive. She's young. She's strong. The bullet has missed her major organs and arteries. You said yourself that she's a fighter. She has everything going for her.'

'If I believed in God, I'd be praying right now,' said Donovan. Despite this declaration, he found himself offering up a plea, begging that Ellen pulled through.

The pain was excruciating. The lights were blinding. Ellen groaned as she tried to move her head. Every part of her body hurt but her shoulder felt like it was on fire. She was aware of a nurse at her bedside, talking to her. She couldn't make out what the nurse was saying but it sounded soft and gentle. Ellen's head lolled to the other side. The voice changed. It was deeper. Tender. Full of concern.

On the third attempt she managed to open her eyes for more than a few seconds and focus.

'Donovan.' She tried to lift her hand to touch him, to make sure he was real but her limb was heavy and unresponsive.

'Hello, angel,' he said. A smile stretched across his face. 'Nice of you to join us.'

The nurse spoke again. 'I'll get you something to ease the pain. Won't be long.'

Ellen's memory started to filter the events back through. Images of the beach huts, Ben lying unconscious, guns and armed police officers filled her mind. Suddenly, she thought of Izzy. She looked at Donovan. 'Izzy?'

He smiled. 'It's okay. Izzy is fine. She's at home with Carla.'

'And Ben?'

'Ben's okay too. In fact, he's here in the hospital, on another ward. They are keeping him in for observation. He's a bit concussed but that's all.' Donovan stroked the side of her face.

236

'Tell me everything, Donovan.'

'Okay, but very briefly. Not good news about Toby. He's dead. I'm sorry. He broke his neck when he fell back onto the stones.'

Ellen was surprised by the feeling of sadness this brought. Yes, he was a bullying, violent and evil man, but she had never wished him dead. She had only ever wanted him to stop. To leave her alone. She mulled the news over several times but other than the sadness, no stronger feeling raised its head. However, she couldn't deny the relief that had sneaked its way to the fore. He was dead and there was absolutely no way he could harm her again. She was finally free. Not in the way she had wanted but, nevertheless, she knew she had nothing to fear any more. She looked at Donovan. 'Anything else?'

'Amanda. She's been arrested and faces a whole host of charges – perverting the course of justice, aiding and abetting, withholding information and so the list goes on.'

'Oh my God, she was involved. That is terrible. How could she?'

'I know. I can hardly believe it myself,' said Donovan. 'Whatever happens to her, she won't be getting custody of Izzy, that's for sure.'

Ellen's eyes filled with tears. 'Kate?'

'Don't cry, angel, it's okay,' Donovan wiped the tear from her cheek. 'Kate's in ICU but she's going to make it. She's got multiple broken bones and some internal injuries. It's going to be a long road to recovery, but the doctors are pretty sure she's going to be all right.'

Ellen couldn't put into words the relief and joy Donovan's words brought to her. She sobbed. 'That's simply the best news ever. Oh, Donovan. I'm so happy.'

He was grinning back at her. 'I know, it's the best.

'So it wasn't that Lampard bloke, after all,' said Ellen.

Donovan shook his head. 'No, but he's been charged with attacking Stella Harris. She's even been able to give a positive ID on him, so he'll be locked away for a long time.'

'That's good.'

'See, everything has worked out okay.' He leaned over and kissed her. 'I love you, Ellen.'

Joy doubled itself within her. 'I love you too.'

The door swished open and the nurse returned. 'Someone looks happy,' she said. 'That's good to see. Now, do you think you can take these tablets? They will help take the edge off the pain. You're going to be quite sore for a few days.'

The feeling was coming back into Ellen's body and she was able to lift her hand and take the container with the tablets from the nurse. Swallowing was a bit more difficult but she managed, washing them down with some water.

The nurse carried out her routine observations on Ellen and completed the chart at the end of the bed. 'All done. I'll leave you alone with your husband now. Ring the bell if you need anything.'

'Husband?' said Ellen to Donovan once the nurse had left the room. 'Not only have I managed to get myself shot, but it appears I've got myself married too.'

'Would that be such a bad thing – being Mrs Donovan? Married to me?'

'That would depend.'

'On what?'

'I'd have to know your first name before I could marry you.'

'There's only one way you're going to find that out.' Donovan looked deadly serious.

'Really. How's that then?'

'When you meet me at the altar.'

'Assuming I agree to marry you,' countered Ellen.

'And will you?'

Ellen grinned as she looked directly at Donovan. 'What do you think?'

Donovan held her gaze for a moment. 'It's in the eyes, Ellen. The eyes don't lie.' He leaned over and kissed her.